CALIFORNIA HUSTLE

A NOVEL

JEFFREY MESSINEO

ISBN: 979-8-9871924-3-6

Swift Media

Laguna Hills, California

To old dogs

learning new tricks.

1
Expo

Something tickled in the back of Grigsby's head, but he ignored it. Probably nothing. It was usually nothing.

The Rosary seemed an appropriate racket on this Sunday, the day the church took the people for their tithe. God, spirituality, all that was fine and good, probably proper, but power and greed had a particular hold on people. And like his Pops always said, "You can't cheat an honest man."

By the time Pacific Coast Highway led him through a few high-end enclaves, past the bay-side yacht brokers, and wide-windowed exotic car dealers, up the coast to the resort hotels lining the beach, he thought he'd figured out a new wrinkle for the job.

Top down on his car, the late August heat embraced him as he slowed and turned his white 1983 Mercedes 450SL into one of those beach resort and spas under the palm trees' gentle sway. Toward the parking structure, schools of men and women in baseball, basketball and football jerseys flowed on the walkway to the large ballroom.

Grigsby pumped his brakes for a quick stop. Three teenage girls giggled in the middle of the drive where they swarmed that just-retired second baseman from back East, his blown-out knee and girls swooning would provide him a payday on TV if the kid was smart. Easy money.

After driving slowly past, he pulled into the parking structure and drove straight to the top, furthermost spot, backed into the space. A check of his watch told him he was an hour early. Being late to an appointment worried Grigsby so much that he rushed constantly, only to be early. Now there was plenty of time for a coffee and some people watching.

Grigsby hopped out of the car, checked his pockets for his keys, wallet, phone, and money.

Son of a bitch. That was the tickle. He left the money in the cookie jar. No worries, he didn't need that much more for today's game. He could make the rest of the cash before the meet-up.

After a check in the car side mirror, he grabbed his bottle of water and splashed a little on his hands, slicked the top and sides of his hair, not realizing he left the back mussed.

With a turn of a key and a button push, Grigsby removed a signed football in a plastic case from the trunk of his car. To the bottom of the case was taped an envelope. He opened the envelope because he couldn't see inside and who the hell knows. What he thought was there, was there.

He peered over the edge of the parking structure. Just as before, a stream of people headed to the hotel banquet area. He marked a few parking guys but not any other security. With the encased football tucked under his arm and envelope in hand, he loped down the stairs casually like he didn't have a care in the world. Game time. Until his knee buckled a little. He cursed the knee the same he had his entire adult life then by the time he reached ground level, he assumed a more dour demeanor. Happy go lucky was not the tone of the day. Grigsby took the concourse walkway towards the dozen story hotel, ocean breeze on his face. The planters held evergreen long leafed tropical plants with a mix of purple stalks, yellow or orange flowers.

Grigsby parked himself outside the automatic entry doors of the resort and assumed a hopeful-eyebrows-slanted-outwards stance and waited.

As a sports memorabilia event, the organizers carried a large list of collectible vendors in what amounted to a small convention hall. This particular event had a lot of football fans thanks to a Hall of Fame traveling exhibit. Packers, Steelers, Rams and even a Dan Fout's powder blue Charger's jersey waltzed past. The average citizen would be surprised to learn the sums collectors brought and would pay for a piece of sports history. Heck, Shohei Ohtani's rookie baseball card was flipped for $30,000 when he'd barely made it to the big leagues. Thirty Gs for a card bought for a nickel? Where emotion and money meet, opportunity is bred. Then, what he knew would show, did: A more salt than pepper guy and his not quite teen son decked out in Patriot’s jerseys. The dad in a Patriots hat, too. They had #12's on their chest and grins on their chubby faces. Dad lead with his belly and his untied $400 Jordans. Just what the doctor ordered.

"Go Pats!" Grigsby said.

The guy smiled and threw his chin up at him. The

boy laughed and gave Grigsby a fist bump.

"Brady fan?" Grigsby asked.

"You wouldn't guess," the dad said indicating the jerseys. "Sure Hall of Famer even with that one he got in Tampa."

Grigsby nodded along, "Well, look. I'm in a bit of a spot and I'm looking for a buyer."

"Sure, buddy. They have those inside," he said and started...

"No, look at this," Grigsby said and shoved the ball at the kid.

The boy's eyes bugged out of his head, "Dad, it's signed by Brady."

"Sure, it is," the dad said.

"I'll keep this short. I coached him in high school and was there on draft day," Grigsby said.

This is where it gets beautiful. Grigsby pulled a picture out from the envelope to reveal him and Tom Brady posing, arms over shoulders in the draft room, big smiles all around.

Grigsby flashed the same smile, "Look at the ball."

On the Super Bowl branded football was written: "Thanks for the help, coach. Wouldn't be what I am without you. #12 Tom Brady - Super Bowl XXXVI MVP"

"I need the cash and want this to go to a fan, not one of these vultures," Grigsby said and hinted inside. "They've already offered me three grand. Brady's a HoFer, first ballot. It'll be worth five times that in five years. I can part with it for twenty-five hundred cuz you guys are real fans. It'll sting less."

The dad looked across his eyes at his kid. The kid held his dream and was sure this talisman would make him a future star quarterback.

"I'll give you twelve-fifty. I have the cash here," Dad said.

"How about two grand."

"Thirteen-fifty."

"Can't go that low," Grigsby said and turned to take the ball from the kid.

"Dad, we could make that back by the time we go home. Shit, some guy inside said he'd give three K."

"Come now!" said the dad with some menace. This is one of those turning points. The whole build-up comes to this.

"Hey, if you're going to turn around and sell it, I'll go with someone else."

The dad said, “Exactly.” Without moving, he kept on, "No, I'm keeping this. Tell you what. Fifteen hundred and we'll call it a deal. But I want to keep my cash. Can I Venmo it?"

Grigsby didn’t like the electronic stuff, digital created trails. Money’s money but this cheap skate wouldn’t part with the extra dough. No way.

"Give me sixteen hundred and you can Venmo it."

Kid had the football tucked under his arm but was messing with his phone.

“Okay, fifteen hundred.” The dad noticed when Grigsby looked at the kid and said, "Stupid games."

"Yeah."

The guy pulled out a wad and counted out $1,000. He reached in the other pocket for a wad twice the size, peeled off the rest.

"Hey, can we have the pic?" said the kid.

"Tommy, stop it!"

"No, that's okay. Sure, you can have it." Grigsby handed the picture over and the kid took a wide-eyed gander. Grigsby hated to give it to them but as often as not it's the picture that closed the deal.

The dad took it away and handed the picture back to Grigsby, "No, you keep it. That's a great memory."

"It sure is." Grigsby felt sweet with the money on its way.

As the dad double counted the cash and was about to hand it to Grigsby, the kid spoke up, "Dad! This ain't the guy," and handed over the phone.

The dad took a look and saw the same pic Grigsby showed them but a vastly different face on the coach.

The dad put a strong hand on Grigsby's sternum and pushed him off his feet, "Almost, player. Almost." The dad mad dogged over Grigsby and the kid threw the case on the ground. The case broke, along with the tension, in three. "You lucky my kid here. Fatherhood made me a different man. Was a time, this wouldn't have ended well for you, but I won't commit violence front of my boy." They walked away, the dad giving the kid a squeeze around his shoulders and a pat on the back as they were already reminiscing about the time they were almost scammed at the card show.

Grigsby got up and brushed himself off. He gathered his detritus and made a turn behind a cement pylon. Closing then opening his eyes with a roll, he told himself he should have enough to pull the job off, anyway. Maybe. He walked back to his car and opened the trunk, removed the bottom of the compartment to get to his spare tire and accompaniments. With the tire iron, he slid the tool along the rim making a full circle and left the tire half off that rim to reveal a plastic wrapped package of bills. A quick count revealed $3,500.

"Shit." By his watch: ten minutes. He worked his way back downstairs and knew he better start roping. He came back to the same pylon as before, leaned against it. A black-haired man dressed in khakis and a polo shirt whistled past Grigsby, not a care in the world. Probably a day job with a paycheck every other week that he saved twenty bucks from each time so he could blow his perfectly budgeted money at the memorabilia show when it came along. Grigsby took a deep breath, forced himself to stand up straight and joined the crowd.

This place had too much of a family feel, the dad and kid notwithstanding. Was a time when all you saw at these places were middle-aged men looking to buy some stuff and bring it back to the shop to make a few bucks. Nowadays, a twelve-year-old from Ohio can put some rookie's baseball card on eBay and sell to a kid in Florida. The world was changing. Hell, it had changed.

Well, no problem, Grigsby was adaptable. He bought a coffee with cash, kept the coins from the change and tipped the server with a paper buck.

He found a guy with dark, close-cut sides with a big cross necklace at a table, eyes on his phone. The guy was definitely a soccer guy. A peek at his phone revealed video streaming off-track betting. The ponies.

Grigsby loosened his tie and unbuttoned the top shirt button, sat at the metal table next to the guy. He dropped his phone and the coins with a racket. Grigsby leaned over, "You watching Del Mar?"

The guy glanced up a little peeved. "Too early. Saratoga Springs."

"New York."

"Yeah," the guy said disgusted as the race ended. He looked over at Grigsby. "The horses just keep me busy while I wait."

"What are you waiting for?"

"Any of the other sports to start." The guy tapped around on his phone. He was moving on.

"It's summer. Bet baseball." Not so fast.

"I can't bet baseball. When the best teams still lose a third of their games? Forget it."

He wanted a sure thing, there was a nibble. "True."

"I got into cards for a while, but those pros are all

doing rocket science in their heads at the table. Too much. I just want to make some bucks."

"Don't we all?" This guy will work.

"You would think," the guy answered.

Grigsby's phone vibrated. He reached to answer and, with a move worthy of Harry Houdini, invisibly dropped something to the ground. It was best if the mark made the discovery, so Grigsby then knocked over and caught his coffee while he flicked the coins toward the mark's chair to finish the trick.

The man followed the noise, looked underneath his chair and, on the ground, was a beautiful bracelet rosary made of emeralds and rubies. He picked the rosary and the coins up, "Ooh-wee, someone's gonna miss this." He handed Grigsby the coins while he marveled at the gems.

A man walked up in sweatpants and tennis shoes but the $3,000 Supreme-type sweatshirt and Offwhite co-lab $1,000 sneakers. With a shoe box tucked under his elbow, he was a true hype beast. A total sneaker head. "Thank, God! You found it!"

Grigsby and Mark, yeah, his name was Mark, looked up, "Is it yours?"

"That rosary is my mama's," the guy with the sneakers said. "Blessed by the Pope!"

Grigsby shook his head, slow and easy, "Wow, lucky."

"Let me give you a reward," the sneaker-head said.

"Nah, man, just take it," Mark said.

"Listen, I'm bringing this rosary to her in the hospital but there were a couple deals I had to close here first." He made eye contact with the two men. "I'm lucky you found it and I want you to feel lucky you found it, too. It's bad luck if you don't take it."

Grigsby shook his head, "I don't know." Mark looked between the two not sure what to make of the situation and tried not to show it.

The sneaker-head continued his story undeterred, "First one, I came here to buy Ricky Henderson cleats and a card, but the guy sold it right from under me." He pulls out $500 and shoves it at them. "Now, it's burning a hole in my pocket. Take it." Neither takes the cash and he drops it on the table.

"No, keep your money," Grigsby said.

Mark looked at Grigsby kinda pissed (that's good) but kept his mouth shut.

The sneaker pimp looked at both of them, smiled and picked up his cash, "Today is my lucky day."

His phone buzzed. He opened and held up his finger. "What?? Now!?! Okay." Hung up and rattled off a text while Grigsby and Mark exchanged shoulder shrugs.

"Look, you guys. You didn't take my money or my mother's rosary. Maybe I can trust you. Can I trust you?"

"Sure."

"Yeah."

The sneaker-head looked between the two of them, "There's a guy I was going to meet right here at this table in an hour, but that call was my sis. My mama just went code blue and she doesn't have long. You know, I gotta go see her before she passes."

"Of course."

"I'm so sorry."

"But that's not the worst of it. This guy I'm meeting. He has five pairs of Nike Air Jordans. Rookie year. 1985. Size 10. Unworn and stored in an Ad exec's house in Portland. Only time they left the box was for him to massage them, so they don't crack and rot. Anyway, he brought them down and isn't bringing them back. I made a deal to buy them for thirty grand, but he wants the money now. It's a steal but if I don't pay him, he's got another buyer here and I'll lose the deal. I don't have to tell you this thing would set me up for the next six months but I gotta go."

"What do you want us to do?" Mark said.

"Make the purchase. Do this with me and we'll split the sales."

"You're going to leave the cash with us?" Grigsby said.

The sneaker pimp opened the shoe box and there were two stacks of twenties with a bank strap detailing a $20,000 bundle. One hundred twenties. 40K. He closes it and sets it down.

"Not exactly. I trust you but not that much. What I am going to do is bring you in on the deal. Can each of you get your hands on five K?"

"Of course," Grigsby said.

"Maybe," Mark said.

"C'mon, man, don't ruin this," Grigsby said.

"I guess I could take a cash advance on my credit card."

"Good, good. This job will make you twice that back."

Grigsby pulled out a wad and counted, "I got $3,500."

"What?" The sneaker pimp eyed Grigsby.

Grigsby grimaced, "I only got $3,500."

Mark said, "That's better. I can get the $3,500 at the ATM right there."

"Then I guess it'll be $3,500," the sneaker pimp said with a pissed off look at Grigsby as they got up and followed Mark to the ATM. “I'll make up the difference, but it lessens your take.”

Mark got his money and Grigsby recounted his stack.

The sneaker pimp took one bundle out of the box, counted out three thousand, put the three to join the twenty grand he left and said, "Now put yours in the box."

“What?” Mark said.

"How do I know I can trust you?" said Grigsby.

Sneaker looked between them both, "I got the most in the pot."

"Yeah, I don't know." This was Mark following the script like he read it.

"Who can come up with a way we can trust each other?" Grigsby said.

“If you can’t trust me,” Sneaker said. "I don't think there's a way."

"There's gotta be a way. We're gonna make a fortune." That’s right Mark.

"I just don't think it can be done. Why don't we just throw in the towel?" Grigsby.

"We can't give up now," Mark said. "Look, we could all watch and make sure nobody takes off."

"No, if we sit and watch, it'll blow the sale. This guy takes no guff besides I gotta get to my mama."

"Well, I just thought-a something, but you'll never go for it," Grigsby said.

"What is it?"

"Okay, we used to do this as a trust exercise in the Army. Put it this way. First, like he said, gimme all the money and put it in the box.” Grigsby gathers the money and closes the shoe box. “Each of us walks around the outside of the ballroom with one other, all taking turns."

"I don't get it," Mark said.

"I'll walk around the ballroom with this guy and the cash, you stay here. Then you two walk around the ballroom then us two walk around the ballroom. It proves that we can trust each other with the other guy," Grigsby said.

"I don't know," the sneaker pimp said.

"Ok, since it's my idea, you two go first. I don't know you guys. If you guys are dirty, I lose my money." Grigsby handed the box to the other two and took a seat to wait.

He always enjoyed this part of it, maybe the most. The anticipation. The buildup. The excitement.

Grigsby settled back to watch some people walk around and walk by.

Shit.

Just as the other two disappeared around the corner Beagle spotted him. We don't have time to get into it here but needless to say there was history and when you were in this kind of work, history eventually turned bad.

"Grigsby," Beagle said as he walked up straightening his policeman's uniform over his prodigious belly and adjusted his utility belt.

"What brings you around here?" Grigsby said.

"Funny, I was going to ask you the same thing."

"Just enjoying the show. Thinking about buying some baseball cards or a jersey. I hear Mike Trout might have a future."

"Sure you aren't working the hot seat on that guy I saw you talking with?"

"I don't do that stuff anymore, Officer Beagle. I'm clean and straight," Grigsby said and smiled.

"Clearly," Beagle said and jiggled his keys.

Grigsby was antsy. They'd be back soon, around that other corner and it wouldn't do to have this copper hanging around.

"Well, good seeing ya," Grigsby said. It might work.

Beagle laughed.

"C'mon," Grigsby said.

"Tell you what," Beagle said. "Gimme a grand and I'll forget all about it."

They came around the corner. Beagle looked at them and at him.

"I don't have a grand."

"I'll come by after."

They were getting close. Beagle smiled his shit-eating, knife-in-heart smile.

"Okay, okay."

Beagle tipped his hat and walked away just as Mark and the sneaker pimp walked up.

"What did he want?" Mark said.

"Oh, they're just looking for a little girl got separated from her dad is all," Grigsby said. "Let's take a walk."

The sneaker pimp took a seat, looking like he had something to say but couldn't, and Grigsby took off with Mark.

The lap passed quickly and, truth be told, Grigsby didn't care to know or had a need to further schmooze the guy. He just needed the cash.

When they rounded the fourth corner and he saw Sneaker Pimp he knew he was close. Grigsby could taste it. He could smell it. They walked up and Grigsby caught the cop in his peripheral vision.

Was he going to blow this?

They exchanged the box and got off on their way.

At the apex of the first corner Grigsby could already see Beagle, who walked up with a Cheshire Cat grin.

"Didn't want you forgetting," Beagle said.

"Forgetting what?" the sneaker pimp said.

"Just fork it over and we'll move on," Beagle looked around. "C'mon."

They followed him into an empty conference room set up for some meeting or other.

"Let's go," Beagle said.

Grigsby took the box from Sneaker Pimp and counted out a grand. He handed the money over and Beagle left with a small salute.

"What do you think you're doing?" the sneaker pimp said.

"He put the drop on me," Grigsby said.

"I didn't agree to that."

"Well, I'm sure you agreed to avoid jail."

"Who says you could negotiate?"

"I took the initiative."

"The initiative? You could've had him for a hundred, ya rube."

"No."

"Yes."

"No."

"I paid the bastard when I got here. He got $100 already, goddammit. He shook you down and you didn't even know it."

"You didn't tell me."

"I am now."

"Goddammit."

"Goddammit."

"God. Dammit."

The sneaker pimp shook his head with something behind his eyes Grigsby didn't like.

"Well - considering we have privacy. Let's settle."

The Sneaker immediately took the bundle he fronted and pocketed it. Then he took the wad of $3,500 and handed it to Grigsby. They were even.

"Now, considering the job was for five grand when we discussed it previously. I am due $2,500 as the original cut." He pocketed the $2,500 remaining from the ruse and grabbed the door.

"The hell you are," Grigsby said pulling the Sneaker's shoulder.

The Sneaker moved quickly. Sneaker twisted Grigsby's arm behind his back, face smashed to the door, then held the tip of a knife to the base of Grigsby's skull. Grigsby couldn't see the knife, but he could feel it, a bead of sweat drizzled down the middle of his back. Or was that blood?

"The hell I will," the Sneaker said. "You've done cocked this up and I'll take my promised share. You came up short and let the mark off the hook at the beginning. You're to have the 5G so he has to match up. You let him off the hook."

"Dammit, Sneaker, I need the cash."

"You're a sweet guy. You'll figure it out." Sneaker palm smacked Grigsby's temple and Grigsby's head pinballed into the door. "Unless you're getting too old." Sneaker released him and opened the door. "Maybe there's a home for used up grifters," as the door closed behind him.

"Goddammit." All of this arguing took too long. Grigsby straightened his pants and jacket, ran his hand through his hair, opened the door himself, looked for the mark and left the opposite way he had come. The marks usually took a minute to catch on but not much more. Beagle was well paid, now. He'll take a report and lose it immediately.

Down the hall and to the exterior doors, a lady in an orange dress opened the exit for him wordlessly. She was the type you don't miss, comfortable in her skin like a jaguar was comfortable in the jungle. In any case, he walked toward the structure and looked over his shoulder as he reached the stairs. The lady stood outside the door, vape in hand, vape smoke all around. Not even a glance his way. She seemed to be talking to a younger woman in an awful purple wig. Maybe he was over-reacting. She must work one of the booths. Grigsby thought about how he had a sixth, seventh and eighth sense about other's eyes on him as he stripped off the suit in the parking lot. He slipped on some khaki shorts, sandals, and a blue Tommy Bahama shirt.

He might as well work his way back to town. There was a steady flow as he passed Azure Cove with its crystal water and craggy, black cliffs in contrast. The closer to downtown of Verona Beach, California, the longer the cars queued. He was forced to slow as he passed art galleries and homes overlooking the ocean from the cliffs below PCH and hills above.

Entering downtown he fell under the shadow of all three stories of the Hotel del Verona and wondered if he should spare the time for a visit. Since a spot was open just in front, he slipped right in. Closing his car door Grigsby decided on the scenic route and worked his way down the sidewalk past the stucco arches and red tile roof of the corner café.

Grigsby crossed the grass strip to the Main Beach area over the railroad tie boardwalk. At the sand, he removed his leather sandals to enjoy the last heat of the day on his feet. Waves crashed and churned on the shore before him, the briny scent all around. He hadn't meant it to be like this, dawdling down the beach, looking for an answer. A friend. A confidant. A mark.

Hook one, then carefully monitor the line for that tell-tale tap and squiggle, like the old man in a small boat on the big ocean. If the right fish bit and held, the reel would spin and smoke for the fight. As he got older, he realized he could cope with much more pain and disappointment than what he cracked under as a young man. Get one on the line, then on the boat. He could make this happen and no one would be the wiser.

Until it was too late.

Back on the boardwalk came a rumble and roll. A handful of grommets slurved through the crowd on their skateboards, laughing, glowing, videoing on their phones. Nothing but nimble ligaments, and Ferrari's in their windshield.

Grigsby approached the hotel from the ocean side, water lapping his ankles. Built somewhere around the turn of the last century, the hotel was an old-world beach resort with crisp chaise lounges beneath blue striped umbrellas. Two attendants in pure white straightened and raked the sand. A set of red Saltillo tile stairs awaited, and, at the top, a poolside bar surrounded by the sweet stench of ice-plant soon overcome by floating summer jasmine.

The under-glow of the pool glimmered as Grigsby passed and entered the hotel bar, proper; deep woods with brass fittings and footrests, low lighting accented with tea candles. The place, nary an empty table, was mixed between the tourists and some locals.

With his sandals still hanging off his fingers like two bass after a day on a boat, he stopped next to the stool adjacent the bar condiment station and dropped the sandals on the floor with a flop. He slipped his toes around the big toe strap and made an almost imperceptible, smooth 180 to the bar.

Without a word the bartender dropped an old-fashioned just as Grigsby lost his sandal to the floor. He glanced down to retrieve the lost shoe and when he looked up the woman in the flowing, low cut orange dress was seated next to him.

She must have just entered from the street because he couldn't have missed her. Besides, with a better look, the woman had the relaxed movements and the perfect skin of someone who could stay up late and wake up late without the fear of missing a day of work.

He looked past her out the large bay window to the disappearing orange globe breaking the horizon. Innocuous jazz echoed in the background.

"If you look closely, you'll see a green flash when the sun disappears," he said.

"Excuse me?" she said.

"There's an old story that if you see the green flash when the sun disappears, new money is on the horizon."

"If that it would," while she actively ignored him. The bartender noticed her waiting. “Pellegrino and lime.”

This ship was going nowhere, he changed tack.

"I must say, it's quite an accomplishment you have there. Your dress matches the sky. Stunning."

"Thank you." The blow off, but as Grigsby does, he persisted.

"Bartender: two tequila sunrises to celebrate the luck of her dress and the sun glowing in the same beautiful shade."

"Oh, no," she said. "I'm fine."

"Please," he said. "This is the only fun I have."

The bartender poured and delivered the two tequila sunrises and a Pellegrino. To break the silence, Grigsby picked up the orange and red drink in a toast.

"May our dreams fly high into the sky but not so high as to burn our wings," he said.

"To Icarus," she said. She didn't touch the tequila sunrise.

"To Icarus," he eyed her. "Not everyone picks up that reference."

She eyed him back, "I am certainly not everyone."

"Not everyone wears an orange dress," he smiled, tilted his drink to her and took a sip.

Now it was time to really see what this woman, who was obviously following him, was up to.

"Are you picking up on me?" she said.

"I... no. Just making conversation."

"Because I'm not what you're thinking," she said, rolling something in her mind, extending the pause as she decided. "That was a tough break today."

"At what?"

"One would think a fish shook off the line if one

was paying attention at the card show."

Grigsby took in the other customers and focused on the mirror behind the bar to cool his jets. He told himself how the mirror was a terrific window onto the others at the bar and tables. Nope, didn't work. "Who <u>are</u> you?"

"What does one do when one isn't sitting at this bar?" the lady in orange said.

"Not thinking. I don't sit around and think about other people's business."

"I bet," she said. Then straight into his eyes reflected in the bar mirror, "One would think you were more active than that."

His look of consternation was entirely unamused and matched hers. "If you're asking what I do for a living, I'm semi-retired." This was Grigsby's fall back.

She turned directly to him. "Ah, yes, you probably have an unbelievable land deal, too."

Grigsby listened to a flute tremolo on the piped in jazz. "Interested?"

"No," with a single shake of her head.

"What do you want?" The highball's cold sweat dripped over his fingers.

"No need to get uncomfortable." She smiled, sipped the fizzy water. "Game recognizes game, that's all. I'm new around here and may need an experienced hand."

"Is that right?"

"Right as rain," she said as she opened her vintage

clasp purse and gathered her phone. "Check your phone. Be there tomorrow and I can tell you more."

"What if I'm busy?" He couldn't, wouldn't, look.

"Don't be cute. I need you to be smart, not cute." She stood, drained her Pellegrino with a single, long draw then dropped a ten spot on the bar and gave him a side glance, no chin. A man walked up and caressed her waist in greeting, "Do you want to go to that fish house the concierge mentioned?"

"That would be great," she said, sweet and warm. "How was the phone call?"

"Just business," he said. She dropped her phone in her purse and stood up with a casual sway on her four-inch Blahniks. As they strolled from the bar, she looked back over her shoulder to our hero with a smile like a cat with the canary and the air-dropped event arrived on his phone. An invite to the rundown theater across the street, tomorrow afternoon.

He pushed away the tequila sunrise in disgust and picked up his old fashioned to think.

"That doesn't happen every day."

A collective gasp filled the room in a wave. A woman gaping out the sweeping window was joined by two couples as they rushed to inspect the beach. Grigsby stood to see a gray whale flail its massive tail and park itself on the beach. He wondered why in the big wide world he would do that? That big ocean out there was his home. Not the land swarming with people and cars and houses and bank accounts. That whale had the life right out in the open water. No stuff to weigh him down. All he had to do was open his mouth and filter out all those plankton and shrimp, maybe a few plastic bottles, and keep on his way. When you look at it, they just chased the sun. Alaska in the summer, Mexico in the winter, road trip in between. There's something beautiful in that.

He descended the stairs of the hotel to the beach, the sandy slippery stairs he considered slipping on for the insurance money, just for a second. A crowd of onlookers the size of a classroom had gathered. A white lifeguard jeep covered with backboards and surfboards was already parked to the side. Two thirty-something lifeguards cordoned the beast off from what would surely become a throng. Both lifeguards, one male, one female, were efficient and orderly. They kept people back and explained a marine biologist was on the way to investigate.

A cry like music and sonorous vocals filled the air. The whale slapped its tail then spoke again.

Grigsby rotated his way toward the front of the water mammal. It was the size of a school bus and took up much of the small beach. Surprisingly, there were small hairs on the skin and no scales. He knew this was a mammal, but his instinct jumped to the scales of a fish rather than the skin, fat, and hairs of a mammal. This thing was going to make a mess. Then he got to the front and made eye contact.

The sodium light from the boardwalk lights reflected but he looked into that deep dark black eye and saw... something. Life. Resolve. He didn't want to say spirit but spirit.

The whale slowly blinked twice and closed its eyes.

He looked around to see if anyone else had just seen what he had seen but the rest had been looking elsewhere or at the lifeguards getting up caution tape. Grigsby had just made a connection with that creature. It had something to say. It landed here on purpose.

Grigsby really needed to find a way to make his house payment.

To be a man between something of this size and the ocean was dangerous, Grigsby thought as he rounded to the other side of the whale between the beach and ocean. On cue the lifeguards removed the gathering few who had situated with the waves lapping their ankles. Grigsby lingered a moment letting the others go before him. The better to investigate them; like the aging man in white shirt, shorts and ample crow's feet who led what looked to be a kindergartner in matching white shirt and shorts. Grigsby wondered if he'd be alive to fleece that desperate little boy when he was a bit older and fatherless.

"I'd be careful if I were you," came a wry female voice.

Grigsby turned around surprised. He didn't like to be caught unaware.

"That flipper could leave quite a mark," said a vigorous woman in strap sandals, shorts, and a one-piece underneath. She was strong and tan and, he could already tell, took no shit. Considering the deference of the lifeguards, she was the biologist in charge.

"I didn't even realize," Grigsby said. He didn’t want to admit he’d thought about the danger but didn’t act.

"No. Obviously you didn't," she said as she elbow

walked him to safety away from the piano (grand) sized flipper of the whale twice the length of a fishing boat.

"Rescued by the gallant scientist," he said with single eyebrow raised, perhaps a twinkle in his eye.

She held his eyes and handed him a contractor's bucket while he took the opportunity, "I'm Andrew Grigsby."

"Bio," she said with a half-amused smile that may have said she'd seen his type before but would allow it. "If you'd like to be useful you could pour some water on this poor thing. They dry out pretty quick on land."

"I-"

"Thanks." She turned, then back over her shoulder, "I'm going to see if I can figure out why we're all here. In particular, why our larger friend decided to be the guest of the hour. Please avoid getting injured."

To his own surprise, he used the bucket to toss water on the beast's body with a dozen other volunteers. He wasn't used to this type of thing anymore. His bad baseball knee hindered physical labor so Grigsby would only fill the bucket a quarter full to be able to throw the water on the whale. Both the lifeguards could manage the bucket nearly full.

On his third trip from the water his knee throbbed, and Grigsby was sure he caught the biologist smirk in his direction. Maybe he would find a way to use his brain and not his back.

The old man had his hand on the shoulder of his young son and gawked quietly, jaws on their chest, as the group threw water and the woman walked around the whale, calling loud enough for the crowd, "I'm looking for injuries or pieces of net, cuts, even massive amounts of mucus. Many eyes are better than few. Please let me know if you see anything."

Grigsby handed the bucket to the kid, "Knock yourself out."

"Thanks, sir!"

As he departed the scene, Grigsby touched the marine biologist on her shoulder, "Good luck, detective."

She didn't offer but barely a humph and he strolled back down the beach in the dark.

He wondered about that lady in orange. Who was she and what was the job?

Once separated a bit, he paused and looked back to the commotion. The spots had been extinguished on the lifeguard jeep and all he could make out was the silhouette of the whale against the marquee of the downtown movie theater mixed with roving headlights of cars and the tricolored tree rotation of the traffic lamp. The biologist shouted directions from atop the hood of the jeep and the crowd gathered like a flock to the priest delivering the gospel. Grigsby turned for home.

2
Brodie Awaits

Grigsby walked the shoreline south back to his house, the short mile made longer by his irritated knee. He always figured walking in the sand would strengthen the ligaments. The ocean was at low tide and by now the sky blended the deepest red and purple ending in a darkness beyond reflection of the gloaming.

The water line was low enough that a boulder, which often as not was surrounded by the surf, perched lonely and dry on the beach just below his property. Twice as tall as he was, Andrew W. Grigsby touched the rough barnacled sides of the rock for luck as he passed on the compact sand of low tide, transitioned to the soft sand then climbed the dozen stairs up the sea wall to his private beach, a perch just about the size of a volleyball court.

He picked up an empty juice packet and two beer bottles then dropped them in his receptacle, Grigsby couldn't stand to see his beach imperfect. He climbed the additional few dozen stairs to the small Saltillo tile patio landing. He waited there and basked in the crash of each wave pounding the sand.

They were small tonight but waves didn't turn off. Shallow fast whitewash foamed and reflected the light of the moon after the break-and-run to the shore. A last deep breath filled his nose with the brine of his beach as he looked and found the big dipper shining in the ink blue sky.

He opened the never locked door and entered a staunch hallway with a half bath on one side and a bedroom / office on the other. The stairs ahead turned square to the left mid-flight where a Spanish rod-iron lamp waited on the ceiling above the landing. As he climbed, he unconsciously felt for the cigarettes that weren't there in his shirt pocket. He hadn't smoked in more than twenty years, but the old habits rise to the surface once in a while. His wife had convinced him to quit with a kid in her belly and he obliged her the way a young man obliges his young wife. He won't mention that she obliged him not half a dozen years later with divorce papers. No need to travel that well-worn road.

He clicked the switch at the main floor, the second floor from where we started, and the light didn't illuminate. He flicked two more times to no avail. With a kick, he then rapped the wall three times flat handed just above the switch and tried it again. Light!

With a plink-plink on the piano in the hall, a swipe of the Virgin Mary statue in an alcove for luck, he went to the kitchen and drew a cup of water from the wall mounted faucet. He drank half and tossed the rest in the sink. Wiping his mouth with the back of his hand, he kicked off his sandals in the corner of the adjacent half-dark dining room. Just next to the door was a China cabinet and a set of size 16 feet with a body to match.

"Hey, there," Grigsby said.

"I don't want to do it," the hairless Sasquatch said.

"Then don't."

"You know and I know I gotta. It's like this is our

ecosystem. You are the sewage and if you don't clean yourself up, I have to," he said. The mook turned on the light.

Next to the big guy a large, faceted crystal bowl sat on a China hutch, glistening and ornate. He picked it up.

"Don't break that. It was my dead mother's."

"Don't you have any of Tony's money?"

"No."

"It's the insurance payment, this vase."

“That thing cost three grand.”

“Means I can hock it for one. Think of it as payment on your health insurance."

"Does that come off my tab?"

"Hell, no, but it lets you keep your toes," the Sasquatch said with a grin.

Grigsby nodded his head, "Sounds fair."

The big guy tucked the bowl under his arm, "Tony wants to know why didn't you drop off this month's payment?"

"Didn't have it." Grigsby had to make a payment every month on the million he owed, and the son of a bitch expected delivery in person. Even if he didn't have it, Grigsby had to show up at Tony's house and explain. And when Grigsby didn't show up, well, you see the result.

"Next time I'll take the car," he said and rubbed his chin. "Or your thumb."

Grigsby held his bunched lips with an answer he was too smart to give.

"No comeback? Maybe you *are* too old for this," the mook said and chuckled.

"Who said that?" Grigsby said. "Who said I'm too old. Too old?"

"Too old but at least you still got a little gumption," the big guy said.

"I'm not too old to slice your throat." Grigsby pulled a pocketknife from his shorts.

"We all reach retirement age," the big guy said as he laughed at the knife. Or Grigsby. Or both and the same. "Or we don't." He looked at the knife, again. And laughed, again.

"I got something tomorrow, Brodie." Grigsby put away his knife.

"Just get the money, Grigsby."

Brodie forced Grigsby's shoulder aside as the big guy walked into the kitchen. The lug spied the water glass, picked it up and shattered it in the sink. He walked out without another word.

"He didn't have to do that," Grigsby said to himself. "You didn't have to do that!" he said out the window to the palooka crossing his courtyard.

He waited until the front gate closed.

Silence.

He grabbed a plaster, orange Garibaldi shaped

cookie jar off the top of the cabinets, double-checked the gate was closed outside then opened. Inside was a bundle of cash wrapped in plastic. Next to the cash was a pack of cigarettes with a couple hundred-dollar bills wrapped around it with a broccoli rubber band. Ignoring the wad, he knocked a cig from the pack, returned the bundle to the jar. He then tapped the cigarette between his left thumb and back of his hand. Grigsby ran the cig under his nose, set it on his lip and just barely kissed it with his tongue while he lit the gas stove.

Tic. Tic. Vroom.

Between his index and middle finger, he held the cig to the flame and let it burn. The smoke and crackle made his nose grow an inch as he suffered the loss of quitting all over again. Then he turned and put it under the water faucet and dropped the soggy cigarette in the garbage can. The broken glass twinkled as Grigsby picked the pieces out of the sink.

It's never boring, this life.

First the big pieces then the smaller ones. He didn't want to cut himself, so he took his time and took that time to contemplate the evening.

He hadn't felt a tail chasing him all night, well, other than that orange chick. Wait, did he miss Brodie because of her? No, Brodie's visit was his usual shake down. Like he said, Grigsby had a sixth sense about people watching him. He made his living watching people. Reading them. Taking in the inflections, eye movement, smiles, hands. Most people think if they lie with their eyes, they convince you. The whole windows-to-the-soul thinking. It's bunk. Every other part of their body gives it away. They stand straight up and look boldly in your eyes, but the veneer ruins it. So do the clenched hands or nervous feet.

Anyway, he knows when he's followed.

He was down to the tiny pieces of glass. The pieces that were merely sand again, if infinitesimally sharper. Dust and sparkle that hadn't been beaten smooth by the constant pounding of waves and other shards. He wet a paper towel and gathered up the last and tossed it in the can. He inspected from another angle and spotted a shimmer. He pressed his fingertip directly on one and two more very carefully like picking up a breadcrumb and held the slivers over the can and dropped.

If that lady in orange had a job, who was she? He placed the waste can back under the sink and wiped his hands of the whole thing.

As he left the room, Grigsby unconsciously knocked the faucet to center to stop the drips. He climbed the third-floor stairs to the bathroom at the end of the hall and turned on the light.

A naked young man soaked in warm water; his arms dangled out of the claw foot bathtub. Blood stained the water pink, a slash oozed across his neck. Crimson blood smeared the walls and dripped from his wrists. A razor blade cutter on the floor, blood puddled around it.

"Aren't you supposed to be with your mother?" Grigsby said after he had taken it all in.

The young man opened an eye. Waited in silence a moment.

Grigsby took a piss.

"Brodie was here," the young man said.

"I saw him."

"You didn't think he did this?"

Grigsby washed his hands, "I'm sure she expects you home." He turned out the light as he left the room.

Grigsby turned the light back on and poked his head in, "And clean up the mess before you leave."

Lights out.

3
Breakfast

Before consciousness offered Grigsby his bed beneath him, the seagulls cried, and the waves crashed like a Debussy cymbal. The sleep receded, he pulled on shorts and, once on the deck outside his bedroom, he took a deep cleansing breath of the brackish air and stretched to the sky. Something moved over his shoulder. His heart jumped. He scanned the corners to ensure his room was empty. It must've been the curtains in the breeze. Had that visit from Brodie shaken him up? If it did, he really was getting old.

He leaned on the balcony rail, his forearms prickled to the rot and inevitable splinters noting, as he did every morning, the need to sand and paint the thing. To his left, far below, were a collection of tide pools half hidden behind a small rock arch. It might be a nice day to take a gander, the tide pools always raised his spirits and sparked his imagination. After breakfast. No, after his thing.

When, what did appear down near the waves, shifting from one rock to another, was the lady in orange. However, now she wore an orange wrap over her white one piece. She laughed at the water kissing her ankles and splashing her arms from the breakers in the cove. What was she doing so close to his place? She was tailing him.

Without a thought, Grigsby slipped his arms through a short sleeve button down shirt and hustled down the stairs all the way to his little patch of sand. She'd come from the tide pools and was nowhere to be seen either way up or down the beach. He beelined to the public access stairs past a few houses and took the first two stairs at once when his knee nearly buckled. He never regretted baseball, but he regretted that slide into second at least twice a day. He caught himself then, more slowly, climbed to the top landing. A salt-bleached surfer stood sentinel checking the size of the break for the day in nothing but his aqua, green, and white board shorts. Grigsby trod past the surfer and his truck full of construction equipment, a surfboard. There was no one on the street or up the hill towards Pacific Coast Highway. At least, no Orange. He missed her. Hands on his hips, he took a few breaths and dragged himself back to the stairs.

"Not today," the surfer said shaking his head.

"Nope."

The surfer shook out a pair of work boots and got in his truck.

Grigsby slipped down the stairs one at a time. He didn't know what it was about that lady, but he didn't like her showing up where she shouldn't. He looked at his wrist. No watch. Wasting time.

He proceeded, carefully, down to the beach, over to the house, back up to his room and showered. No need to rush, he had plenty of time before the appointed meeting.

Dressed in a gray suit, not too nice, a colorful bright blue tie, scuffed black shoes, and a Timex, he whistled his way downstairs to the middle, main floor, of his house, and settled back into the rest of his morning routine. Each step an intricate dance with habit: Espresso (grind, brew, steam the milk), fresh orange juice (cut, juice), a quick egg (sunny side up), whole grain wheat toast (margarine).

He ate and drank in the small dining room as he checked his phone. Nothing from the kids. Never anything from the kids. He guessed college kept them busy. No texts, no email. No social media dm's. Grigsby set the phone on the table face down with a thousand-yard stare at the horizon outside his ocean-view window. After a moment, his phone blinged then another. He picked it up to his lock screen: "You have 8 notifications waiting for you." He opened the Facebook app, and all were posts from some spammy site with motivational sayings he followed in a moment of weakness and three trending posts from some friend of his daughter's that seemingly competed with the Kardashians. All he ever got from the boy were those weird murder set pieces like he was that kid in "Harold & Maude" while, from the girl, silence. He locked his phone again then efficiently cleaned his dishes surrounded by the echo, tinkle and clink in the bright morning kitchen and dried his hands.

4

The Theatre

Just across the street from Main Beach, Grigsby parked his car. The old white and blue lighthouse shaped lifeguard tower stood centered directly in the middle of the panorama. A railroad tie walkway bridge sat adjacent for flash floods that raced down Verona Canyon Road in the winters (that actually had rain).

An early morning volleyball game was under way on the sand and a motley crew of oldsters and youngsters played pickup basketball on the two half courts that face east away from the sunsets.

Down the beach just out of sight, the whale, whole but dead, invited onlookers.

He breathed deeply and tilted his head up to read the marquee on the building: “Thanks for the memories!”

Grigsby passed the island ticket booth floating in sea-foam-colored tiles to enter the open door into the lobby of the dilapidated movie theater.

The place sat closed for a few years now. Originally, it had opened as a movie palace in the 1920’s for townspeople and vacationers. Purple carpets and grimy chandeliers led to plush velvet chairs with a balcony and gargoyles overlooking the main seating. Now, the smell of the place had a deep mix of mold, rotting fabric, dust, and popcorn: classic movie theater.

She, Orange, stood center stage before the large, not too large, silver screen and clapped a slow clap.

"You made it!" she said and waited in front of the movie screen at the end of the walkway.

"That I did." Grigsby held his position at the top of the walkway, she at the bottom, a bit like a Mexican standoff.

"Do you like movies?"

"Considering the profession, one has to love a good story."

"Fair enough..." She moved towards him slowly.

"Do you have a good story?" He succumbed and did the same.

"Oh, I do, I do..." She smiled.

"Don't be shy."

"First, the set up." They met in the middle, facing each other.

"I always love the set up," he nodded.

"A film festival."

"Oh, for Christ's sake. I'm not working a fucking film festival," he turned and walked back up the tilted, carpet covered walkway.

"You will for this one."

"No, thanks," he reached for the door and opened

it.

"The score is five hundred grand."

Grigsby let the door close and took two steps back, "500 G's?"

"That's the cut." Her arms wide as if she addressed an entire crowd.

"Bullshit."

"Why not?" She closed the distance between the two, less than two arm lengths. Personal space.

"With a team you don't know?"

"This fell in my lap, and I have a team. But I need a local." Now, she sat on the back of a chair, propped her feet on the seat.

"Me."

"You."

Grigsby still stood but shifted his weight from one foot to the other. He needed more. "The mark isn't the john I saw you with the other night?"

"Oh, hell, no. Don't worry about him. We've got a big fish and we need to land the big fish with a small boat."

"Okay, what do you want from me? Wait, first, who's this mark?"

"Bao Gong. He's the son of a billionaire industrialist from mainland China who fancies himself a duke of some sort."

Grigsby took a seat two rows from her, leaned forward, "What's his flaw?"

"Besides delusions of grandeur? His dad's factories are the ones with fences all around in an attempt to stop people from jumping off the roofs."

"That means he's the same as many factory owners around the world."

"Some of those people are kids."

"Right. Child labor. That's legal in their country. I want to know who the kid is and why he'd do this?" Grigsby leaned back in the chair, maybe this was something.

"He's rich. He wants to be famous."

He leaned forward again, "I don't buy it."

"He's the seventh son. He might as well be a servant in the family. He wants some attention."

That's pretty thin. Whatever. This was going nowhere fast, but it looked to Grigsby like there was cash on the line and if there was one thing he needed, it was cash. This lady didn't seem quite as seasoned as she presented herself to be. Maybe he could take her for a ride. "Famous. Okay, I'll put out the feelers and see who's available."

5
The Boys

When Grigsby left the theater, he walked past his car and down Coral Avenue through the tourist crowd. In the early 1900's, a group of artists had branded the town as an artist colony and attracted some of the finest California naturalists. Now, a small number of the galleries propositioned airbrushed mass-produced posters they could sell as numbered prints. Then, not for the first time, he thought, "Why hadn't I thought of that?"

He had bigger fish to fry.

As he passed the candy store, a toddler ran out, saltwater taffy in his hands and Grigsby nearly ambled over the child. He exchanged smiles with the father, patted the kid on the noggin and kept on.

The main drag was filled with bars, restaurants, breweries, chocolatiers, and art. The street t-boned a quarter mile later at the fire station and City Hall.

He walked into City Hall and it smelled of a scramble between septic one-hundred-year-old building filled with one hundred-year-old paper and environmentally safe soap. That blend hit him straight in the stomach. It was definitely that smell or it was Councilman Cox and the Fire Chief walking at the other end of the hallway with their self-important sticks up their asses. Grigsby slowed. He wanted them to get where they were going without realizing he was here, then Grigsby passed through all the offices to the back maintenance area. Where the real people work.

He slapped a few hands, and a knowing smile crossed the receptionist's face, "What are you doing here?"

"Hi, Delores," Grigsby said. "Is he around?"

"Nacho's out. Ron sent him out to handle some debris at Sicomoro Creek."

"Got it."

"Don't bother him - He's working."

"I would never."

"And give him this, he forgot it." She handed Grigsby a white bag with a burrito inside. "Don't eat it - it's his lunch."

Grigsby waved as he walked down the hallway and back out to the street.

As soon as he was outside, he broke out the burrito, chorizo and eggs by his nose, and ate it as he walked back to the car.

He headed to the south side of town and turned off PCH to the side street and Sicomoro Creek. Up the arroyo a bit was a restaurant and a small golf course known to relinquish birdies and feed deer.

He stopped well before the golf course, a few turns up the road, where a city truck and its driver looked over a fallen eucalyptus tree blocking the road.

Grigsby parked on the dirt siding. The fresh camphor, honeyed smell of the exposed roots and earth filled the air as he approached a man in a city maintenance shirt, "This what they got you doing now?"

The man standing adjacent to the tree didn't look up at the comment, just grimaced, took a drink of coffee and said, "My guys are on the way."

"Don't you have a bigger mess at Main Beach?"

Now his big brown eyes met Grigsby's, "The whale?"

"The whale."

Back to the tree, figuring, "I needed to get away from the crowds. The thing doesn't stink, yet, but that much rotting meat is going to stink like a son of a bitch. Híjole." Back to Grigsby, "You got my burrito?"

"Right here," Grigsby patted his belly.

"Pendejo," he laughed. "I already got something anyway."

Two trucks pulled up: a pickup and a big box like truck with a tree shredder behind it. All the guys were practically out of the truck and running a chain saw before they even rolled to a stop.

"I gotta thing," Grigsby said.

"Do you?"

"I don't know quite yet how but I'll need your expertise at the city."

"Okay - okay. I'll be ready," Nacho said then he turned his attention to the tree cutters, yelled over the whining chainsaws. "Hey! Let's get the road clear first.

Forget the top on the hill. Stupid pendejos." He waved to Grigsby.

"Good luck with the whale, Ahab," Grigsby said and got in his car.

"Very funny!" Nacho said. "Ahab. The least you could do is bring me Starbucks if you're going to make whale jokes," and took a drink of his coffee.

Grigsby drove back to PCH. He spent a moment to soak in the ocean ahead of him at Sicomoro Creek Beach as he prepared to turn right. The waves pounded the beach with a heavy, churning shore break. As a matter of fact, at one time there was a pier here. A distinct pier with a diamond shaped end that suffered one too many storms and had to be demolished because the waves accomplished their task while the pier couldn't.

He punched the accelerator, and the rev of the engine was nearly replaced by the wind in his ears as he headed downtown.

A police car waited at the light coming out of the Collage hotel, a swanky five star whose construction rolled over what used to be a mobile home park on the beach. The traffic light Christmas treed from green to yellow to red and Grigsby hammered it.

Steering got tight and he slot-carred through the late morning light traffic. The police car lit up and pursued.

In the rearview mirror, Grigsby could see the cop rip straight down the median. The middle-of-the-road turning lanes were empty. Slick. The son of a bitch was catching up.

Grigsby held his speed until he reached a minor fork

at Dizz's Place. He turned onto the street, bottomed out on the dip, and rocketed up the hill into a residential neighborhood, no sidewalks, old trees. The sirens disappeared. He slung a few rights and lefts then parked gently in a hedge hidden driveway before a beautifully cared for beach cottage.

Grigsby waited, listening to the silence. The pop and crackle of tire and gravel was the only announcement of the police car as it rolled into the driveway behind him. The policeman exited his car with his hand laid gently on his pistol and swaggered up to Grigsby's driver side.

"I oughta kick your ass," the policeman said.

"Then you wouldn't know we've got one on the line," Grigsby said.

"Is that right?"

"Well, fixin' to be on the line."

"Okay. Okay. Good, I'll be waiting." The policeman turned and said over his shoulder, "But could you use the phone next time?"

"Right," Grigsby said.

The policeman wheeled gently to the street and away. Grigsby lit up with a grin as he backed out, popped out of reverse, and did an F1 pass around the police car with a wave and a honk.

"Asshole."

6

Now He Had One More Stop

Grigsby traveled to the furthest south end of town, passing the hotel and fallen tree again then turned into Xerces Bay. Pulling up to the guard shack, the guard glanced up and passed Grigsby through instantly. He took a right and a left after driving three blocks through the tree lined streets. A gardener was loading his truck in front of the house in question as Grigsby slowed.

"He already went out," the gardener said to Grigsby. "He left when I started across the street."

With a hang loose sign, thumb and pinkie out, for the gardener he gunned it down the street when he saw something. Stopping, he hopped out of his car and grabbed a newspaper in its sprinkler protected bag from a driveway and got back behind the wheel. A mostly empty parking lot awaited him as he passed the last of the homes. He stopped with a skid.

He parked in the lot next to a platinum pick-up. Grigsby grabbed a Sharpie from under the registration in his glove box and brought the newspaper along.

A sand crusted ramp awaited him as he strolled a long semi-circle around and down the hill toward the ocean. To his left was Robles Point thrusting into the Pacific guarding the land. Before him was a patch of tide pools and clusters of rocks at a much smaller outcropping into the sea.

Not too far out was a bright orange safety buoy bouncing in the passing waves.

Pulling the newspaper out of its bag, Grigsby took a seat. He removed the rubber band and slid it over his wrist. Then, he wrote a five word note in big print across the front page, tore it off, folded it neatly, tucked it back in the bag and tied it off.

A not-quite baseball sized rock fit the bill as he picked it up and placed the paper (with text visible) and rubber banded it to the rock. With a test of the weight, he looked out to the water and slowly worked his way out to the tide pools on the jumble of rocks, hopping big one to big one until he couldn't go any further without getting wet.

Grigsby chucked the rock. It bounced off the buoy then sank.

"Just like throwing it into second," then he leaned back on a rock the same height as him and waited. He had time.

A few moments later Ali's mask covered head popped out of the water and he yelled, "You coulda hit me!"

"But I didn't."

"You couldn't wait for me to finish?"

Grigsby shrugged.

"One's on the line?"

Grigsby gave him a thumbs up. The diver gave a thumbs up back, flipped Grigsby off and dove back under water before he would see Grigsby wave back. That done, he moved happily along his way.

At the crest of the hill Grigsby found Brodie leaning into the long wait from the front fender of Grigsby's SL.

"What?" Grigsby said.

"I see you running all over town," Brodie said. "And the suit? You got something?"

"I believe I do."

"Well, you better."

"Jesus, Brodie," Grigsby said. "Listen, this is a big one. Tell him if it hits, we'll be all square."

"This one or another. Don't matter. Because if you don't... Look, you know I like you but, if you don't settle soon your pal is going to make you fish food."

"Jesus, Brodie."

"It's not my call." He ruffled Grigsby's hair like he was a little kid then got in his car.

"C'mon, Brodie. Do you gotta do that?"

Brodie laughed and drove off.

7
Projecting

When it came to beached whales, one thing nobody wanted to talk about was the stench. It wasn't a smell or an odor but a downright stench that attacked Grigsby. Of course, 60,000 pounds of rotting flesh will do that.

Grigsby parked in front of the movie house and despite that waft of bouquet de dump, he had to look. At this point, the carcass was out of view. He left his car and walked to the crosswalk to wait for the light. In Verona Beach you wait for the light. It is not an unfamiliar sight for a tourist to leave their shoes where they were struck and have their body deposited 100 feet hence to become the same meal for the same bacteria as our friend rotting on the beach. The lights work if you wait for them. When Grigsby was a kid, they had yellow flags sitting in a box at every corner to be held high so people wouldn't be struck. Sometimes it even worked.

A straggler car ran the light while Grigsby watched the car keep on its unfettered way. The boardwalk was dotted with benches on which tourists beheld the sunshine sparkle off the ocean like bubbles bounced in champagne. What the hell kind of choices had gotten him here, waiting every day for the hammer to fall from a loan shark. If he was lucky, all he'd lose was his house.

Down the boardwalk, a family relaxed on two of the boardwalk benches. He studied the man, wife and two teenage boys, two to a bench, with that contended look, not a worry in the world. The boardwalk reached the terminal point at a small outcrop in the beach and the hulking, stinking culprit came into view. For now, the whale looked to be sleeping, nothing more.

A team of scientists worked diligently around the beast. They weren't wearing lab coats, they had on typical active beach attire, shoes, strap sandals, shorts, but they moved with purpose and excitement. They were measuring and slicing and poking and investigating all under the watchful eye of Bio, the lady he met the other night. She was the boss and matriarch, no doubt about it. He stopped and admired the fluid movement of the operation for a moment. The attention to each detail of each task by the staff was apparent even from this distance.

It bothered Grigsby that he couldn't, and Orange wouldn't, pin down the motivation for this con. Everything pivoted on the reason. Two things needed to be true simultaneously, the mark needed to be willing to risk their money for an unbelievable return and have a reason keeping them from running straight to the cops. Grigsby had an idea start to brew and wanted to get some additional information. After kicking off his sandals, he covered the rest of the way on the sand to the spectacle. As he approached, Bio looked over, "You found your way back."

"Don't worry, I'm not back to bail water."

She looked from him to the whale and back, "I don't think that's going to be a problem."

"No, it wouldn't seem so. How long before they

haul this thing off?"

"Sometimes it can take a couple of weeks between all the meetings, approvals and simple logistics."

Grigsby wondered whether and to what degree Nacho would be involved. To her, he said, "Doesn't this type of thing get attention?"

"Oh, yeah - the news will be here soon. And so will the people."

"Lots of people."

"Until the smell gets bad."

"This isn't bad?"

"Nope, and it sticks to you."

"That must be some powerful perfume. Gets you lots of dates." He didn't mean to say that last part.

"Are you asking me out?"

He wasn't but now that she mentioned it, "Are you interested?" She was cute and from the sound of it, wouldn't be a bad date. He could use a break from all this worry.

"Can I take a rain check?" She motioned to all this around her.

"Um. Yeah. Of course." God, this never changes. Asking a woman out still felt like he didn't know what he was doing. Grigsby could scam a man of his life savings but got nervous asking a woman out to coffee. Emotions are weird.

"I'm serious, I just need a couple of days before I can even think about anything else."

"Sure thing. I'll see you around."

She smiled all the way to her eyes, "You know where to find me." Bio went back to one of her team who was grad-student age. The student wore a sly grin and, by that point, he didn't want to see what transpired next. He had nothing to contribute anyway so he offered a not quite grim wave and headed back to the old theater. Which he found empty. The floor stuck to his feet, but the smell of the whale outside faded against the place's ghost smell of popcorn from days gone by. And, with that, he recognized his hunger and stopped to imagine what he could eat.

What leapt to mind was from decades before. This little shack sat on an empty stretch of PCH like any thousands of roadside stores in the rural west surrounded by hundreds of acres of dry, yellow grass. It was dirty, dusty white with a picket fence. By the time Grigsby visited, the place was like a strong faction of Verona Beach at the time: it was a hippie joint. Their best stuff came with alfalfa sprouts on deep raisin dark bread, turkey, avocado, cucumbers, and tomato. The smoothies had bee pollen and frozen fruits, frozen yogurt, or carob. Earthy. Crunchy. Delicious.

Across the highway his Pop's girlfriend had a horse she used to ride on the beach and up into the hills following trails for miles until the sun finished waiting for the earth to turn its circle.

Grigsby wanted the sandwich. That place. That time. A girl with sun-kissed hair and light lipstick, in a flowing white dress on a horse on the beach, laughing with the freedom of the smooth rocks tumbling in the waves. That place and the acres around it were now rolled over for mansions and restaurants, a golf course, and a state park to satisfy the coastal commission. Another boondoggle he lost out on.

Once he turned the corner, the Greek gyros and fries killed the stench and lit his appetite. At least he'd get some cucumber on the gyro and nobody made better fries.

How was this job going to work?

Grigsby kept running situations through his mind. This theater was an interesting take on a place for a big store. (For the uninitiated, a big store is a location to run a big con on their victims. There's a whole history to the name but let's stick to our story.) Now, Orange's big store seemed so in the middle of everything. It was in. The middle. Of. Everything. This isn't Cannes for Christ's sake, we had a run down theater. He dipped his fries in ketchup and Tabasco and wondered what the hell scheme she was up to. He'd seen a a lot of scams but not usually in those bigger numbers. Good big numbers.

When he got back to the theater, Orange was directing the installation of a digital projector.

She sat with legs over the seat back in front of her as "Cinema Paradiso" played and adjusted and shimmered on the screen: *A perfect little Italian boy popped "vafangùlu", hand on biceps, at an old guy in a church.*

She laughed and took a hit on a cigarette. "I love this film. How can you not love this film?" she said.

Grigsby looked between her and the screen and her again.

"Have a seat," she said.

"Watching movies," he said and sat in the row behind her.

"Now you don't have to go and do that," she said.

"Do what?"

"You damn well know. Knock off the power play bullshit. Sittin' behind me. Making fun of the movies. This is my show, you're along for the ride."

"You don't have a show without my help."

"We both know I do."

"But it's easier with me. Now don't you go on with the power play."

"What do you want?"

"I need to know why this mark is going to buy in. Why's he doing this?"

"I told you: He wants to be famous."

"No, he doesn't. And if he does, if that's his motivation, our little job ain't going to work."

"He's also moving stolen art and needs a place to launder the cash."

"Now you're talking. You better not hold back on me. If you want my expertise, I need to know the whole story. What's the play?"

"Basically, we set up a festival of one where Gong bids for the rights to the festival winner. It's Sundance without all the stars. We just need some characters to fill the room and drive up the price."

He could see it. Like The Sting, a big store set up with the whole audience made up of Grigsby's people, moving in and out like a well oiled machine. Maybe they could run it like The Wire with a twist. (The Wire was another old-time con used for stocks and horse racing.) In reality, this reasoning still wasn't enough but Grigsby had more immediate problems.

"I need some starter funds," Grigsby said. "Nobody starts without them."

"Let's settle down. I'll show you something." She took Grigsby into the lobby, up the stairs and into the projection room tucked up high above the rest of the theater. Between the large film projector and the projector hole, a young bleached blonde kid with tightly cropped hair screwed a platform in place with a digital projector the size of a box of chocolate. A line ran from a laptop on a lower shelf. The kid put her screwdriver in her pocket and scratched her freckled cheek. Was this that purple wig chick from the card show?

"A projector," Grigsby said. Maybe it was. Whatever.

"It's digital. No film."

"So. Isn't that the way now-a-days?"

"Yes and no but, this way, we can make changes on the fly," she said. "I love the romanticism of film, look at the movie." In the movie, the little boy sat and watched a movie flicker on an old silver screen from the projector's booth same as Orange and Grigsby (and the tech). "But we need the flexibility."

"Ok, but what about the funds?"

"I can Venmo you 5G. That's my limit."

Grigsby shook his head. "No trails, even digital. Besides, I need $7,500. 2,500 for each of them."

Orange dropped the cig on the floor, ground it with her orange Chuck Taylored toe and from the duffle in a worker's locker she pulled out a stack of bills. She counted out $7,500 in hundred-dollar bills and handed them over.

"Thanks."

"Don't thank me, it comes out of your share."

"They're in on this, they get a cut."

"Of your share," she threw the bag back in the locker. "You don't like it: walk."

She walked out and down the stairs.

The projector kid smirked and took a hit off her vape mod.

"What the fuck are you laughing at?" Grigsby said and followed Orange down. And he thought about how he could handle this.

Orange stopped in the middle of the stairs and looked back at him, "Already counting your winnings, huh, Grigs?"

"Listen-"

"Probably already spending it," she said. "Now I know why you never graduated from the short play."

"C'mon. I know better than that."

"Keep your eye on the prize, old man. It'll work."

"It goddamn better."

"You're goddamn right." She banged through the swinging doors to the theater. "You know your way out."

Grigsby stood in the lobby; his feet stuck in place.

"It's the popcorn," he said to no one. "And soda," as his sandals stuck to the carpet a little as he left with an unconscious pat of the cash in his shorts pocket.

He got some cash. Things were looking up.

Grigsby hopped in his convertible, pulled an illegal U-ey and wondered if they'd be waiting at his place or if he needed to go bend a knee.

Best to bend a knee. Besides, he looked at his watch, it's that time.

8

ON BENDED KNEE THEN THE NEWS

This part is just ludicrous. But people are full of contradictions. Things, too. We learn that, don't we, as we age? Grigsby had taken a few turns right and left in his car as he wended his way up the hill to St. Francis by the Sea, seat of bishops to the American Catholic Church. The tiny little white adobe and red tiled church was built from the rubble of the 1933 Long Beach Quake. That was the one that convinced the Midwesterners who had moved here that California was earthquake country, even more than the 'Frisco quake in '06. 1906. Southern California: land of opportunity.

He walked into the intimate sanctuary; Jesus suffered at the other side surrounded by bible scenes in colored lead glass. The old bastard he came to see was on his knees praying the rosary and Grigsby took a knee next to him. That old guy looked over, did a double take, but finished his prayer. "...and lead us not into temptation, but deliver us from evil." He genuflected, jerked his head towards outside and got up.

Grigsby followed in silence.

The old guy had come to this place because the old priest at the Roman Catholic Church on the other side of town retired and the new priest wasn't having it with his antics. The priests expected him to repent and stop with all the mobbing, so to speak. He wasn't doing that. What would he do if he stopped mobbing?

"I assume you have good news," the old guy said as he straightened his silk shirt that made him look a little like he was on a bowling team.

"Yeah, Tony." Grigsby reached in and pulled out a wad of bills from his back pocket. He had added $2,500 of his money to Orange's $7,500 and kept a little spending money for himself. Never, ever give them everything. "Here's ten grand. Sorry it's late."

"I'm glad. I'd hate for Brodie to hafta change the nature of our relationship."

"You're telling me."

"Yes, I am, Andrew. I can't let this go all the time, it's bad PR."

"It doesn't get out."

"But it does," Tony said. "It reflects poorly on me."

He was right. People see and, those with more power, judge. The gossip was: some new kid was making waves in his territory. Tony's protected territory. And the guys back East weren't doing anything about it. You ever try standing on a board on top of a ball? It's shaky and if for some reason you can do it without falling? You still look like a clown.

"What can I say?"

"Nothin'. But what can you do?" Tony grabbed a peach from the tree in this little garden. It was time.

Grigsby felt like a school kid, "Jesus, Tony. It's a church."

"It's ripe and I'm hungry. God doesn't make fruit to rot on the tree."

"The church might see different."

"Well, we both know I don't see eye to eye with them," Tony said and took a bite. Juice exploded down his chin and he jumped back to avoid getting juice on his shirt and shoes. "You can learn from this. You aren't too old to learn," he said while chewing and wiping his mouth with the back of the peached hand.

"I don't know."

"You're never too old to learn. Life finds a way."

Grigsby eyed the peach tree. Maybe there was another ripe one. That looked pretty good.

Tony grinned and looked Grigsby in the eye, "Okay, pretty good. I'm glad you came through but I'm expecting as much by Friday." He motioned to his pocket with his elbow. "If not, Brodie's taking a piece of your - whatever he feels like. There's been a run on thumbs and toes. I don't get it but he's effective."

"C'mon, Tony. Friday? Two days from now."

"Forty-eight hours. This payment was already almost a week late. I could make it twenty-four?"

"Will do."

"See that you do."

Grigsby got the hell out of that damned little church, without a peach. He forgot to grab a peach.

From the hilltop in his car he looked out on the stucco and tile beach town and sparkling ocean beyond. "Look at all this." With that many people down there, there was money down there. He just had to find a way to get it from their pocket to his.

Adding up what he had, there was the money in his cookie jar, $8G, and the $7,500 from Orange. Well, $10G just went to Tony, so he really had about $5,500. In the worst-case scenario, he needed about another $5,000 by Friday. Remember, never give them everything. Gotta find something though.

As he rolled his way toward downtown, Grigsby

drew around a small outcropping in the road to reveal the beach below. Something became very clear. The whale. The very big whale on the beach. Grigsby's idea slowly formed around that big-as-a-bus beached thing. The idea clarified as he watched the scene from his car seat high above. The amount of activity surrounding the beast reminded him of ants or, what surely would happen soon, crabs crawling all over and around the thing feasting.

Of course, there were two other distinct groups besides the helpers and lifeguards now. One group had big cameras with big lenses recording the whole spectacle in still and video. The second group had two subsets: they either stood for a few moments and moved on, or stood in front of the animal, took a picture with their phone, and moved on. That whale had a distinct ability to draw the curious, and morbid, in equal numbers.

He pulled up to Main Beach and his sneaking suspicion was right. The half dozen news vans were set up over behind the café off of PCH with the satellite dishes deployed. Grigsby nodded approvingly knowing the vans brought the onlookers in even greater and greater numbers. When a camera was pointed at an object, many people immediately assumed it was important.

That brought up an important point, he hadn't even checked what went around on social media. He cycled through and found Facebook full of links and articles about the whale, Instagram already had influencers and their selfies, Twitter had spun a whole conspiracy linking the military, industrial shipping, and the oil industry to the destruction of the whale's ears, food, and reproduction.

Interesting.

Grigsby quickly created accounts in each social media app plus a TikTok (China needed to know) and registered a domain. All the accounts linked to the Film Festival, Verona Beach style. He quickly posted some starter posts and a few #VeronaBeachWhale shout outs.

Manic excitement rattled his imagination. The quick release and responses of social media fueled a high-level energy he hadn't felt in years. The likes and shares and #'s mixed with the gifs and pics for a jambalaya of what makes social media fun and interesting. He texted his guy in TJ, Juan Gustavo, with the domain info and some short instructions to get a website up immediately. "No problemo, padron." Fifteen minutes later a small, but working site was up.

Gus text: It's up

Grigsby: It's up? So fast - How?

Gus: I do my magic, you do yours.

Grigsby: You cloned another client, didn't you?

Gus: Don't you worry about it.

Grigsby: You rock!

Gus: It won't cost you any less ;)

Now that Grigsby laid that foundation, there was work to be done, work that could only be done right now. He walked out to the beach; Bio was giving an on-camera interview.

The cameras and their operators swarmed the site, more or less careful to stay out of each other's shot. But Grigsby noticed a young producer to the side eying all the bystanders. He perched himself a dozen feet from her and coyly made eye contact. She immediately grabbed her cameraperson and the on-air talent and approached him.

"Would you mind being interviewed about the whale?" the producer said.

Grigsby demurred, "No. I don't think I'd be a good interview."

"Just a few words. It'd be a huge help," the on-air girl jumped in, flashed her smile and did her best to hide the tiger in her eyes. Grigsby knew that look all too well, from his side. He worked hard to hide his tiger while on the job and everywhere else for that matter.

"Well, if it'll help you."

"Great," the talent took over from here. "What's your name and something about yourself, like your job."

"Andrew Grigsby, Director of the Verona Beach Film Festival."

"Is that right? Very cool."

"Yes, this whale may be real trouble..."

"Hold on," she said. She could see the story now. Much better than just a whale. She had a hook now, "Film Festival ruined." He could see cogs in her head spin a little faster. Now, the newscaster had a way to link this grisly scene to the human element. It's all the audience, or anyone, really wants, after all. Think about it, how many songs aren't about love, sex, or depression? Self-centered species. "Let's get this on camera."

"Oh, right," he said.

The talent dove in, "Mr. Grigsby, could you tell us what you saw?"

"Well, I was here the other day when he - is it a he? When the whale beached. We were all intrigued and hoped to help. Now that he's died and is rotting, everyone is wondering what to do with the corpse. I'm most worried because our Film Festival may not be able to fight the whale."

"Fight the whale. Why is that?"

He was getting into this now, "Well, the smell and the attention is all headed to dealing with the whale and all the air has left the room in our town. If he was alive, I'd call him my Moby Dick." What the heck. It was a little on the nose, but local news would eat it up.

"And there you have it, Moby Dick ruins not only the beach but the small businesses, tourism and the local film festival. Back to you, Brock."

As Grigsby rolled through what he'd said and if he covered all the bases to get this festival off the ground, he walked straight into a tall, strong blond dude. The guy removed his aviators as they met and mad dogged him for a full three Mississippi. Reading that, it doesn't sound that long but stop right now and count to three-one-thousand. That's a long time.

And imagine with someone you don't know.

Grigsby actually considered clocking him in the face but something about the guy kept him from doing it. He finally worked his way around the weird blond guy to land in front of the most put-together and driven twenty-year-old he had ever seen in his life, who approached him.

"Did you say you're running a film festival in town?" she said.

"I did."

"Look, I like the way the whale conflicts with your festival and the effect on the community. Can I get a picture and take a short video with you for my Instagram account? You'll just need to stand next to me."

"Sure," Grigsby said. Some youngster wasn't going to cost him a minute even if it would never reach as many people as the news.

She held her camera above them and her demeanor completely transformed from kick ass businesswoman to cheery smiley-face.

"Hey guys! The whale washed up here is doing more damage than just the stink. Our local film fest is being ruined. I believe in saving the whales but this one is gone.

"I want to tell you: we need to save the arts and save this festival. I've included their web link and @VBFF - give them a follow and do your thing TiffTeamArmy get them known. Save the little guy. Save the arts! #PoorDickie. BeachieGurl Out."

She thanked him and left for more whale pics. But before he got back to the crosswalk, he had to silence his phone. The follows and mentions on the Instagram account were spinning up like numbers on a slot machine.

He looked back for the girl, but she was gone.

He clicked through to her account and the girl had 105 million followers. There are that many people on this app?

Well, he guessed he knew where to find her. And her followers.

9

Some Bullshit

The lobby of the theater was illuminated by the slice of light through the open door as Grigsby paused and entered, the door catching open. The lights weren't on. Orange stood in front of the scratched windows of the disused popcorn machine.

Orange was not happy.

"I'm not happy," she said. "I didn't tell you to start publicizing."

"I saw an opportunity and I took it," Grigsby said.

"My people don't like publicity. Not yet."

"Bullshit. They want to get into movies, of course they like publicity. Get over yourself."

Grigsby wouldn't allow the whole show to run through her and not have a say. It just wasn't his style and her little con wasn't going to cover the nut he needed. Besides she didn't have this thing all worked out. That much was clear.

"Did it ever occur to you that I have steps in line for this job?"

"Sure," Grigsby said. "But I improvised. I saw a shot at free promotion and a couple hundred thousand more people know about this than did an hour ago. And not just ratings, look at the account." He showed her his phone and swiped through all the hundreds of notifications of new followers lined up on the screen.

"These are before I turned the notifications off."

Grigsby kept the notifications because he needed to make the point. He knew after thinking for a minute that she'd be pissed he did this. It might gum up the gears, but there was an opening and he took it. It would work out.

Grigsby pushed on, "People know now. Did you see #PoorDickie and #SaveVBFF were both trending? We can make some operating capital. I grabbed the domain. I already gave my geek the info and he set up a site. We'll start taking money. We can get paid for the festival applications. We'll target the film schools and the damn things will roll in. Make it tiered. Pay more and we'll review it quicker. The rich ones will always pay more. Plus put in a script category. The writers always have one in the trunk they want to promote."

"We don't have anyone to review them."

"Who cares. We'll take the cash and pick one at random."

Grigsby was feeling it again. He'd been so scared lately, it felt good to think on his feet and make a decision. It was going to be alright.

"This isn't alright. I have to think about what I'm going to do. I'm not sure I want you on this job."

"You're stuck with me, kid. You said it yourself, you need a local guy and now my face is attached."

His phone rang. Grigsby didn't want to talk to the face that appeared with caller ID but he wanted out of this conversation with Orange, "I have to get this."

He walked outside, swung the door closed behind him,. and accepted the call. Before he could say a word, a voice on the other end of the line said, "What did you do?"

It was Nacho, the city guy. "Talking on TV about a festival? You don't have any permits for that. The city won't allow people in that old dump."

"I'm sure you can find a way."

"Grigsby, I just don't think this one will be possible."

"Don't forget your cut, it'll be fine."

"It'll be fine. It'll be fine," Nacho said. "Pendejo."

"See you later," Grigsby said and disconnected. With his hand on the door, the phone rang again. "Shit."

He accepted the call, "Hi, Posie." His ex.

"Did I just see you on Channel 5 news? Since when are you running a film festival? Since when do you even know what a film is?"

"Posie, I'm going legit. I have a partner with connections. It'll be huge."

"Next month?"

"Just as summer ends. People will love it."

"Well, with the job I guess you can give me some money for the kids' school."

"They're grown. I don't have to give you money anymore."

"College, you asshole. I pay for their college."

"School's for the stupid to prove they're smart. Our kids are so smart they don't need to prove it."

"I'm glad you're taking an interest in them. They are coming to stay with you for the month. Kent and I are redoing the house and we don't have room. I wanted to give you a heads up: they'll be at your place when you get there."

"Posie, this isn't the time."

"It never is."

"You're not listening."

"Nope. Just not caring. Make do."

"Posie. It's a bad time."

"I know, Andrew. I know. It's always a bad time. Just don't embarrass the kids, again."

"Why would I do that?"

"It's your only talent." Off.

He touched his chest unconsciously looking for a cigarette in his shirt pocket that wasn't there. Not for twenty years.

The kids.

Grigsby turned around to take a peek at the ocean and ran his fingers through then grabbed his hair.

Three cop cars rolled up at the front of the theater and parked in a line.

Grigsby turned around and, in his head, nearly ran inside but, on the outside, he kept his cool. The officers and the police chief exited their vehicles. A fire truck rolled to a stop behind the police cars. The fire engineer dropped blocks behind the tires as the others climbed from the cab.

The police chief with two officers flanking each shoulder passed the ticket booth, underneath the formerly grand marquis, over the art deco patterned tile courtyard to the pair of glass entry doors.

Orange met them at the entrance, “Good morning.”

Grigsby rotated and took Orange’s shoulder just inside the entry. He looked around and Bob, his copper boy, wasn’t there. Grigsby swallowed but found his mouth dry. He reached for a cigarette in his shirt pocket again and felt a tremor. Was that an earthquake? At least that would’ve helped.

“You’re not having a film festival at this dump,” the chief said.

Grigsby’s head got light.

“We have a lease,” Orange said. “We have a right to open to the public.”

Good. Good.

"Not here," the fire captain chimed in as he waved a sheet of paper. He handed it over. "This building is a fire threat, a tinder box. No public performance. "

Bad. Bad.

"Shut her down, Grigsby," the police chief said.

"Just wait a minute," Orange said.

"I wasn't finished," the fire captain said. "I'm condemning this building." Two of his fire crew walked up with their turn out pants on, suspenders over white t-shirts. One had some chains while the other had a lock, some keys, and a smirk. "We'll give you a moment to gather your things but this building is unsafe for humans until a series of improvements and inspections can be completed."

Orange squinted then relented.

"Freckles!" Orange yelled. "Git yer shit!"

Orange marched into the theater itself under the watchful eye of the police, fire, and a new arrival: Councilman Cox. Orange sauntered to her seat halfway down the purple carpeted, tilted walkway and grabbed her bag and laptop.

Grigsby stayed silently in the lobby running all the ways to get out of this with no workable ideas. Lawyers. Payoffs. Where the hell were his dirty cop and dirty city guy?

"Nobody here to help you, Grigsby," Councilman Cox said.

Grigsby couldn't stomach another fail. Cox was still pissed he didn't get paid on that one. Hell, Grigsby didn't get paid either.

"Is that what this is about? Not participating in something new?" Grigsby said.

"This is about public safety," Cox said with the look that said it wasn't about that at all.

Freckles came down the sweeping lobby stairs as Orange came out the theater doors. They met at the bottom of the stairs, Freckles with a duffel bag over her shoulder and a projector under one arm and a toolbox in her other.

"We'll follow you to your house," Orange said as she bumped past Grigsby.

"Shit," Grigsby said as the firemen chained the door closed and the cops posted condemnation notices on the old brick walls of the Olympia theater. How was he going to explain this to the kids? And the kids to Orange?

10

HOME. AGAIN.

And what was he going to do now?

Grigsby stewed as he drove his car alone back to the house. He half hoped Orange and her acolyte would get lost on the way but there was way too much cash at stake to let it happen. So, he slowed whenever a stoplight turned red behind him, or a pedestrian crossed PCH stopping traffic.

He hit the remote and parked his car to the right side in the two car garage. The hard top was hoisted near the ceiling and awaited placement on his SL in the middle of his garage. His perfectly clean and nearly empty garage. The floor shone with only a single, dusty 5-gallon paint bucket in the corner and the exposed time-worn wooden studs framing the walls.

Orange pulled right in like she owned the place. And Freckles knocked her head on the hard top when she exited Orange's orange sixties mustang.

Grigsby waited for them, then opened the private garage door on the left side of the wall into the courtyard.

They entered that cloistered courtyard, deep green grass, white walls, border flowers and the two women screamed. Hanging from a large limb of the Ficus tree near the center of the courtyard was a young man. A noose around his neck.

"Grigsby!"

"Oh my god!"

"Where's your sister?" Grigsby said and walked straight into the house. Orange and Freckles looked at each other.

Grigsby slammed the door behind him.

The young man opened an eye. Black makeup darkened the underside of his eyes, his cheeks were rouged, and his lips painted a purplish color.

"No shit," Orange said.

"Pretty good makeup, actually," Freckles said and followed Orange inside.

"I suppose I should give you the tour," Grigsby said as he waited. "Let's start below."

"Grigsby," Orange said.

He walked through the entry, took a right, reached over and plinked the stand-up piano key like an eight-year-old, because he couldn't resist, then headed down the stairs. They followed him past the Virgin Mary in the alcove wall shelf to find a young woman in tight black plasti-leather jumpsuit at the bottom of the stairway. She let loose an arrow down the hallway, out the back door and through an apple placed upon the head of a mannequin already carrying five arrows.

"Didn't I ask you not to shoot that thing in here?"

She ignored him and walked to recover her loosened arrow plus the others.

"My daughter-"

"It's Katniss," she interrupted.

"Right, Katniss," Grigsby said. "To the left is my office and out the door past - Katniss - is the beach."

"This is all very nice but what the fuck...," Orange said waving her hands. "...are we supposed to do now, god dammit."

"Let's head back upstairs," Grigsby said and showed

them to a bedroom on the main floor off the living room. It opened onto the courtyard with French doors. The bedroom was sixties tiki and surf themed. An ancient teak surfboard nearly the length of the wall hung with a Gidget movie poster and the famous silhouette of Endless Summer facing from the other walls. "We'll figure something out."

"Goddamn right you will. I've got a mark coming into town without a big store!"

"Not to worry," Grigsby said. "You brought me in for a reason. I have connections, we'll have something."

Orange looked at Freckles who sat on the twin bed, bounced, and immediately got up and pulled a trundle from underneath.

"We'll have something," he repeated. "Get some rest," and closed the door.

Freckles looked at Orange, "It's three in the afternoon."

A strain of syncopated music cast from the piano in the hallway. Freckles looked at Orange and they walked into the living room to find an old ragtime tune under Grigsby's fingers.

Still playing, Grigsby said, "It helps me think."

As her eyebrows bunched under the weight of her thoughts, Orange took in the room and view then said, "I hope you are pretty good at thinking your way out of problems."

His fingers kept on running as Grigsby said, "You have no idea." He focused on his music and ignored his guests.

While he played, Freckles settled on the couch to listen and swipe her phone while Orange stepped onto the balcony and pondered the ocean. Working through the notes of a song his fingers knew better than his conscious mind, Grigsby meditated. He allowed his mind to roam free. This relaxed concentration always allowed him to formulate his next steps. He moved off the main melody and began dancing around the song's key of F and imagined what he wanted the end game to be. How this could all come to fruition. An arrow only has a chance of finding its mark by aiming for that target. Magical thinking wouldn't cut it, but creative faith would. Hope backed with action made dreams concrete. Picture the money, the kids and the grifters, even the boys, all celebrating the payoff. Imagine the feeling of having made it all happen, sitting on his patio. Everything just beyond his mind's eye while his fingers rallied over the keys.

A bonk broke his train of thought as he looked over to Freckles with Grigsby's acoustic guitar in her hands and a whoops in her eyes. She had picked up the instrument and unintentionally hit it on the table adjacent.

"It's there for playing," he said.

"I don't know how," she said as she investigated and plucked a few strings.

The hammers battered the strings of the piano again as Grigsby said, "You only learn by doing."

Freckles plucked and Grigsby did the same, although with a more practiced approach. He pictured his scene of success and worked his way backwards, following each strand of the braided rope to the string from which it began. The rope that would either tether his boat to success or hang him.

11

Morning Mayhem

Grigsby opened his eyes to the shrieks of seagulls outside, stomping feet downstairs and pots falling out of the kitchen cupboard.

He instantly regretted allowing all these people into the house. Allowing. That's a joke. As if he had a choice. He rolled to his feet without another thought and headed dead red, straight downstairs.

All four of these extra people had foraged in the kitchen. Coffee grounds were spilled on the counter, three empty dirty pans sizzled on the stove and wasted orange peels piled in the sink. Grigsby turned off the burners then he closed his eyes for patience and opened them as he crossed into the dining room.

There was a full breakfast spread. All the mess from the kitchen was laid out like a cooking show on the dining table. Plates of huevos rancheros, pulpy fresh orange juice, warm tortillas, and cups of hot java.

The large painting was off the wall and the beginning of a movie flickered over the plastered white. Katniss had set up a mini projector to her phone with her brother, Orange and Freckles gathered to watch.

"What's this?" Grigsby said.

"Have an eat, Grigsby," Katniss said, pausing the vid.

Orange laughed, "She shot it for class and we wanted to take a look."

Grigsby grabbed a plate and a tortilla and turned to watch. "I never see these."

"You never ask."

"Bullshit."

"Well, not like her."

"Just hit play."

A black casket lay on a small hay wagon pulled by a fleet of turquoise, white and salmon Vespas surrounded by lichen covered headstones and ground hugging fog in an old cemetery. Introduced by the hum of the stylish mopeds, a short horror film mixed Gothic and beach culture telling the story of a corpse and a graveyard and a carriage. Eventually someone gets brained with a shovel and the executioner knows every soul in the place.

"Funny and scary. It's not half bad," Grigsby said.

"I call it Surf Goth," Katniss said.

Grigsby laughed, "I bet you do."

"Not bad, kid," Orange said.

Freckles hopped up, "Can I check out that projector? Is it Bluetooth?"

"Yeah, check it out," Katniss picked it up, "and I can carry it in my little pocket purse. The quality is fine up to about 20 feet."

"Slick."

With a smirk, Grigsby cleared some dishes to the kitchen running the images of the flick through his memory. At the sink, he only slightly frowned at the effort to find a spot for the plates amongst the hurricane that had landed.

He felt eyes on him.

A glance into the courtyard revealed Brodie there, silent in the corner leaning between a folded ping pong table and a potted dwarf lemon tree.

Grigsby went out, "For Christ's sake, I gave him an installment yesterday."

"And you owe another tomorrow," Brodie said. "Nice table."

"Fuck you. Why don't I play ping pong with your eyes?"

"Hey, don't blame the messenger. I figured with a full stomach you'd have a better disposition."

"Well, I do have an idea..." he said changing gears. Grigsby tells Brodie they've got a new con but he's got an extra idea. Why not? This will get Tony off his back for a minute. "We're making a movie and isn't Mary, Tony's daughter an actress? Maybe she can star?"

"That's what you got?" Brodie said shaking his head. "I'll run it by him."

“That’s all I ask.”

“But you still got two days.”

“I thought it was tomorrow.”

“Whatever,” Brodie said and picked a green lemon. “I’m just the muscle.” Then tossed the lemon to Grigsby and slipped out.

Grigsby followed him out with his eyes, “You didn’t have to do that.”

He looked at the tree and grabbed a few fallen leaves out of the pot. Grigsby shined the unripe fruit a bit on his shirt and started inside. “It’s not ripe. He didn’t have to do that.”

Now Grigsby had to figure out how to produce a piece of shit movie and a film festival. He’s gotta stop improvising.

Orange waited for him in the hallway, “You’re in the lurch to some big shot, too?”

“No, no. I got it. Trust me,” Grigsby said, eyeing the Virgin Mary in the alcove. “I’ve got money that is better in my hands than his. This money works for me. It’s my retirement. People don’t pay off their mortgage with their 401k, why would I get rid of this debt?”

“Because he’ll kill you.”

“Corpses don’t pay, Orange. Never forget that.”

“For fuck’s sake.”

Grigsby changed tack, “This is perfect anyway, with Tony involved we’ll have funding so your mark won’t be as spooked."

"Who said my mark was spooked? Don't start making things up to cover mistakes already. Besides, my mark doesn't share," Orange said assessing that Virgin May statue.

"Well, we'll work it out."

"Will *we*?"

"Of course," Grigsby passed into the kitchen and set the green lemon on the window sill.

"What makes you think you are going to stay in it?"

"You have nowhere else to go, Orange."

Grigsby had done some digging and for all her bluster and talk, she had talent and some skill but her track record was, lets say, she hadn't hit the trifecta let alone the daily double. This was the biggest j.o.b. she'd ever sniffed and the largest target Grigsby had seen in a very long time. This fish was gonna get boated. He had the team and a place to run the job was the least of their worries. They were in one of the most beautiful places in the world. If they couldn't find a spot here, they couldn't find one anywhere. In fact, if they couldn't find something here, they should just get out the game because they weren't worthy of the game.

And if there was a truth to all of these cons, it was that you had to be worthy of the game. You can't cheat it. A good mark wants to be taken. They think they can get something for nothing and it was our job to make them pay for what they wanted for free. And then some.

"The game costs. It costs us and it costs the marks

but if you put your mind and heart and soul into the game, the game just might pay you back for your attention. Your love. Your life. And I'll be damned if losing a tiny theater is going to keep me from this score. We will win. We have to win. We will win or die."

"No, you'll die. I'm not in the lurch."

"That's not how these things work. We're all in it and the merry go round never stops. Life doesn't stop. It won't stop when those pert little tits of yours drop below your waist just like it hasn't stopped when my balls started dragging in the sand. Get busy living or get busy dying but don't think your beauty will last forever. Beauty won't tell you which way the wind blows."

"You're an asshole. I use my assets but it takes brains to do what I do. It's not my fault there are men who smell perfume and roll over like a puppy for a belly rub. Getting them to roll over takes a certain type of coercion you men have never understood, and you wouldn't, anyway, because you don't care to understand. That would require self-reflection. A realization that you, that all men, don't pull the strings."

Grigsby's phone rang. He looked at her with an 'are you done?' and took the call. Tony wanted to talk. Now. Go to him. Of course, now. Always now. Tony waited for no one.

Back to Orange. "Don't mix this up, Grigsby. My mark doesn't play well with others. Do not fuck it up. And find us a place, mother fucker."

After she stomped off, Grigsby thought for a sec. He really didn't know enough about this movie business. He headed to his office laptop to spend a moment hunting before he left. He needed to buy some time and interesting movie facts for Tony might be just the trick.

12

LET'S GO SEE TONY

Tony hadn't told Grigsby where to go. Grigsby figured, considering the time and day, he would head to the little church on the hill. Talk to Tony after confession. You read that right: confession. What a world. Tony's car wasn't out front of the church, so Grigsby changed course and drove over to Tony's house on the north side of town.

It didn't have to be this way. Grigsby started out with dreams. He could've been an actor or a singer. A dentist.

Instead he got involved in real estate. Which wasn't bad at first. He read the books like "Think and Grow Rich" and Tony Robbins motivational tapes, Zig Ziglar, Seth Godin. Tom Vu. He went to the seminars on how to buy real estate with no money down. So, he flipped a couple duplexes and was on his way.

Until that place over on Superior. He had found a building for sale next to the mechanic. It was a dump. Up for a song, Grigsby saw how he could fix the property a bit and sell it again. He had a perfect person to buy it, too. So, he set it up. He got the place tied up in escrow and contacted the guy he knew would buy it. Turns out he was hot and ready. Grigsby sold it to him before Grigsby even bought the joint. The escrows closed one day after the other, this was before all this technology. And, Grigsby found his business model.

He started cruising around the county tying up properties and flipping them. Well, he got through one more and the next one, then the police let him know that this was against the law. Himself, Grigsby felt it was a gray area and got a lawyer.

He called them phantom flips. The cops called it fraud.

The guy got him off with a couple felonies, served some community service, and Grigsby got a taste for the game.

It was a lot of work, but it had juice. Maybe there were more ways to make money without any risk. Other than the risk with Johnnie law.

The fraud conviction locked him out of the official financial world but, Grigsby enjoyed getting away with something, and the cash. He never looked back.

What you need to know here and now is: the money he made on those early jobs got him the house he lived in now.

It, the house, was worn and weary when he found her. But like all the beauties, she had good bones. He grabbed the place off the tax rolls when he was flush from those couple jobs then buried it in a couple double blind trusts and a maze of holding corporations that did nothing but keep the wolves at bay. Hell, his ex-wife couldn't even take it from him in the divorce. And that was all she wanted. Other than his head on a pike.

She wanted it because she thought that house was all he cared about.

She was right.

He did screw around with a couple ladies while he was learning to be a real estate agent. But Posie hooked up with that Kent prick anyway. Then moved out taking the kids.

He only cared about the house because it was all he had.

The point was though: she didn't get it.

But all the legal hiding didn't work on guys who don't care about the law. After all, Grigsby kept working loans on loans to kill off other loans. When he hit that rough patch after Posie left, well, the lean on the house wasn't with the bank. It was with Tony. Regardless of the fact that Grigsby was tight with his shark, Tony couldn't allow slackers on his loans. Tony would have his balls and his house.

It was just the law of the jungle. You pay and if you don't, you've embarrassed the boss, and the boss can't have people questioning his resolve. Everybody knew you wouldn't die in your sleep. Your eyes would be wide open, even if they were going to tear off your eyelids to do it. No open caskets.

Well, it wasn't going to come to that. Not now.

All this worry about the past didn't help the present. He parked on the crowded street a block away and walked down the middle of the road because there were no sidewalks and too many cars. At the proper house, he walked along a tall, plastered alabaster wall with a secure entrance at its center. He knocked avoiding the iron clavos dotting the arch and panels on the old world Spanish dark oak door. At that port's center, a peek-a-boo door opened with Brodie's mug looking down through the space. Grigsby smiled mouth unopened, toothless in greeting. Brodie opened the door revealing a beautifully lush courtyard. Grigsby had to convince Tony of a number of things: (1) that Orange's mark was funding a movie, (2) they were bringing in their own director and (3) wanted a young ingénue to play leading lady so why wouldn't Mary, his fourth kid with his third wife, be perfect for the breakthrough role?

"Yeah, you think she'd be good for it?" Tony said. "Have you seen her work?"

"Does she have a reel? I could use it to show her around."

"Of course, she's got a YouTube channel with her reel. I'll show you."

While sitting at the iron café table in the courtyard, Tony brought YouTube up on his phone, watched her name pop up as Waitress in some credits then a cut to her delivering a hamburger to the star of an off network syndicated show. Then a scene from a community theater production of Oklahoma.

"What do you think, Grigsby?"

"Well, she's got something there, Tony."

"You really think so?"

"Yeah. Sure. Definitely."

Tony smacked Grigsby on the back of head, "She can't act, you asshole."

"Well, c'mon, Tony. She can do something in it."

"The girl spends her time waiting tables so she can be a waitress in a shitty TV show? Why would I encourage that. She can work for me and make REAL money. Fuck no, am I putting her in anything."

"I'm just trying to help."

"Jesus, Grigsby. You disappoint me. You think you can buy me off that easy?"

"Well, Tony, maybe..."

"Shut up. I didn't get where I'm at by being stupid and a sucker. *I* pull the strings here, kid. Nobody else."

"Well, sure, Tony. Maybe I could get you in on this production."

"Hmph." Tony rubbed the bald crown of his own pate.

"We've got a top notch crew here, Tony. Sure to make a killing."

Tony grabbed a lime from a bowl on the table, considered the wedge in his fingertips. "Thing is: the only killing I see in your future," he squeezed the juice into his Pellegrino, "is yours."

Grigsby grimaced and soldiered on. “Look, Tony, these things can make serious money.”

“Yeah, but I ain’t funding Spiderman.”

“No, it’s the little ones that make money for nothing.” Grigsby needed him to get on board here, “You ever see ‘Blair Witch Project’?”

“With the snotty nosed girl crying in the camera? Disgusting.”

“C’mon. People loved it. They made it for like 60G.”

“It looked like it.”

“Do you know how much they grossed worldwide?”

“How would I know that?”

“250 MILLION DOLLARS.”

“You’re fucking kidding me.”

“No. Real money, Tony.” Here we go, “Little Miss Sunshine? 8 mil in, 101 Mil take home. Clerks, Napoleon Dynamite.”

“Those are all old. The 90’s were a different time.”

Not so fast. “Napoleon Dynamite was 2000’s.”

“Old. Times have changed.”

“’Get Out’ cost 4.5 mil and made 255 mil. That was just a couple years ago.”

“I like that one. Like the old Twilight Zones.” Tony said shaking his head. “People should read short stories more."

"Yeah, sure, Tony." Let's get back on track but he's picturing it. "Picture it, Tony. Your name on the big screen; four-feet tall big white letters on a black background." Grigsby paused for dramatic effect, summoning the credit right there with a sweep of the hand. "Besides, look at the multiples they made on those things. Just have a few things fall right, and we're in the money."

"Rolling in it."

"Rolling in it."

"Another cockamamie scheme."

This meant he was coming on board.

"Not with what we've got set up."

"I looked up your girl and asked around."

"You did?"

"It's not my first rodeo, kid. Besides, I could see this from a mile away."

"Okay." He's gotta know she's in the game. I'm dead.

"She has some hot Hong Kong director coming out to do this flick."

"She does." Or not.

"I want to make some money and I got a soft spot for you. Use some of the money you owe me to invest. I'll take 25% of gross and we'll call it even."

"I don't think I can negotiate that without everyone

involved."

"Just make it happen."

"Tony, I can't say it'll work this way."

"That's why I like you, you try to get out of it all by telling the truth. Most of these other guys lie. You just twist the truth until it fits your needs. Like a writer. You may have a future in this after all. Now go make me some money."

Grigsby got up to leave and that big blond prick who mad-dogged him at the whale news van, in his shitty aviator glasses, showed up again. Grigsby wanted the hell out of there before Tony changed his mind but that asshole took off his glasses, mad dogged him on the way past. He oughta kick his ass. Something he don't like about that guy. Whoever the fuck he was.

Grigsby looked back and Tony rose to greet him. What?

Brodie opened the door from the courtyard back out to the street without a word. Grim. Brodie looked real grim. He closed the door without even a look.

13
GRIGSBY GOES TO NACHO

Losing the theater was a considerable wrench in the gears of this job. Orange was not pleased and now, solid breakfasts notwithstanding, he had the kids, Orange, and Freckles in his house. Grigsby was used to his privacy; besides he didn't like the kids in the line of fire. For the moment, his home was ground zero.

First step: get back the theater.

Grigsby caught Nacho walking out the brick facade and cement archway of City Hall.

"Yo, Nacho," Grigsby said.

"I don't have time, Grigs," Nacho said, as he walked right past him.

Nacho had on his sunglasses, city work shirt. He carried one of those metal clipboards that opened up to all sorts of documents.

Grigsby followed Nacho as he walked down Coral Avenue. They approached an outdoor café filled with tiny 2-tops. One in particular, Grigsby eyed two sweating red, craft-cocktails and purple cabbage covered tacos that, more importantly, sat between an elderly couple with straw hats protecting them from the sun and from the eyes of passersby. The huge brim on the lady blocked her face and shoulders, the old guy had his own hat tilted charmingly like in the old black and whites.

"Nacho, we gotta get that theater open."

"Not gonna happen."

"You gotta do something."

"I can do a lot of things, amigo. This is not one of them."

"Nacho."

"Grigsby, it's way over my head. You pissed off Griffin on City Council again. Cox, we all know about Cox. Fire and Police both signed off - out of my league completely." Nacho walked, "Think of something else."

"Something else. Shit." Grigsby settled his eyes on the old couple again, the wife must've had a hard time lifting her drink with a rock like that on her hand.

"Nacho, nothing else will work."

"It's gonna have to."

Maybe... He'd circle back. Nacho wouldn't budge right now. "Where are you going?" Grigsby said.

"Something about the whale. I'm meeting that biologist, the City Council, and the City Manager down there. Go away." They reached PCH and the traffic sped past in both directions.

"Maybe I can help." Grigsby figured it was a chance to impress the rest of the City Council.

"Go away, Grigs." Nacho walked right through the traffic stopped at the signals.

Grigsby looked both ways. He wasn't risking his life for this, Grigsby knew that.

Well, not this second.

Just as Nacho hit the other side of PCH the lights changed and that pack of groms rolled through on their skateboards like a flock of seagulls. One kid popped an ollie while another rolled up the streetlight pole and flipped off it with two more kids swerving in and out. The last had his phone out filming the entire time. Filming - what a word. Not quite videoing - he captured the moving image, you know, a mov-ie. Was that just a colloquialism for a moving picture. They didn't call photographs stillies, did they?

When who does appear but Bio, right next to Grigsby, carrying three bags of bagels, a coffee jug, cups, a couple OJs and two waters.

"Quite a load, " Grigsby smiled.

Bio gathered herself and gave a sideways glance, just as she almost smiled, Grigsby took leave with a small salute, 23-skedoo, back towards city hall and she stumbled her way into the crosswalk on a green light.

14
JAH LOUNGE

The awning shade relieved Grigsby of the last of the evening sun and even before he entered the door, the smells of roasted coffee and ganja floated around him. Jah Lounge was a coffee and hookah joint, a comfortable California beach town bungalow with a mix of the bright colors of the locals with the amigos from the south and the teaks and koas of the island bruddhas to the west. Guarding the entry was an eternally young Bob Marley statue holding either a relaxed peace sign or a missing spliff. Grigsby strolled in and gave a swipe on the two fingers rubbed clean of paint and polish.

The place split evenly between the enclosed inside and the covered outdoor living room space. Café tables and chairs, comfortable sofas and armchairs blended to provide a pleasing area to visit quickly or linger longer, whatever suited you.

A small stage for bands and readings was tucked in the back corner with lights strung across the ceiling providing a glowing ambiance. Presently, a band softly tuned their instruments and warmed up for the evening show as a steady stream of customers rolled in. Before Grigsby knew it, the place was half full. The band must be pretty good.

With the kids staying at the house now, Grigsby

thought he should warm himself up to the idea they'd be around. Also, maybe he should get that quality time in without those other grifters around.

Adam and Katniss were seated on a couch mirroring each other with some sort of coffee drink in one hand and phone in the other, quietly thumb swiping. Obviously, they hadn't gotten him anything, so he ordered a cappuccino and joined them on the couch.

"Hey, guys," Grigsby said to barely a glance up. He pushed the corner of his mouth in for resolve and sat. "Is there anything you need at the house that I can pick up for you?"

Silence.

"Schools back in soon, do you need anything to go back?"

Only scales from the musicians. He didn't know how to do this dad thing. Posie always did this stuff. Hell, maybe he should just be himself.

"How about a bowl?"

They both looked up surprised and Adam popped up. "I'll go get it."

Grigsby rolled off a twenty and Adam looked at him questions in his eyes.

"I grew up in a beach town, kids. It wasn't the 18-year-olds that made pot legal."

They both accepted that, and Adam went to the front counter.

Apparently, this was not new to them. Katniss pulled a pipe and lighter from her bag as Adam came back with the biggest bud Grigsby had ever seen, that deep army green, oily with orange fuzz. Straight out of *High Times*. To be honest, Grigsby hadn't smoked in years. Really, since before the kids were born. Not because there was anything wrong with it, but it made him paranoid when he was high and depressed after. He had to be quick on his feet.

This was different though. It was some version of breaking bread. Well, let's be honest, it was literally a peace pipe.

Adam crumbled the herb, packed the bowl, handed the lighter and pipe to Grigsby with an expectant smile.

Mercifully, as Grigsby took his first hit, the band started into its first song. A Foo Fighters ditty from their first album, "Learning to Fly". How appropriate.

He passed to the left and leaned back to listen to the music while the kids smoked, drank coffee, and did their best to ignore him. Or maybe he ignored them.

His mind was spinning about how he got into this mess. The house. The kids. His marriage to their mother. Jr.

It always went back to Jr.

Grigsby paused to picture it.

"We were just stupid kids at the time," he thought to himself.

Tired of the short games and scoring just a couple hundred at most, they wanted to score real cash. Cash to pay for something more like a car or funding a long con.

They didn't really know what they needed the money for except they longed for more.

So, like teenagers who always think they are the ones who invented sex, they thought a good mark would be out in the wide open. After a few weeks of looking around, they decided on the diamond district guys. Jr. had gone with his dad to DTLA to get the second wife a gift. After checking it out, they decided these diamond guys must carry pounds of diamonds and those things're worth thousands instead of a duffel bag full of cash like at the bank. They'd seen enough movies to know getting caught at a bank involved the feds.

Grigsby, they called him AW in those days, and Jr. waited for this old guy. They cased him to come out of the building carrying a paper bag they were sure had the diamonds. Cuz he always had the diamonds in that bag. When they were casing they had watched him from the hallway up on the eighth floor through the glass walls that locked everyone behind that double paned bullet proof stuff with buzzers and intercoms.

All the physical security in the building, Jr. and AW knew they weren't going to get anyone or anything inside. It had to be some other way. When they watched that building up on Hill Street across from Pershing Square that week, the old guy clutched that bag tight every day. He left the place at 11 a.m. and had to be going to make those trades they do. An exchange.

The old guy came out of the building and AW and Tony, Jr. met him just at the door as he came out and each grabbed an elbow and started walking him to the alley past a quinceañera dress shop and a cheap electronics place. At this point, something didn't feel right but this was the plan, so he stuck to it.

The electronics store must've had its share of bangers stealing their boom boxes because they had a security guard Grigsby and Jr. hadn't paid attention to; an old guy eating a torta with beans dripping on his chest.

As soon as they reached the guard, the old guy yelled, "Artie, they're robbing me."

Old guard guy looked up and in a single motion pulled his gun and shot Lil' Tony right in the chest. AW didn't know what to do.

He let go of the old guy and grabbed Jr., who was already bleeding a gallon a minute, blood came out his mouth, like some stinking Saturday matinee.

The old security guard got his gun on AW, now saying, "I ain't got a gun to maim, puto. I shoot to kill, so better not move."

AW was crying. Tony was crying. There were sirens coming down the street and AW smelled it.

The old diamond guy, he's cursing at them and on the ground next to them is the paper bag, a tuna fish sandwich burst on the cement, oozing out of the bag in a pile of mush and stink.

AW would never forget that stench. Tony dying in his arms and his blood all over him AW couldn't even wipe his hands. He was crying and Tony was crying.

And AW wants the diamonds, "Where did he hide them?"

There is honor among thieves. Grigsby wasn't going to leave Tony.

Any decent robber would have left him on the sidewalk and saved his own skin, but AW wasn't going to do that. AW knew it was right. There was honor among thieves.

They were just going to make a score and now the cops came and cuffed AW. The ambulance carted Jr. away but those paramedics just went through the motions. They already knew the end of this tale.

To make the matter worse, they did the job up in LA and Big Tony's got no pull. Nobody was in his pocket there. On top of that, Jimmy Cap was pissed because they did this on Jimmy's turf without approval and just to ratchet it further, the old fucker from the diamond mart paid his protection every month, on time, no complaints.

Everybody's pissed off. Everybody's embarrassed and Big Tony's sad. AW is crushed. The only good for AW is since Tony Jr. died, Jimmy Cap doesn't have to finish AW, too, to prove a point.

Grigsby was carted away in cuffs, but Jimmy Cap owned the cops and things worked fast. Grigsby wasn't taken to the station; he was on his way straight to Jimmy, but Big Tony's boys intercepted on the way and paid those cops off in a way that they both took early retirement in Rosarito. Those two coppers never lifted a finger down in Mexico but to open a cerveza or bait their hook. Grigsby would never shake that one. He could never get over the fact that they screwed up so bad.

"Dad!" It was Adam who knocked him out of his

reverie, "Dad, you that stoned?"

"What? No." Grigsby pulled out of his slouch shaking his head and focused on the guitarist, how he fingered the solo on "What I Got" down near ten and twelve instead of near the fifth and seventh frets like he did and ignored the kids.

15

First Unpleasant Meeting of the Day

AW Grigsby strummed his acoustic guitar, set his left-hand fingers and plucked an arpeggio with the right; danced those fingertips over the rise and fall of the cascading strings, then - boom - he burst into a percussive, hand-muted chuck of chords, the one of every measure in time with the explosions of the waves below.

The commotion of the people on the beach and the waves crashing against the sea wall drove the music until there was a rustle inside the house that made Grigsby's gut lurch.

He set down his guitar, got up. It had been quiet in the house. All his visitors were out somewhere else.

Why are people always in my house?

That huge blond guy Grigsby saw around town with the aviators had a smirk, arms crossed with his ass leaning on the solid-state living room turntable from the 70's. The guy Grigsby'd seen everywhere. The beach, Tony's.

Ah, shit. Things were about to get rocky.

"We haven't met," the blond said removing the sunglasses, eyes steeled. "Officially." He had a touch of Southern accent but the sniff of Ivy League.

"Why are you in my house?"

"You could say this is my house. Well. Not yet." Now he offered a Southern charm smile that didn't then the unwelcome visitor stood up and crossed the room. "It's nice. This house has good bones." He paused to look out the bay window at the setting sun, hands clasped behind him. He turned, "I am Sorenson."

"This is my house," Grigsby said.

"Yes, but I own the loan."

"That's Tony's loan." Who was this guy and where was this going?

Sorenson paused and reached into his jacket pocket and out he pulled a blue and gold pen, "My whole life back home, my father was infatuated with pens and calligraphy." He turned the cap off, "Even removing the cap is a joy with these instruments." He pivoted the pen to Grigsby revealing a nib tip, when he turned it over a drop of ink coagulated on the split and rounded business end.

With the setting sun, it was getting dark in the room.

"Many people don't know this but the type of ink used in these pens does more than change the color." Sorenson considered the instrument some more. "It's thickness, the viscosity, its whole configuration affects how the pen will write as well as how long that information lasts. Some inks fade in months. Some lasted thousands of years." He looked at Grigsby now, "You know inks have been made of sap, precious metals, even squid ink? Some vibrant, some dark."

He broke his own revelry for a moment, "Is it getting dark in here?" He crossed to the hallway light switch and flipped it. Nothing happened. He looked at Grigsby silently, who returned the silence. Sorenson nodded once and continued, "I prefer rare inks. That rarity gives my documents gravitas and documents are important. An agreement between two people who have struck a deal, the signature on that deal representing the pact. A solemn pact to fulfill the duties outlined within said contract. Each party agrees to do what they say they are going to do. Often, the remedies are defined within that contract but, really, most contracts are not worth the paper they were written on. Do you know why?"

Grigsby shook his head.

"The reason a contract is worth nothing is because one of the people making the agreement is worth nothing. A contract is only as good as the people signing it. Don't you agree?"

Grigsby shook his head.

"You mention Tony's loan. It WAS Tony's loan. It is mine now. I own it."

Okay. New strategy. Let's dance. Grigsby started, "Well, I just renegotiated some of the terms with Tony. We..."

"That's done now. We, you and I, are renegotiating

our agreement. I have new rules."

"I'm sure we can come to an understanding."

"Oh, we will. The understanding is: You will pay me in full by October 1 or this house is mine and..."

"How do you expect me to do that?"

Sorenson held up his finger, "I am not finished. I have anticipated your displeasure and intent to plead your case. I have another paragraph for your contract. Would you like to hear it?"

Grigsby's turn to steel his eyes.

"Good," Sorenson paused for effect and spun his pen on his thumb. "You will pay me in full by October 1. If you don't, this house is mine and your daughter or your son will die an uncomfortable death. Your choice."

Grigsby's insides melted and a charge almost pushed his heart through his ribs with the thump.

"You'll be more apt to complete our transaction if you must choose which of your children will live. Or die. Depending on how you look at it."

Grigsby didn't move.

"Many children have it hidden in their hearts that their parents love their sibling more than the other. I'm doing you a favor. Now, they will know who is most loved."

Sorenson walked through the room, "If you do not pay up, in addition to your child, I'll take the house. As I am new to town, I hate living in a hotel and why rent when I can own?" And out the front door. *Click.*

Like a statue, Grigsby didn't even move his eyes to follow him. He fell back on the sofa then listened to the constant pounding of the waves attacking his sea wall. That persistent march against his battlements would fail. Grigsby's foundation was solid and he would handle whatever came next. He had to handle whatever it was the tide brought in. The day ended with Grigsby alone in the dark.

16

ANYTHING. SOMETHING?

Grigsby peered through the darkened glass pane doors to the theater, his hands cupped around his eyes to cut the glare, "Isn't there something you can do?"

He talked with Bob, the cop, and everything about his friend projected the negative: chin, arms, eyes. Anything to do with the theater was outside of any pull the cop had. Nobody at the city listened to a beat cop on that type of thing and Grigsby lost any goodwill there long ago.

"You know, we used to be more than this," Bob said, partly hiding himself from street view behind the ticket booth island.

"What do you mean - more than this?" Grigsby studied the condemnation notice again. Maybe there was an angle.

"We used to be friends, Grigsby. I was more than a contact."

"C'mon, Bob. We go way back." Really? Now?

"Yeah, well, when was the last time you came to the house? When you reached out for more than a favor? Besides the gigs." Bob moved next to Grigsby for more of his focus.

"It's not like that." Still reading.

"Isn't it?"

"Jesus."

"Time passes. Old bonds fray."

Grigsby put his focus on the cop, "Poetic in our old age, Bobby?"

"You know what I'm getting at. We used to have a lot of fun. We meant something to each other. All of us. Nacho and Ali, too. We were more than a crew. Now? This? It's just business."

"C'mon. Something's gotta give." Grigsby looked around at the theater, at Bob, at the world. There had to be an answer.

"It's okay, AW. Life's like that. I just had to get it off my chest." Bob's radio squawked and he got a call about a dead body on a residential street. "Probably a skunk. See ya, Grigs. Don't worry, against my best judgment, I still got your back." They slapped hands. "See you Tuesday," and Bob left Grigsby whose text blinged. Grigsby answered back: Be there in 10.

Mid-morning on a Monday. There was a touch more traffic than normal, the air with the slightest touch of heat. Comfortably warm, jasmine and salt air floating in equal parts with car exhaust. Grigsby cruised down PCH in his convertible.

Despite this warm summer glow, Grigsby held that undercurrent. His gears churned over all the moving parts of the deal, the list of problems growing, the least of which was Bob's complaints. He had the con with Orange with no place to run it. It was good but not going to be enough to save him. Grigsby had to believe the deal he set up with Tony was still good and that it appeased Tony for the moment even though it pissed off Orange. Not to mention, the festival he also just made up that pissed off Orange. Orange seemed to be pissed off a lot.

Wrap that all together and he's got no way to pay off what could be the real problem. Sorenson. So far, Sorenson didn't seem the type to actually follow through on the threat. Grigsby didn't think so, at least.

Forcing Grigsby to choose a kid. That's real God and Abraham stuff. Grigsby's no savior. But he could be out there on Highway 61 at the crossroads with a choice to make. Fact was: Grigsby did best when times were the worst.

Shit, you know, he had less than thirty days. Each time he did some figuring, he came up short on the math.

He arrived on the threshold of Jah Lounge, the morning aroma of roasted coffee and stale ganja washed over him. The Bob Marley statue had a chalk board leaned against it with September 5 and some specials, he gave the peace sign a swipe as he sauntered in. Ah, Labor Day. People have the day off, that's why there was some more traffic and some more people dotted around the lounge.

This place was a little different in the daylight, the tropical colors popped, the dark koas mellowed, the essence, and incense, created more of a yoga vibe than the rocking band / bar vibe of the other night. Books and games were stacked on bookshelves, which had fallen into the shadows before. Of course, all the band equipment was gone and a lectern sat center stage for those readings they did here, too.

Lisa, behind the counter, gave him a wave and pointed Grigsby to his boy already seated on the sofa with his own Café Mocha, a chai, and a perfectly quaffed cappuccino for Grigsby on the table. Where was Katniss? Did she not show? Is this happening already? "Where's your sister?"

"Bathroom." Adam looked up from his phone, "How did you get BEACHIEGURL to pump this film festival? And what is this film festival, Pops?"

"I don't know." This worry about the kids was gonna be too much. Grigsby's gotta get this thing settled.

"Well, it's getting traction. Have you even looked?"

Grigsby paused. His kid was talking with interest to him. Did Grigsby miss something? Grigsby pulled out his phone and with the numbers on the Instagram and email newsletter sign ups, he was sure the phone weighed more for the digits. He had forgotten he turned off the notifications after that run in with Orange.

Katniss plopped on the couch next to him, "What

did you do, Dad?"

Oh, thank, god. Was he going to be on edge about where the kids were from now on? To the kids, Grisgby said, "What do you mean?"

Looking Grigsby in the eye, Katniss said, "This festival. It better be for real. I know these people." Is that where Grigsby knew her from? BEACHIEGURL was that one who showed up on Facebook all the time. Once Grigsby focused back to the conversation he realized his daughter wasn't in that Katniss get up, either, just a tank top and shorts.

"It's real." Katniss was interested in what was going on, too? What happened?

"It should be real. Your numbers are REAL," Adam said.

Grigsby flipped through the rest of the social media he'd set up and all the platforms were flipping users and engagement. He better have Gus start managing this stuff more closely.

"I got all this from one news interview?"

Katniss looked to her brother then to Grigsby, "No, Dad, you got all this from BEACHIEGURL."

"Great, whatever. It was just a riff. I don't even think I'll follow through on it." Grigsby put his phone on the table, face down.

"Dad, you have to."

"Nah, it's a distraction."

"Do you realize what you can do with this amount of traction?" Katniss leaned in.

Adam did, too. "What a following like BEACHIEGURL's 100 million people means?"

"It means money, Dad."

"Yeah, right. Followers are just numbers. It doesn't mean anything."

"No, it does."

Adam looked to Katniss, who took the ball, "Look, you've heard about 'influencers', that's BEACHIEGURL - they control and influence what's popular on all the apps. Which means the people on the apps get excited about the stuff they are pumping. And they get paid to do it. It's a road to fat sponsorship."

"Sponsorship from national brands. You can't control what's viral and this," Adam held up his phone. "This is viral. You have lightning in a bottle."

They all looked at each other in silence.

"One in a million," Katniss said. "More. It means real duckets, Dad. Big bucks."

Maybe Grigsby was coming around. Maybe his improvisation hit. "Maybe, we could ride this wave."

The kids looked at each other, then Grigsby, and said at the same time, "If you don't, we will."

Two smiling and engaged kids looked at him expectantly. He hadn't seen that in years. Probably before puberty. *What's to lose?*

Well, everything. Everything's to lose. But there could be some winning buried in here somewhere.

"Okay, you two start to figure out what we can do with this thing and bring it back to me. Gus is on this, too. I'll send his info."

"Bitchen."

"Cool!"

If what they said was true, about stuff going viral, about all the people, this thing may get them through this, yet. First things first, however. Grigsby scraped the last of the foam out of his cappuccino, "We'll see. I have to go meet Orange."

17
THE BIG STORE

On a bench in the small courtyard before the Olympia Theater, Orange sipped some sort of coffee drink with two more steaming cups beside her.

Ali, our Real Estate Diver guy, approached from the opposite direction and Grigsby joined him in front of Orange. She gave them each a coffee without a word and waited. Grigsby's heart would pound out of his chest if he had more coffee but he wasn't going to turn her down, she was pissed enough at him.

"The theater isn't going to work. Not in time for the job." It was Grigsby.

"That's why we're here, I don't think this is going to work out. Give me those starter funds and we'll agree to meet some other time," Orange said.

"No, no, no," Grigsby said.

"Starter funds?" Ali looked between the two of them.

"Yeah, I was trying to buy off some permits. It's not important," Grigsby said. Ali let it go but Grigsby could tell that wasn't enough to appease him. He would hear about this. "We're going to a place that will solve some of the problems and add a little mystery to the job."

"Great." A statement from Orange that meant everything but.

"He's not wrong," Ali said, always the professional. "This place is special. We can only enter the property with one car, but when you see this lot, if not this particular job, your imagination will take off in directions for a million others."

"I don't need a million others. I have one. This one is on the line and it needs to be on the boat."

"Come see."

They drove south through town past the big whale art gallery guy, taco and pasta shops, a certain prix fixe restaurant Grigsby liked, the ocean view hospital, and pulled off the ocean side of PCH directly to a gated driveway the length of a car. Behind them, cars sped past on

PCH whipping them with their wind draft as Ali punched the code into the security pad. Over a hump, and inside the gates, nearly two unblemished acres touched their noses with the earthy, herbaceous scent of dry grass, sage and scrub oak. In the upper area of the property were two basic rental houses. Fifty-year-old, utilitarian wood frame containers of drab beige. In the lower area, down on the water there was a jewel. A home that started on a small cliff but finished on stilts with a balcony that extended into a pier touching the water.

Grandfathered in, this place did what no other house in Southern California did: it allowed the occupant to fish from a pier on their own home stretching into the Pacific. To top it off, below was a cemented-in ocean fed pool. Built into the hill and basically part of nature now, it functioned as both a swimming pool and tide pool. It was deep enough to swim in and contained an array of crabs, anemone, squid, some small fish, barnacled purple abalone, dark bluish-black mussels.

"This is all great, but how does this help me?" Orange was unimpressed.

Grigsby said, "We'll shack them up here, then wine and dine them."

"That's your answer. Wine and dine," Orange said. "You are a fucking amateur. I have a big fish on the line and you think something like this will impress him?"

Grigs and Ali stood in silence.

"He eats gold bricks for breakfast. He doesn't give a fuck about his view."

This wasn't the reaction Grigsby wanted. "No, but

he can stay here while we wrap him into the festival."

"Now, the fucking festival. You were a mistake, Grigsby. My big mistake."

"It's the way." Grigsby was convinced this could work out. It had to.

"It is a distraction. Before you, I had a lead, a Big Store and a closed system. A festival that was meant for one, with a guy who would bid against himself in a film auction racket and put all his money in my pocket. Now, I have the world knocking at my door, the mob invested, my lead wrapped up in a different story than I pitched and, now, a fucking house on stilts on the beach. Grigsby, this is a distraction."

"Partially, but let me tell you what I'm thinking."

Orange needed to be on board. He launched into his plan for the film festival competition. What their start was and where he imagined it going. Orange stood and listened.

At least she didn't leave.

"Here's the play: Pocket Movies."

"Are you kidding? That Quibi thing already took a shit with this short movies thing. And they had backing from the studios, Goldman Sachs and Google."

The way she looked at him, Grigsby couldn't tell if she was getting ready to poke a knife in his jugular, getting used to his riffing or flat out preparing to skedaddle. "Not like that. We aren't selling the shorts. We're selling a competition and access."

"So, we make money on the entries." Orange was

manipulating the pieces of a deal in her mind as she watched the ocean breathe.

"More importantly, we make money on advertisers." Grigsby needed this buy in.

"Ads?"

"Yep. Absolutely. Ads run the internet anyway." Grigsby moved a little closer.

"And the public votes." Orange placed another piece of the puzzle.

"Exactly." Grigsby loved the convincing. "We've all made money on March Madness. NCAA basketball is worth billions. We'll come up with a catchy name and promote the same way."

Orange faced him, "Sports are different. Art isn't sports."

"Awards are."

"Not wrong." Ali said and they both looked and paused.

Grigsby pushed on. "The top 64 compete against each other in brackets creating rounds of 32, 16, 8, 4 and until there's a final winner picked online and by the audience at the festival to be shown at Main Beach under the stars and streaming live."

Orange shook her head. "You're an idiot. I have a guy on the hook to produce a movie offering money with which we can abscond. We just need a place to run this con and we need some characters to fill it out."

"You are talking about one guy's money. I'm talking about everyone's money."

"I'm not ready to walk from my player."

"Don't you get it? You don't have to. If this goes the way I see it, we can work him for more. It makes us even more legit."

"Who says I want to be legit?"

"Nobody, but don't you want be remembered?"

"I just want to be rich."

"We could be legends."

"We could relax and retire."

"You're too young for that. I'm too young for that, for Christ's sake. They'll tell stories about us. About how we reached for the stars."

"And burnt our wings. Icarus, remember?"

"Better than grasping mud."

"I just want the cash."

"No, listen, we scam your guy. But we can scam all these little suckers and scam these advertisers, too."

"Too much. Too many people."

"That's where you're wrong. All these people create our cover. It'll seem like no single one of them is such a big piece of the pie when everything else helps to fund it. The focus scatters."

"I think you're full of shit."

"Get your investors here. We'll get this rolling. They'll get excited. It'll buy us time." Grigsby stopped. He had a deadline. Like: Dead. Line. "But not too much time. We gotta close. Everything done by October 1."

"Now you're finally talking."

"Let's get some cash."

It would work. By the time they were done, they all had those little $$ symbols in their eyes like an old Merry Melodies cartoon.

Grigsby hoped it was enough.

18
THE SNOWY PLOVER

Every first Tuesday of the month at the Snowy Plover was Jazz night. It was a night Grigsby looked forward to more when things swirled like they'd been swirling. A chance to check his mind out of his problems and enjoy the music. The place was mostly empty when he arrived and, as he sat at the piano, a soda and lime appeared on the table next to the instrument. It didn't really 'appear', Sharma was adept at coming and going without you barely noticing, like she had done now.

Grigsby took a sip and gave her a wink as she worked her way back to the bar and gave him a smile. The place was small and all wood. Rough wood walls that absorbed more music than just about anyplace else in town but the hotel. Generations of drinks and dancing made the comfortably spaced chairs and tables shiny and smooth. He dropped a paper set list on each of the three music stands next to the drums, bass and an empty chair. The others must be in the bathroom.

As Grigsby began to tinkle the keys, Bobby took a seat at the drums and knocked the tap and hiss of a beat for him. Bobby had barely finished two bars when Nacho laid down the bass line on his stand up with a grin and a nod to Ali as he sauntered in with his sax already hanging off his neck. By the time Ali made it to the center of the small dance floor he was noodling around the melody Grigsby had been playing for Take Five. Bump bump baaaah bah bump. They knew the arrangement and settled into the song like putting on an old hat. It just fit. They worked through the head chorus once in perfect unison when Grigsby decided this was jazz not music class.

It was time for some improvisation, so he broke away from the melody and started running all over the place with his right hand allowing Bobby and Nacho to hold the bottom together while Ali took a back seat and provided fill. Little in life gave Grigsby the joy of wandering off the written song and dancing his keys between the melody. Jazz and the blues, the spirit around the notes left room to find that hook: you show them the thread then work your way through as many different combinations as you could imagine, until you show the audience the thread one more time right then and there. It was time he brought it back around to that last time through the main melody and they finished the song.

"Hello, boys!" Grigsby said.

"Hey, Grigs," Ali and Nacho said in unison.

Bobby just looked at Grigsby.

"What?"

Bobby started in, "Do you always have to just run off the reservation like that?"

"C'mon, Bobby. I was just having a little fun."

Ali and Nacho sat silent. Not this again.

"We've got a written song. We're all here to have a little fun but in the first song, we haven't even warmed up yet and you're breaking into some crazy improv."

"Sure, why not?" Grigsby looked to the other two for help. None was coming and there was nothing to be gained by picking sides in this fight.

Bobby nodded, lips pursed, knowing, too, that this was useless, "Could you just let us get our feet first?"

"Yeah, sure. Next time, Bobby. Let's take the A train." And they took off on the A train with Bobby shaking his head, Nacho and Ali meeting eyes, and Grigsby in all his glory.

Delores from the city tilted her glass to the boys. Glowing LED candles were dropped into the glass containers on the tables as a small group and three sets of couples took their seats, and the band played on. Tony came in and took a seat in the back far corner with Brodie seated at the table with him, but Brodie kept the door in his sight line.

The band worked through a few numbers and took a break. The guys went to the bar to wet their whistles and Grigsby went to Tony.

Grigsby dove right in, "Who's this guy?"

"Which guy, Andrew?" Brodie went to the bar and Grigsby took his seat.

"This guy who just came to my house, threatening me and my family. This guy who seems to take great joy in giving me shit everywhere I go."

"Yeah, that guy is now my Co-Captain." Tony didn't even look at Grigsby as he said it.

Grigsby squinted like he was trying to read something without his glasses, "Sounds like bullshit to me."

Tony nodded and, before he took a drink, "Yeah, me, too."

"Sorenson is your Co-Captain." None of this made any sense to Grigsby, he continued, "What are you going Corporate?"

"Jesus, it's a new world AW."

They were silent for a moment lost in their own thoughts until Grigsby knew it was quiet for too long. "I appreciate you coming out." Grigsby also knew Tony'd get sentimental. The boys always reminded him of his first son.

Tony pushed the corner of his mouth deep into his cheek, thinking. "Watching you guys up there, I was thinking about you and Jr. I don't know, maybe I was too overprotective of him. With his mom dying on him so young, it made me a little soft on him. Maybe he thought he was invincible."

Grigsby wasn't having it. "I was thinking about him, too. I always think about him. But, we were stupid and young. When we were that age, we thought nothing bad happened. Not to us." He wagged his chin side to side. "We did think we were invincible. Like in the movies. Who knows, kids now probably think they can dodge bullets if they concentrate hard enough."

"Yeah. You know, Grigsby, I'm not sure how long I can protect you. You see the pressure coming. Shit. They made me a fucking Co-Captain for Christ's sake." Tony took a drink, lifted an eyebrow. "The power flows until it doesn't. And I gotta protect my flank. The pressure's real. They don't like that I've given you leeway all these years but they're thinking they want more power around here and a young guy will listen to them. Me, I don't give a fuck."

With a twinkle in his eye and a smile on his lips, Grigsby met eyes with him. "Well, Tony. You know I appreciate your trust all this time, especially after what happened. But I won't let you down. This stuff's gonna work. I can feel it."

"Yeah, AW, I know, I know. That's why I like you, you're always an optimist. Not enough of those around anymore."

"Okay, Tony. I got a thing," he smiled again and knocked his head toward the piano and the three guys waiting for him, "but we'll get this right, you just wait."

"Right, Grigsby. You better get this right."

19
A DIFFERENT CON ALTOGETHER

As it happened, there was an advertising conference up at the Convention Center, so Grigsby saddled up and traipsed on over to Downtown LA. You see, there's always some sort of con going on up there.

Not quite an hour drive, he had the chance to strategize and review all his options on the way. He had the kids getting this contest started with all these shorts and people and social media. They were good at it and were going in the right direction, but he could already see the need for some people to start meme-ing on it. Maybe Gus down in TJ had some insight. There was more money to be mined here.

Orange and this investor would work but he still hadn't seen how the score would be big enough on this guy for all her consternation. She told him $500k but Grigsby still didn't believe it. She had something else in her head and Grigsby didn't have the bandwidth to figure that out at the moment.

Of course, this crazy idiot Sorenson. Even if Orange could pull it off, his share minus the cuts for the guys didn't even give him half. There had to be more lettuce out there because this Sorenson guy might actually do it. Nobody really offed people for the money all that often. When they did, it was fast. It wasn't out of any sense of morality. It was business. A corpse doesn't pay bills. A scared sucker does.

Grigsby felt like the sucker he was.

But he was on his way with the new direction. If he used all these pieces to settle his score, he could make everything right. He was on the right track. He felt it. He hadn't felt the juice in so long, he almost forgot what it was like to actually trawl a big one. That fish on the line was fighting for its life, but so was he. And AW Grigsby was sure he had more tricks up his sleeve than some stupid fish. He better have more tricks, or he was going to be swimming with those fish. Fuck, one of his kids would be.

The Convention Center on Chick Hearn Drive past Staples Center was Grigsby's favorite approach. Banners for the Kings were flying everywhere readying for the beginning of the hockey season. Grigsby liked hockey. The speed, power and precision couldn't be touched by the other sports, baseball included. Each sport had its beauty. Besides, he loved the trick of an ice sport in 100-degree summer. That's some tight showmanship and effort right there.

But who are they kidding? It's a Laker's town. There's a statue of Gretzky (and Luc) but there's also Kareem, Magic, Kobe, Shaq, Elgin. Dr. Buss was a real estate guy who bought the Lakers for like $3M. They must be worth $5 Billion today. Now, that? That is a deal. The other guy who owned the Kings awhile back, the one who scammed all those coins all those years? He was a gem. Understood the fun to be had, even swung that deal for Gretzky. That guy did his time in the slammer and sold the team. Gretzky even visited him in jail. You know he's a good guy when a star comes to jail for a visit.

He forgot Bob and Chick had statues. Those teams

were nothing without a voice to promote them. But De La Hoya? Boxing ain't what it used to be. Grigsby loved the fights and, despite his chosen vocation, he hated the fix. Nothing in life matched the excitement of one athlete against the other in a test of their abilities, pushed to their limits. The excitement was out there on the ledge, that's where you learn what the core of a person is; on the precipice.

It's like seeing those kids during March Madness. Nothing more exciting than watching teams climb the brackets to get to the Sweet Sixteen, Elite Eight, Final Four, National Champions. The people who care about those things get so caught up in it they ignore work, travel to the games across country. Sports create community. Sports create fans. That competition creates dedicated, interested fans.

Anyway, Grigsby parked in the underground garage, walked the intermittent striped walkway out past the Staples Center concourse to the Convention Center. The glass main entrance always reminded him of a huge aquarium. Like they set the whole thing up just to watch and grow the biggest batch of animals, the greenest batch of things you've ever imagined. Fish, plants, widgets, money. They all sparkled under the huge banks of LED lights.

Groups of men and women teemed into the main room like schools of fish colored by their particular cotton blend logo-ed polo shirt trailed by their rolling cases. These were mostly product and service vendors ready with the brochures, PowerPoints, and tchotchkes for the masses.

Spotted between the corporate groups were two entirely different species. One group consisted of individuals who looked and peeked but rarely struck. Like the sea basses of the world, they mostly just bided their time. That batch were probably the reluctant freelancers who knew they had to be there but couldn't bring themselves to swim with the groups.

And then there were those who were clearly sharks. Fast, clean and strong. Ambitious with the killer instinct. Not too many of these but the keen observer could pick them up moving with purpose through the crowd.

Double checking the branded event app, Grigsby discovered where the social media panel was. The room was well attended with agency types, who discussed influencers and branded content, blah, blah, blah. He got it. They became a little famous then conned an advertiser into paying them for an endorsement.

Then he went to some room discussing the new world of advertising where authenticity was key, blah, blah, blah. What a bunch of blowhards spewing buzzwords to impress each other to a room filled with desperate people looking for a tiny clue to climbing out of their pit of debt, misery and frustration.

Here's the clue Sherlock: get out in front of them instead of wallowing in the crowd.

He spent enough time in each panel to get the gist. Their slant. When you know the rules of the game, there's no drama in the outcome. No big reveals.

New game, same rules. The human heart wants what it wants. Despite all our protestations of rationality and analysis, eventually, our decisions always come down to emotions.

Star Trek's Spock was a beautiful dream, but alien. Grigsby would never have made it this far in the life he led if people didn't eventually default to hair-trigger, deep-seated emotions. In any case, always diligent, looking for new information, he walked the floor full of software-as-a-service companies and cheap offshore produced direct marketing toys, pens, mouse pads and the like.

What a waste of time.

The last panel he slipped into was about movie marketing and tie-ins. Basically, they bragged about how the movies get free stuff from marketers and marketers get their stuff in films so they can be cool-adjacent. There's no endorsement like Tom Cruise drinking a Pepsi while saving the world from terrorists. What may have been the most important thing he learned in the panel was Kate Schroeder. She was the head of production at Warner Studios and this woman kicked ass. She was wrapping up, "In the end, what I find intriguing is not how we can make money off each other, that is readily apparent. I love the fact that we can create some sort of synergy, brand building, that will elevate both of our products by association with each other."

"What a terrific thought to end on," the panel lead said. "I'd like to thank our panelists..."

Grigsby dipped. But before he forgot her name, Grigsby looked up the production head and sent an introductory email to her at the studio. He found their naming convention, which happened to be first.lastname@ and sent her his pitch about the festival. You can't go swimming without getting wet. He saw that one in a movie once and that guy made it out alive, so Grigsby had to believe there was hope even if he knew life wasn't a movie.

It was too early for a drink, so Grigsby went to the coffee bar. He got a small coffee, black, and surveyed the space.

Sitting by herself was a lady he had exchanged some small talk within the Ad forum earlier. She worked for a large, packaged goods company that had more money than Bezos, which in turn meant they had more money than God.

He thought he'd try something out. See if he could apply some of all this newfound knowledge.

"Lawanda," he said standing across from her. "Do you mind if I sit with you? There aren't any seats available."

"Oh, sure." She went back to her phone, swiping the emails that surely piled up while she was away.

"I don't mean to be presumptuous, but I like to say what I think."

"Okay." She looked up with a question in her eyes.

"You seem so comfortable in this setting."

"I've been doing this for fifteen, no, eighteen years now. I've seen it already." Lawanda went back to her phone.

"Well, I'm new at all this and I was wondering if I could ask you something?"

Surely. She didn't look like she was going to take the time for this, but Grigsby had never lived on low hanging fruit.

Grigsby set himself and took the shot, "How do I get started?"

"Well, you're too old to go back to school!" She laughed. Good. Let's loosen things up.

"No, what I mean is," he couldn't be too self-assured here, not yet. "I have an event that we've been setting up and we'd like to get some sponsors."

Anybody who has done anything for nearly twenty-years likes to be an expert, "Well, usually for a small event like that you can engage with local places like restaurants and construction companies. They are often happy to help."

"That is a good place to start. However, we're looking for a more substantial partnership."

"Is that so?"

Here's where it starts to get good. But wait for it. She's now transitioning from expert to questioner.

"Our event is blended online and in person. We have significant traction with followers and influencers."

"What type of traction?" She doesn't know it, yet, but exactly the kind she needs. Let's set the hook.

"We've launched and have over a million followers across each of the different platforms with endorsements from KewtieBae and BeachieGurl driving engagement."

"That's impressive. How long have you been promoting?"

"A week."

She almost jumped out of her shoes. This was what she needed. Viral. Hot. Engagement.

The reel spun. *Vvvvvvvv.*

"What is it you're promoting?"

"Pocket films."

"What is that?" She leaned forward now. She engaged and the hook felt good.

"We have blended a film festival with a tournament competition like March Madness."

"So, you've matched competition with a deadline." She had leaned in and now she sat back. Wanted to fight the feeling. Wouldn't give in.

Reel her back in.

"Yes, but even better, the prize is fame and fortune. We have a big-time producer on board to develop and produce a feature film from the winner."

"Really?" Lawanda sat a little straighter.

"And our most engaged market is 15-45."

"Really?" Her head tilted.

"And what we need is a partner to share the spotlight."

"Really?" A tight grin.

"Someone with the clout to enhance our image and be made cooler by association with a vibrant, new, underground competition that will highlight a younger demographic."

"Umhm." Now an eyebrow.

"Our competition has traction, eyeballs and will be the American Idol of movies. Full user engagement, all tied together with content, interaction and voting. Trust me, the number of impressions is astonishing."

She had the sparkle Grigsby knew so well. He continued, "Did you know that, already, our users not only return multiple times a day, but our analytics show that they spend up to 2 hours per visit?"

"That's better than Instagram and twitter."

"Nobody's seen this since Friends and Seinfeld. Pre-Internet. It's like having the golden age of television back." Grigsby heard that one today.

"It is."

"A place to promote and impress a group of people that will never return to television, distrusted social media and needs a place to entertain themselves while soaking up stories and myth." When a boulder rolls downhill, there's no stopping it.

"Wrapped up in a package with a built-in climax."

"You got it."

"So, do you. What are your prices?"

If he wasn't a pro, he'd celebrate inside but no hurry, no pause. "Our gold sponsorship starts at $150,000."

"That's nice. If you have what you say you do, we want a premier sponsorship that also includes branded skinning and exclusive advertising. Send me the links."

"Well, exclusivity raises the stakes. We could do it for $1 million."

"Send me the paperwork. And the links." An alarm bee-booped on her phone. "Oh, shoot. I have a meeting that was to start right now in the tent. Here's my card. Send me contracts. We'll get this going, Grigsby."

Lawanda hurried off; Grigsby watched her go.

Did he just close a million dollars?

On the boat before he knew it.

He'd worked scams before but never like this. Why did he waste his time risking jail and death when he could have been having two martini and steak lunches?

Holy shit. He had to figure out how to write a contract.

20
INVESTOR

Grigsby rolled back to Verona and went to this new Big House. He wanted to get a better feel for the place. Make sure he knew it inside-and-out on the off-chance something bad went down while there.

Know your Fire Exits, kids.

Parked in front of the cliff-side mansion was a convertible Bentley and two guys on each side of the entry, clearly packing. Mainland China guys and built like they didn't use those guns. They didn't need to. Hands as lethal weapons type dudes.

Orange walked out the front door with a gentleman, probably early thirties and soft around the middle but eyes like razors.

He wasn't impressed with Grigsby but didn't seem to write him off, yet.

"Mr. Gong, this is AW Grigsby," Orange said. "My partner in this venture."

Oof. She used his real name? He thought she was experienced and she used his real name?

He eyed her but she was oblivious. Maybe she thought this whole time he was giving her a front name? That nobody would give out the real thing, no matter what.

Was that what's going on? Had everything really passed him by? Was there no honor among thieves?

"Orange has told me you are doing some very good things for our project." Mr. Gong offered Grigsby his hand but it was a limp shake.

Grigsby shook and gave a short bow, "Yes, I just returned from an encouraging meeting, as a matter of fact."

Was he supposed to bow? Was that too formal? Why the fish hand?

Mr. Gong offered a curt bow in return as he released Grigsby's hand. Okay. Whatever was right, there was reciprocity. A con with a foreigner was a different tune.

"Very good," Mr. Gong answered. "You can tell me

more about it upon my return."

He was already in the car. Mr. Gong quietly waved as a single parting exit and was driven away.

Grigsby looked at Orange, "You brought him?"

"I figured we might as well move forward."

"He's not walking?" They were still in front of the house.

"Not yet. He's made money in many ways in China and tech is one of them. He wasn't scared by the expansion."

"Wait until he hears I already signed a million-dollar sponsor."

"You signed what?" Grigsby sure liked to see that smile on his partner in crime.

"Well, promised by a big time marketer. This stuff is way easier than the crooked way we've been doing it."

"Apparently."

"I'm a quick study," Grigsby grinned. "By the way, do you know how to write a contract?"

21

INFLUENCERS

Looking at it, Grigsby had some runway left but it was tight.

Based on Sorenson's deadline, he had twenty-three days to pull off all of this or he would lose. He could handle getting taken out. Great. So be it. But this thing about taking his kids out? It just ain't right.

Grigsby took some solace from the idea that this online route might be the answer to closing the gap. At the very least, if he could swing the cash from this advertiser, his runway expanded from an aircraft carrier to an air strip in the jungle. Bumpy and difficult but not impossible.

The next important step involved Grigsby looking online for contracts, piecing them together like piecing together a broken vase with glue. Orange was no help. Then he realized he didn't have to do it.

Maybe he could even help out another local. Arlo was an old-timer Grigsby knew from the hotel. They had spent a fair share of nights sitting at the bar, drinks in hand, laughing at stories together. One time, Arlo brought in some sea anemone from a dive and convinced Grigsby and the barkeep to eat it with him. Arlo loved it but it tasted like slimy, sandy tide pool to Grigsby.

When Grigsby decided to asked Arlo to write

something up, Grigsby figured it couldn't cost more than a couple grand. Plus, he'd only need one contract with it being an exclusive deal.

A hanging bell rang as Grigsby opened the prefab dark wood door to Arlo's office and before he even shut the door, "Grigsby?" A man with white hair and a voice that sounded thirty-five met Grigsby in an empty reception.

"Arlo, I have something for you."

"Did you get yourself in trouble? I'm not a criminal lawyer, Grigsby." Arlo led him into his office proper.

Grigsby followed, "This is legit. I have a film festival in town."

Arlo took a seat and indicated one on the opposite side of his desk for Grigsby, then said, "I'm not one of those trust fund kids. I still have to earn my way."

"This is paid, Arlo." The office was tidy, not layered in dust like so many movies. Arlo had pics of his family on the beach, in the mountains, grandkids, a law library bookshelf, some puzzle-type knick-knacks.

"If it's paid, I'm listening."

"I have a big sponsor who wants on board but what do I know about contracts?"

Arlo laughed, "You know less than a con in court."

"I know that. It's the reason I'm here. Can you write up a contract that'll look like I know what I'm doing?"

"No." Here Arlo leaned forward and got serious. "But I can write up a contract that'll look like you know how to hire someone who knows what they are doing."

"Well, that's what I need, Arlo."

"And, that's what you'll get. Lay the details on me."

Grigsby had been running the details through his mind but besides Orange, he hadn't pitched the job. He hadn't worked out the flow of the story yet, but he jumped in. "We're running the film fest and most of it is online. They compete against each other like in March Madness."

"Not a bad idea."

"Right?!" He couldn't help liking the positive response to his idea but he kept on. "So, we got a heap of attention because of the whale."

"That smelly thing?" Arlo said as he pulled out a yellow legal pad and settled a pen over it.

"It does smell awful, Arlo." Grigsby started the ball on one of those pendulum things that transfer the motion through six other metal balls, knocking the one on the end up and down, then the other side did the same. "Well, I went to a conference and met this lady at a major packaged goods manufacturer." Arlo was bored. He didn't need the tale, he needed info. "Long story short: She's pledged a million bucks for a site skin and banners and I promised a contract."

"Fair enough." He hadn't written anything, yet.

"This week. We need the funds and..."

Arlo set down the pen. "You need the funds."

"Yes, Arlo, I need the funds but we also need it to

pay for the technology."

"How much trouble are you in with Tony?"

"It'll be fine, Arlo. If I can get this contract and the check from this lady."

"Are you incorporated? Did you do that?"

"No, I'm not incorporated. Why would I do that?"

"She's not going to write the check out to Andrew W. Grigsby."

A pause while Grigsby thought about how to fix that.

"You can't think of everything, Grigs. I'll set up a Corp real fast with you as the officers then write up the contract. Come by tomorrow to sign the papers for incorporation and give me another day for the advertising contract. I have a good draft in my archives but want to nail down some of the finer points."

"Just make sure she knows she's gotta pay the million."

"That's one thing that will be in there for sure."

Grigsby stood out of the chair, threw a real smile at Arlo. "Great. Thanks a million, Arlo."

"It won't be that much. The incorporation is $2,500 bucks and the contract plus negotiations will be in the five thousand range," Arlo said as he got up and ushered Grigsby out of his office.

"Just make it happen, Arlo."

"Don't you worry."

What's a couple grand out of a million? Grigsby thought as the bell jingled to the open and close of the office door.

Next, when he got home and down to his office, the kids were there working. The French doors were open onto the Saltillo tile patio, Adam at Grigsby's desk and Katniss in the shadow of the blue and white striped umbrella; the ocean breeze just cool enough to soften the sun's sparkle.

Grigsby got his chico in TJ, Gus, on the horn. He put him on speaker in case the kids had something to add. The kids, Katniss and Adam, were scraping entertainment sites and writing content on their own but Grigsby needed Juan Gustavo to expand this thing. Gus told Grigsby with the astonishing amount of traffic, with the additions and changes, Gus needed to up their technology: Web hosting, SSL, CDN (set up a content delivery network) with more than their own server stack for the videos. They needed more bandwidth. They were going to be carrying big images, huge video files, in addition, a million users at a time means a heavy load on content and the databases. Maybe another couple grand a month in tech. No problem. Another 50G in developer and engineering time. So be it, gotta spend to make, right? Cost of doing business.

Grigsby was getting pulled off course to someone else's needs. Hold on. "Gus, the reason I called: do you have anybody who's a meme factory? We need people to promote this thing," Grigsby said. "We have a solid start but we need to go viral."

"You're already viral, padron."

"No, really viral."

He could hear Gus shake his head over the phone, "Bro, just get the users to do it for you. Make a game out of it. If they get enough likes or karma or some other type of online thumbs up they get different kinds of badges, stars and shit. Not all the users do it but the ones who care, really care. They go to big lengths to get that in-app stuff. Exclusivity. Those things, the badges, are like Gucci and Ferrari to them."

Katniss came up behind Grigsby, "Like Reddit."

Then Adam piped in, "No, more than Reddit. Have you seen how they gamify the apps? Old ones like Clash of Clans and Fortnite? Let alone Mob Boss and a million other games. Honestly, did you know Minecraft sold to Microsoft for $2.5 Billion?"

"No shit. There are things you have not even dreamed of, young Grigsby." Katniss.

"No shit," Gus piped in. "That stuff is better than social media. The users invest their creative energy, receive social recognition and carry badges of social proof."

"So, these people are making a billion dollars based on gold stars from their teacher?" Grigsby said.

"In a word, yes." Adam grinned. Grigsby had been doing this all wrong.

"On that front, Grigs," Katniss said with a daughterly grin at Grigsby's scowl. "BeachieGurl reached out to me. She wants some money as an influencer to be pimping the fest."

"She's getting us a lot of attention," Adam nodded.

"We can't have the spigot turned off, Dad. Plus she got a line on big players like Kim Kardashian and Christie Teagen. They cost big money but are worth it."

He told the kids to make the deal. They were going to be rolling in it with all this attention. In no time, they'd have singers and stars on this train. No one will be left out, jumping on his fame bandwagon.

This momentum was good. Grigsby didn't want to have all of his eggs in one basket. He would spread the work around. Multiply the chances to make money. One of these schemes was bound to hit. Grigsby could keep Sorenson at arm's length until he could figure out how to get rid of him. For himself and for Tony.

22

ORANGE AIN'T HAVING IT

Grigsby came up the stairs to find an electrician working on the light switch in his hallway, "What are you doing here?"

"Are you Grigsby?" The electrician put his needle nose pliers in his leather utility belt and reached into the back pocket. "Sorenson told me to give this to you." He handed an envelope of high-quality paper with AW Grigsby written in a calligraphic script in brown ink. "He says he doesn't want his house burning down so I should fix this electrical problem. You know, he's not wrong. Faulty wiring-"

"I get it," Grigsby said. "Who's paying?"

The electrician, pliers back in hand, tugged a wire sticking out of the wall, "He already wrote me a check."

"Fine. Fix it and get out."

Walking to the balcony, Grigsby wondered why Sorenson needed to add insult to injury. It just wasn't how things were done. When he tore the letter open, there were two perfect symbols and writ large: *22 Days*.

As if he didn't know.

Dropping the letter on the patio table, he looked to Orange on the outdoor couch flipping attention between swiping her phone and watching the ocean sparkle. Did she just let that electrician in the house, no questions? He asked her.

"No, he was messing with the panel outside when I got here. I figured you called him out," Orange said. "Faulty wiring is dangerous, you know."

"I know, I know." Grigsby focused on the simple motion of each wave following the other down below.

Orange focused her own attention on him, "Gong plays it close to the chest."

"I can see that."

"But he's skittish with this competition. That skittishness is making me skittish."

"I've been saying all along, everything can work

together, Orange."

But still Orange ain't havin' it.

She said so. "I ain't havin' it."

"C'mon. What's changed? We've been over it. Some movies are single shot, some are animated. Horror, comedy, drama, romance."

"Good. Great." She swung her feet solid to the ground. "And Gong might like the exposure, but he wants to make a movie."

"We can fund it with this. People're paying a hundred dollars to enter. Think: with a million users, that's a hundred million bucks! We could make one of those superhero movies for that."

Orange was at the end of her rope. "You are an idiot."

Grigsby just kept on. That's all he knew how to do. Hustle was all he had. Persistence. One step then the next.

"On top of that, we're auctioning off a spot in the top 64. For charity. It's easy enough. Like the old rag, they can make the check out to the Catholic Association of Sister Helena. C.A.S.H. for short."

"Are you for real?"

"Of course. The highest bidder. Tracked in real time. Online auctions are gold. Just ask eBay. Shoot, ask Google about those AdWords."

"You are so off course." Orange's eyes were on the ocean, pondering. Removed.

"There's more," Grigsby said. "The kids thought this

up: We also charge the advertisers for short films. 'Consumer Generated Content'."

"To get ideas for their company."

"We sell them competitions along the way. They pay extra and they get pocket ads for their product. The kids get a portfolio piece, the sponsors get content and we get cash. The less to deal with those ad agency shmucks I saw running around that conference center."

"Are you capable of focusing and implementing one idea at a time, Grigsby?"

Walking inside to avoid answering the question, Grigsby saw the *22 Days* letter on the table. That son of a bitch. Grigsby picked it up and put the letter in the junk drawer next to the sink in the kitchen. Sorenson was going to eat these letters when Grigsby made his payment then he unconsciously centered the kitchen faucet to stop the drip, drip.

He wandered out of the kitchen.

Orange studied him, exasperated once again, "Haven't you ever heard of focus? You know, Warren Buffet says focus is the key to success."

"Warren Buffet has always had money. Family money got him started" Grigsby pointed at her from the middle of the living room. A little hot. "When you're like me, you have to make a lot of bets. None of us is Midas. Not everything you touch will turn to gold. If I focused on one and it fell through-" Then cooled. He raised an eyebrow. "XX's for eyes."

"The plan B's are gonna screw this deal."

"The plan B's are the reason we will seal this all up. I wouldn't have made it this far without doing it this way."

"But what got you here may not get you there."

Enough of the roundabout with her. "How're things with Gong? Really. Not the pussyfooting."

"Like I said, he holds his cards close to the chest." Orange got up and came to him in the room. "I can't tell if he likes the idea of a Hollywood studio or if it gives him indigestion."

"Depends on what he had for breakfast. He'll buy. In the end, he'll buy."

"He doesn't even know what he's buying anymore." She patted his face, walked past. "Focus, Grigsby."

Grigsby nodded his head in the affirmative. "Focus."

She continued toward her room. "Of all the schemes I've been wrapped up in over the years, you have created the most hell-bent mess I have ever had the displeasure to experience."

"Ain't it great?"

She closed the door.

Grigsby walked downstairs and mulled the situation some more. All of this was okay, but still not enough. He flipped all the ideas around. Moved each chess piece in his mind. Grigsby made the decision he wasn't manipulating Orange enough. Maybe, he had too much respect for her. Orange needed to dream about more than money. She needed to dream about movies. She needed to dream about making a mark in the world instead of working a con.

Orange would need to want to be somebody.

23

GRIGSBY GETS A MEETING

Grigsby scoured the trades and industry websites lately, looking for some sort of connection with the movies. He emailed that executive, Kate, from the movie panel, as well as the rest of the executives on that panel. No answers, of course. He kept searching for a person, even a name he could use to get in the door with one of these studios. As he was ready to move on, he got an email from the competition website form and a dm on 'gram from some little joint about the festival. Some type of new media production company. The contact even used the term he coined: pocket movies. They bounced a couple quit hits and they confirmed. No shit. He got a meeting. Maybe he should keep Orange out of it.

He'd sell and deal and negotiate himself.

Didn't think he'd tell the kids either.

But he had one meeting he was going to hit first.

Tony.

Grigsby had to keep that plate in the air. He couldn't tell him about the sponsorship money, yet. Not until he had it. To Tony, the money wasn't real until the money was in your hands. If it was a check, it had to be cashed.

"Tony, I've got a meeting."

Tony sat at the painted white iron table in his walled garden and looked at Grigsby. He sipped his espresso (with a twist of lemon) then looked away in silence.

Grigsby breathed deep and decided to try this whole 'be present' thing he saw from the Buddhists. He focused on a lavender bush. The spindly leaves. *Are they needles?* He tried to smell it in his mind and watched a bee buzz the flowers. A butterfly flitted through.

This made the silence easier. *Silence is a tool. Never forget that.*

"What the fuck are you waiting for? Tell me more."

Silence is also power.

Grigsby grinned, "Some guy in Culver City. He wants to talk about the festival. The rights. How we can fund a deal."

"Is he for real?"

"He has some credits in the Internet Movie Database."

"What? In IMDB? Shit my kid has a credit there from her cousin's student film." Tony picked up his phone and dropped it in disgust. "Apparently she's a casting director, too."

"Tony, these are real. I checked the credits running on the movie." Grigsby typed to bring it up on the app.

"Any awards?"

"No, they're B movies." Didn't even look up.

"Don't waste your time. Not enough money. The studios - or awards- or nothing. And I mean real awards you can't buy. Most of these festivals are as corrupt as yours." Tony was following the flight of a hummingbird. It darted a bloom at a time.

"I'm chasing the studios, too."

"Oh, I'm sure you are." Tony motioned to Brodie. "Now, get out of here, I got a meeting."

Brodie brought a laptop and set it on the table. "It's a Zoom." Tony shrugged, *whaddya gonna do?* "See ya, Grigs."

Grigsby ignored Tony about blowing off the meeting. Grigsby was going to the meeting with the production company. How else was he going to get a feeling for the film world?

He figured it would be better to be a little more prepared. With a few hours before he needed to leave for Culver City and that meeting, he went to the house and looked through the festival website. No kidding. It really worked well.

The first two films that came up: One had a Swede playing chess with the grim reaper, and in the other, an Italian father stole a bike or something.

At least they had an international flair.

He clicked to the leader board; clicked number one before it even loaded.

Fade up: A black casket laid on a small hay wagon pulled by a fleet of turquoise, white and salmon vespas.

What in the world? It was Katniss' short. It was winning?

Grigsby was equal parts proud, impressed and incredulous.

Were they gaming this damn thing?

He looked at the comments and likes. These were real people. When he checked on the users, most had used their google or Facebook account to tie in. He could tell they were real people. Not the bots they'd have to use to drive up the like counts and bullshit comments.

No shit. She had a good run going.

*****

Grigsby parked in a shitty lot behind a dog-eared chain link fence surrounded by crumbling re-purposed factory buildings that looked like they used to be garment shops.

Great. This guy's gonna be full of shit.

An intern-aged girl lay on the purple swirl couch in the entry watching a movie on her phone.

Before he said anything, he peeked at her screen. Nice. She was watching that bicycle thief one. Maybe there really was some traction.

He cleared his throat.

She looked up, tapped a pause and scratched one of her pigtails in one motion, "You here for Dylan? Hold on."

She texted then went back to her movie.

Another young lady fluttered to an interior doorway. She wasn't much older than Katniss with silver dyed hair, knee high socks, a plaid skirt and crop top; slight shoulder slump. "This way."

She walked him through room after room of either dilapidated sewing machines or small sets with three lights and a couch. Looked a lot more like porn than film.

But at the moment he thought that, the woman said, "I know, it looks like porn. But it's not. Most of these are podcast sets. We record the audio and post the video to YouTube. Some people still like to watch them talk." Then after a few silent steps, "Plus: search." The assumption was that he would know what she meant.

They climbed a flight of wooden stairs to what would've been the manager's office in an old factory. The room was fronted by a full wall of wood paned windows with three slatted, open windows and one swinging one, also open.

The office was empty.

She sat behind a desk that probably came with the place.

"So, what's your deal?"

"Are you Dylan?"

"Why wouldn't I be?"

Grigsby thought the boss would've had a plebe come grab him. In truth, they had only emailed. Grigsby had assumed Dylan to be a man. Moving on. "I didn't think you would have been the one to fetch me."

"I would've had Eunice bring you up but I was in the can. It's right by the entry. To be honest, since we're being honest, at first, I pegged you as a little younger. This festival is a pretty fresh approach."

"We are getting solid engagement."

"I've noticed."

"Why did you want to meet, Dylan?"

"Like I said, at first, I pegged you as younger but when you accepted a face to face, I was afraid you were an olde. Our age, we just hop on a video chat, Zoom, WebEx, Teams, you know. But the oldes, you like to see people in the flesh." She looked at him, disappointed.

Grigsby wasn't what she hoped for. The meeting was over the moment they set eyes on each other. The rest of the meeting was politeness and posturing in case one of them was worth the meeting down the road.

Some meetings were like that.

But because of the meeting itself, he realized something else: this chick was full of shit. No power. Hell, she couldn't punch her way out of a paper bag. This girl was a player? Or was this an example of how little juice Grigsby's fest had? Fuck.

24

KATNISS IS A FAVORITE IN THE FEST

The heat of the summer sun beat into Grigsby's living room as the ocean breeze gently pushed the gauzy white curtains.

"Did you think you could place it and no one would find out?" Grigsby looked at Katniss on the sofa. Out of direct sunlight, she carried a look on her face like she was a toddler. One time Grigsby spent half an hour putting a child-safe catch under the kitchen sink to keep her from the chemicals. After he finished, she walked up to it; pulled. The catch stopped the cabinet from opening so she reached in, unlatched it and looked inside.

Now, her flick was the favorite in the fest.

But she can't win the fest.

She's running the fest.

"Whatever, AW." She looked at him with a sparkle. Katniss had a Holly Golightly vibe today. Hair up, perfect, pert earrings, and a little black dress. Even the sunglasses. She was feeling it.

"No long cigarette holder?"

"I don't smoke," Katniss said. "Cigarettes."

She kicked off her shoes, side-crossed her legs under

herself on the couch. She inspected Grigsby thoughtfully, "Why would you be concerned about impropriety? You aren't going straight on us now, are you?"

"Jesus, if people find out, they won't spend any more money entering the damn thing. We also can't get more sponsors."

"Square." She even made the shape with her fingers. "Perhaps I'm just a wild thing. Don't put me in a cage."

"Yeah, yeah, I know. We've all seen the movie. Very clever."

It was useless. She wouldn't win. He'll leave her movie up and let it all play out. What did it matter, anyway.

Besides, she was right. Was he becoming legit?

"Did you see what we got rolling on TikTok?" Katniss held her screen up for Grigsby. It showed an anime-type clip full of action blur and racing cars promoting the Verona Beach Film Festival.

"You didn't do this?"

"I'm going to take some credit." Katniss smiled.

"You did the animation?"

"I came up with a promotion. I took Gus' idea and had him implement a social function on the site. The users get a special promo badge on their avatar that progresses to different colors. The different colors are linked to views and likes. We have a handful of users that have already surpassed the diamond level for this promo."

"Good?"

"Yeah, Dad. Good. Those five users have brought us over five million views in the last two days."

Realizing all of this was over his head, Grigsby tried to simply enjoy whatever small signifier of progress appeared. "That's amazing! Does that mean that the promotion is over because they accomplished it?"

"No, it means we created another challenge. Adam had the idea to create competitions in each genre. Now besides the general one, like you saw, each entry gets the chance to compete in horror or comedy or drama. Whatever. Some hard core users have attacked it and are creating shorts every day. It's a small group but they're creating massive amounts of content. We are racking up engagement."

"It's getting better."

"It's only getting better."

Grigsby wasn't exactly clear but she seemed pleased. "Keep it up."

"But all those users are taxing the servers. Gus had to upgrade our contract with the CDN and we upgraded the CPU and RAM on our virtual servers. It was only another five grand so I told him to go ahead and implement it."

Every step forward continued to cost him more money. It was like everything stayed exactly the same. He started getting money in and that money created more traffic which cost him more money. There was an old saw that the only ones who got rich in the gold rush were the people who sold the picks and shovels. Grigsby began to see why.

25
The Arts Festival

Grigsby cleaned up and got right through downtown and halfway up Verona Canyon Road.

Verona Canyon Road had changed over time. Not too long ago it was a two lane twisting canyon road that flooded in the lightest rains and was filled on each side with dusty mom-and-pop car repair or antique joints. Speckled within were also clapboard homes and, if legend is true, caves in the hills that the hippies used to live in. The caves were still there; to Grigsby they looked too small and too sparse for anyone to have ever lived in them.

There was also a drive-up zoo where the animals were loose and approached the cars. One time Helen the Hippo escaped to bathe in the roadside pond.

Now the road expanded to as many as five or six lanes in parts and was cut across by a toll road surrounded by a county park with an art school and lots of city parking.

But an enduring fixture through the changes were the multiple art shows each with its own area.

There was the Cuttings Fest, named for the sawdust left from building the booths, now full of permanent structures. This part of the summer festival was an arts and crafts area. The type of things you buy mom or dad for Hallmark holidays. Very fun, always clever, what some might call folk art but certainly not high art.

Then there was the Verona Beach Arts Festival. These works (paintings, sculpture and some photography) sold for more than three months of most people's rent. Some aspired to the higher callings of art blended with commentary and philosophy while others were bland enough to match the bank executive's splotches for her empty living room wall.

The crown jewel of the Festival was the brainchild of an enterprising lighting designer who recreated famous paintings on stage. In front of a thousand people, they used live models, dressed and made up to look like the originals. When the proper lights were struck, the three dimensional people transformed into what looked like the canvas of the painting itself. It really was a terrific spectacle.

Grigsby strolled up to the ticket gate of the Arts Festival. A second gate further in held the Jubilee. He checked with a hand in every pocket as he approached the ticket taker, who smiled at him.

"I can't find my ticket," Grigsby said.

The old guy in a dark jacket and slacks smiled. "Of course, Andrew. Go on in."

"Thanks, Clarence."

As the Festival neared the end of its run, at summer's end, the town folk got nostalgic and the crowd blossomed. City Council members yukked and guffawed with each other by the wine bar. Real estate agents discussed the latest cliff-front mansion for sale, and who listed it.

All these people were here for community, and

recognition, but it wasn't necessarily about the money. But we all know, right now, for Grigsby, it's all about the money. He needed someone on the line and he wasn't going to get one on the line unless he got out and looked for one.

Tony caught his eye and gave him an eyebrow as Grigsby surveyed the crowd and his options.

Grigsby wasn't sure if that meant *what are you doing here* or *are you looking for marks* or he was going to have Brodie eat his liver. Grigsby just knew he didn't want to deal with Tony tonight. Not just yet.

Giving Tony eyebrows back in greeting, Grigsby turned around to find another row of paintings and patrons, and there was Stewart with his cohort of purple hairs.

Stewart always had a group of older women, mostly widows, with whom he held court. They liked to invest in young artists and Stewart knew who to buy, when, and for how much. As an art broker, he kept himself in a steady income, he kept the artist fed and the ladies loved to both lavish money and be lavished with attention.

"Stewart," Grigsby said. "How's tricks?"

Stewart smiled his mischievous smile, dipped his chin and shared a secret, "One of the damn artists didn't even show up to his booth tonight - But we'll blame that on the artist's temperament. There are times it works."

Grigsby nodded his understanding and Stewart turned with a wave of his arm, "C'mon girls! I have someone over here you have got to meet. He's new to our community so nobody has his work. And he works deliberately so there are only 4 works per year available. Supply and demand, ladies."

Stewart smiled at Grigsby and the gaggle followed with excited chitter chatter between themselves.

Grigsby found his way into the amphitheater to watch some of the show and its paintings. This year, the focus was California Naturalists. He loved the work but didn't feel it suited the show itself. For the magic trick, you need people in these paintings.

When intermission came, he sneaked back out and, as he rounded the corner, he ran right into Bio with the contents of her wine glass spilling on his chest.

"Whoa, slow down turbo!" Bio said.

Grigsby stopped and smiled at her, "Come now, look what you've done."

"Oh dear. Well, I am sorry. It seems I've thrown nearly as much wine on you as you were tossing on the whale."

Grigsby wasn't sure if that was a dig, an apology, or a joke.

"That's right," he said. Two can play that game. "You're the biologist with the whale." As if she hadn't already imprinted on him. He had never had less game than he did with this woman.

"And you were the man with the pail," she said and, as the bashful type, immediately embarrassed herself.

"We never had a formal introduction. I'm Andrew W. Grigsby."

"If we're to be so formal, I am Dr. Violet McGrath." Grigsby offered a slight look of confusion. "They call me

Bio because..."

"Oh, yeah, because obviously..." He opened his palms to everything.

"Yes, a perfect combination of the job, and loss of an entire syllable."

He smiled. "Expanding your horizons?" he said, breaking the silence and, now, indicating the amphitheater with his hands.

"Well, yes, but the colleagues thought it might be wise to rub shoulders with some locals. We still have considerable work ahead of us and I'd like to gather some useful information. Make sure the contribution of this whale beaching will be more than simply a carcass to the community."

"That is noble."

"Well, the stench is pronounced but it could be really great for the habitat. You wouldn't believe the amount of calories a whale adds to the food chain."

Grigsby could only nod in agreement. There was nothing pithy to add to the thought of rot as food.

"Luckily, it'll be gone soon," she said, sensing she said too much or was too excited to be cool. "It's quite a load."

"Yeah, I guess so."

"You'll see." Her colleague came out of the restroom, and the lights flashed and the bells rung for the restart of the show, post intermission. "Well, good to see you."

"Good to see you."

"Sorry about your shirt."

He looked down again at his shirt decorated in red wine. "Yeah, I'll send you the bill." He laughed and waved her on.

With a sly grin, she left with her friend, and he got out of there feeling like a kid skipping school.

26
First Deadlines

As the technology continued to become more and more expensive on this festival, Grigsby took a look and Gus was holding back on some of the billing for sure. They still blew through the fifty grand and another twenty-five since they started. In billing. Of course, Grigsby hadn't paid him, yet.

The contracts were sent to Lawanda at P&G, but he hadn't heard back right away. On follow up and follow up again, she just told him to sit tight. That's how legal worked at a company her size.

She wanted him to wait? He already got rid of the extra rounds. He adjusted the timeline to make October 1 the Finals date. No more 64, 32, 16 stuff - straight to the Quarter Finals, Semis and Finals. Clean. Elegant. In time.

The Quarter Finals would come and go with nothing to show from this huge company at this rate. He needed cash, and she was the source of those funds. He'd already spent a bunch of that money, as you know. Tech, influencers, code, design, marketing, printing, rentals. Shit, this better work. People who collect paychecks never understand the passage of time. Their money comes every two weeks without fail, whether they really do their jobs or not. When a person like Grigsby waits on a check from one of these huge companies, he dies a little every single day. The irony was someone *was* going to die if that thing didn't come in.

Worrying never fixed anything, action does. So, Grigsby decided to plan for some other infusion of capital.

He stepped back and surveyed the town in his imagination, face by face, door by door. Someone had to be doing something to make easy money. The more he thought about it, the more he realized old Stewart seemed to do good business with the blue-hairs. Grigsby called him up.

At their meeting they sat on a bench at Main Beach in front of the beach volleyball courts. Two pairs of women played a match. They served, set and spiked like pros because they were. They were local kids, at least county kids. It's tough to find adequate competition, so they met up here for practice and camaraderie.

Grigsby hoped the friendly rivalry might spark some of the same spirit in Stewart.

It didn't.

"Grigsby, you want me to cannibalize my money train for a movie?"

"It's a slam dunk, Stewart. The movies make money.

Your pack of mistresses and widows have money they want to spend on the arts. It's a perfect fit."

"That's pathetic. That's your pitch?"

Grigsby didn't like how this was going.

"You're going to have to do better than that. 'We'll make money'. Even my old bags are more sophisticated than that. Where's the intrigue, the story, the hook?"

Sometimes there was more to this gag than Grigsby had realized. Just because he believed and was interested, Grigsby hadn't really thought that another person couldn't, wouldn't, automatically be interested. He did need to set the hook. Why would this be any different than the con?

"Look, AW, I like you. I won't take this lack of preparation personally. But you need to do better." Stewart pushed up off the bench and wiped the sand off his hands. "Come to me when you get your shit together. You'll need to do better for me, and you'll definitely need to be better when you get out and pitch to the real pros."

Grigsby had been entirely focused on the money. Not on the job. Doing the job right always delivered the money. Fucking Sorenson and his choice. Grigsby was off his game.

He needed to settle down. One pitch at a time. One shot at a time. Know your goal and work your way towards it. Worrying about the whole amount, worrying about what was going to happen, didn't fix it. Working on the steps to solve the problem did. One. Step. At. A. Time.

But this was one of those stupid steps.

Every bit of money they collected on the festival went back in at this point.

They decided to call the first round the "Early Bird" and extended the chances for more entries while increasing the price for the ones who hadn't come first. At least the festival would make more incrementally.

The technology forced Grigsby to understand the festival faced a new paradigm. Grigsby came from a generation that believed fame was doled out by the big companies, networks, corporations, magazines, newspapers, radio stations. The new kids built their own opportunities, and some of them made it big. Digits of money with multiple commas and their own form of fame based on likes, views and followers instead of ratings, box office and Billboard charts. More of this new shift included endorsements of a different vein. A long time ago, a place like Mr. Coffee paid Joe DiMaggio, the greatest player of his generation, to drink their brew on national television to millions upon millions of viewers, but now? Now they paid an influencer known by a fiercely dedicated group of sometimes only tens of thousands of viewers to drink Bullit coffee while they hawked their own training seminars about startups. To Grigsby, it seemed like everyone got in on the hustle while he wasn't paying attention, and that the hustle went legit.

More to the point, what Grigsby knew was that the users getting involved with the festival needed more. He had to ensure that they would get a kick start for their hustle on his platform. This festival would have to feed the big social media machine. Give all these dreamers fame, but, then, link all of that fame to a golden chalice. Offer these hustlers what they couldn't get themselves: Big Budgets. Like all of their heroes. The chance to be a general on set. To be Billy Wilder, Hitchcock, Scorsese, Lucas, Tarantino, Kubrik, Speilberg, Ridley Scott.

They would get the opportunity to run a real set with hundreds of cast, crew, tools and toys that only Hollywood can provide. Trucks, cranes, helicopters, gaffers, grips, dollies, make up, hair, art direction, props. All of the things that can only be done by a team of very talented, very skill-specific people. And all of it paid for with other people's money. Those YouTube kids paid for all their own stuff.

Grigsby needed the money from the studio.

The kids needed to dream of working with a studio.

The festival needed a development deal with the studio.

Not just for Gong, but for the festival itself. If he could provide that deal, he could provide the jumping point he needed for this whole thing to blast into outer space.

He was going to make American Idol for pocket movies. Would he need celebrity judges? Some sort of Simon Cowell?

He was sure that he needed to star-build these players. He would also have to lock them up for years. Both their work and their ideas. As bad as a boy band, these players faced a future beholden to him.

He would have the power. And he would have control.

At least, he would have the money.

And his house.

And both his kids.

He would be whole.

The very first step was a spectacle. This festival needed to draw crowds and he needed a place to hold the Quarters, Semis and Final. He sat on the bench looking at the beach wondering where in the wide world he was going to be able to hold this festival without the theater.

27

Who does he think he is?

"Who does he think he is?" Tony said. "This is my job. My book. My place. I'll handle this shit my way. That little shit isn't my boss."

Grigsby came to see Tony at his place. Grigsby didn't know who to believe. Or more importantly, who held the power. He needed to please both of these jerks or split up Sorenson and Tony completely. "Where's the power, Tony? All these years?"

"They don't care. Nobody cares. The kid took over back East and now they push me." That old man who ran the show back East for fifty years, who came up hocking goods that fell off semi-trucks and dumping bodies from trash trucks, died peacefully and his kid, who went to

Princeton, of all places, took over.

"What about Sorenson? How does he play in?"

"He's not even Sicilian. They run it like a company now. I swear he turned in a resume."

"But our deal is good, right?"

"With me it is. But look at the writing on the wall, kid. I'm not young anymore. Shit, you're not young anymore. They do it different nowadays."

"Tony, you've carried their load."

"I have carried their load all these years. But this MBA type kid. They think you only learn things in school now."

"Instead of the streets."

"Yeah, instead of the streets. Little do they realize all those rules in school are written by pencil heads watching the real people do the work. Theories are for classrooms, but the real stuff, the real stuff happens in the real world. And the real world doesn't always follow the laws and theorems they create to explain the unexplainable. This stuff out here. With the people like us. It's not all that different from the rest of the world. It's survival of the fittest. Dog eat dog. The universe keeps making rain and rocks and flowers and beavers. Everything just keeps ticking along. That piece of beach you love so much won't ever know you're gone. The crabs will keep crawling." Tony looked like he was gonna have a heart attack, face all red and splotchy, but he came to a decision only he knew the answer to, and said, more to himself than Grigsby, "Yep. There comes a time when we meet our maker." He looked up. "That's fine. I'm at peace."

"Tony, you kidding me?" Father time: unbeaten. But Grigsby wasn't prepared to give a pep talk. He needed Tony to take charge, though. "The guy's gone somewhere right now, Tony. I haven't seen him. You ain't done for."

"Doesn't matter. Him, someone else. Cancer. Heart attack. I won't live forever. We all gotta face mortality, Grigsby. Something is always the end of us. Don't forget that. We always get it in the end."

"It'll be alright, Tony. Like they say, it'll be okay in the end, and if it's not okay, it's not the end."

"You don't get it do you?" This meant Tony would go on one of his monologues. When he does this, you just shut up till he's done. He mostly talked to himself when he did this.

"The times changed. Take the old days. Waste management didn't just launder money, it provided for disposal."

"Of all the bodies." Grigsby should have kept quiet.

"Of course, the bodies. It was easier to pay off the poor sap who worked for the dump for a couple bucks an hour than it was to have a boat and sink the body - who knows, somebody could get lazy and not go out far enough when they ditch it. I even had a stiff float to the surface after it slipped the chains we tied around it." Tony turned to face Grigsby. "Good thing we waited around for a little bit to be sure. We smoked one of these, me and Larry the Lug."

Tony pulled out a cigar, clipped the end and held the cigar in his teeth while he patted all his pockets, "Using the dump, the place already stunk, and it don't get turned over. Once it's buried - and believe me the whole place is full of rotting food - which rotting steak and pork is the same as a rotting human - nobody ever knew."

Landing on the lighter in his back pocket, Tony showed it to him, lit the cigar with the chrome Zippo's *vrump* and *clack*, puff-puffed, then kept on. "But killing people gets harder and harder with—nobody does it as much as in the old days. Just too hard to get rid of the bodies with cameras and the people and the ethics. New school."

He spit tight through his lips, seemed to consider the changes for a moment, then Tony was done philosophizing. "As it is, I'll need another payout from you just to keep the wolves above me at arm's length."

Grigsby didn't see this coming, and didn't like where this was going. He couldn't be paying two of these guys off, Tony with his crap and Sorenson with his threats., "Tony, Sorenson tells me I gotta pay him."

"What did I say? Don't you worry about Sorenson. Besides, he's in Georgia for a funeral." Tony was still thinking about the dumps, or the old days.

"That's why he's not bugging me these couple of days. You sure?"

"He told me himself while he's twirling that damn pen," Tony said and fiddled his empty fingers in disgust.

Grigsby nodded. "I don't see that son of bitch going anywhere for a funeral."

"I hear it's his father."

Okay, with Sorenson gone for a little, maybe Grigsby would buy more time. "So, I got a minute."

"No - I just told you, you gotta kick some more cash my way. And fast." His attention was fully on Grigsby here.

"Tony, I just had a meeting. I got another one coming up. At a studio. And I got this festival ramping up. We'll have the money. It's like we're building the machine that prints the cash."

"I don't give a shit about the machine, just get me the cash. I'm looking for $15G from you, Grigsby."

Hell. Where's he going to get that?

He asked him, "Where am I going to get that?"

"Not my problem."

"How about five. I think I can get you five grand."

"Okay, tomorrow morning, bring me the five," Tony spit again and put the cigar in his mouth.

The meeting was done. Grigsby didn't want him dreaming up anything else for him to do, so Grigsby took his leave and contemplated this next mess as he got out to his car.

As if Grigsby needed another task. He didn't have any of that kind of cash to cover his ass. Dammit. He needed to blow off some steam. Maybe, he'd go for a surf. But he'd see people and this shit was making him feel like he'd rather not see anyone.

No, he'd go play some golf. Nobody'd bug him if he was a single out there. Besides, it would make him feel better hitting a little white ball as far as he could. It's like baseball, except you don't need seventeen other guys to play.

28

AROUND A ROUND WITH GRIGSBY

"You can't cheat an honest man."

His Pop's favorite phrase. And it stuck with Grigsby all these years. Pop'd been gone more of Grigsby's life than he was here. Fact was, AW Grigsby was older now than his Pops was when he died.

They'd never been members of the country club. Even when Pop was flush, he wasn't going to drop the thousands it took to be a member of a club he could get invited to for free. Just took a few well-placed words and a few well-placed balls. Golf was a gentleman's game and gentlemen prefer to wager. Gentlemen also prefer not to lose and that's where Pop came in. He could swing a club with the best of them but most of those guys wouldn't let a non-member play with them. Unless it was for money.

This particular country club had fallen on hard times during the last crash. This southern California beach town had money, but the town don't have *money*. Besides, even the normal rich suffered during that crisis, if suffering meant not playing golf or selling their memberships. Rather than sell out to a developer for a run of condos, the entirety of the club voted to open the course to be played by non-members and the clubhouse to be rented out for weddings and such. These two changes pulled the ends of the strings together so they could tie a knot. Weddings are another opportunity where emotions and money meet but that's a different story altogether.

On this day, Grigsby had kicked his leather sandals off and played the first nine of the eighteen holes barefoot and by himself as a single, if you will, behind the threesome. Playing two balls to keep himself off the tail of that group before him had two benefits: he could work on his game by hitting the differing shots each strike inevitably provided him and, secondly, to keep that group ahead in his eye.

Grigsby already heard one of that leading group blather and scream when he won a hole. Watched him bully an extra mulligan off the fourth tee over the gully, that free shot saving his score, and drop his "found" ball when passing each other at the sixth / seventh fairway, when, in reality, the only way he would find that ball was if the bully went in the pool of the gothic mansion over the hedge.

Those three were an interesting crew. Not only loud and playing music off a Bluetooth speaker in their carts but throwing hundred-dollar bills around after each hole. They didn't have the class to settle up at the 19th over a cocktail. They'd count the money out each time. Most importantly to Grigsby, they clearly had cash and Grigsby knew the loud, proud, drunk and stupid tended to be easy marks.

At the turn between the ninth- and tenth-holes Grigsby figured it might be time to get serious. The foursome two ahead of Grigsby were two couples, man and woman pairs that Grigsby watched. The men teed off the golds and women teed off the silvers. In the old days what were called men's tees and women's tees, the men's further from the hole than the women's. Eventually, the big golf companies in the sky tried to simplify a little for duffers, most people out there can't play a lick. Removing genders was meant to remove the stigma of an easier option. Not with these types: men still hit off men's and women still hit off women's.

In any case, at the turn as he tied up his two-tone black and white shoes, he watched the couples tee off. The threesome who had been in front of him had taken a detour to the clubhouse and aggressively rolled up with splashing beers and loaded brats. The loudest of the three addressed Grigsby, "Hey, you're the barefoot single behind us, why don't you join us?"

Grigsby smiled inside, definitely not outside. "Oh, I don't want to encroach on your game."

The brash one again, "Then don't play," as he worried his brat like a dog on a bone.

The two couples ahead had finished their second shots and cleared the fairway, making room for the next group off the tee.

"We're up," said the fatter of the two others as he pulled a driver from his bag and approached the tee box. Then, to Grigsby, "You should play. More fun than chasing two balls around the course by yourself."

"What the hell," Grigsby grinned, and held out his hand. "I'm Grigsby."

The brash one smiled at his friends, "Billy," he said,

ignoring the offered shake, "we're just playing a hundie-a-hole." He pulled his driver and went to the tee box. "Join us, but you don't gotta pay to play," he said as he tongue-cleared the last of the bratwurst from his cheek.

Oh, he would play. Grigsby kept a stash of a couple grand in his bag for days just as this. "A hundred bucks a hole can add up quick, but I'll manage." Or had Grigsby already pulled that money out of his bag? Whatever, Grigsby had this.

Grigsby took his turn on the tee, placing a dimpled white ball atop a deep blue tee. Now the games began. He took a deep breath, smelled the deep green grass and found the brown earth underneath, felt a soft ocean breeze on his arms, a slow backswing, then struck the ball and placed a beautiful shot right down the middle. Keeping his wits about him, he played conservatively and kept everything close to the vest. When necessary, Grigsby made sure to create a push by tying the score on the hole when one of the others might win the hole. Over the next six holes they ended up carrying over the scores, and the pot, of every hole up to 17. The seventeenth hole was a par 5. Not the longest on the course but a long one that required the most strategy and skill, forcing an array of differing shots with the tree placements and a creek. Grigsby nutted a drive down the fairway, then pured a three wood. Now when you "pure" a shot, you've hit a perfect, "pure", just-like-what-the-club-was-designed-for shot. Grigsby pured it to 10 feet from the pin which he then sank for eagle. Two under par. Tiger would be proud.

Oh baby, Grigsby thought, that hole was worth $1800 and enough for a good day. Then the windbag started his bitching.

"You guys never should have invited him," he said. "Fucking blood in the water."

Blood in the water. Like Grigsby was a shark. Well, there was blood in the water but the guy was a dick. And the loud and proud ones are always worth an extra take, especially when they're up against it. Their ego can't take it.

"Tell you what, I didn't come to the course today to take your money," Grigsby said. However, he was at the course for that exact reason, just lucky he found these losers.

"I'll give you a chance to win it all back on eighteen," Grigsby said with a sip and twist closed on his water bottle. "Double or nothing. I pick a club out of my bag; you pick a club out of yours. No putter. We play with the other guy's club for the entire hole tee to green. You win, we're even. I win, the payoff's twice what I just won."

"Why don't we make it the pot for the round? I mean for all of us."

This guy was too much. That put the stakes a little over five grand. Grisgby better win, he knew he didn't have that much.

"$5400 it is," Grigsby said. "Sure you don't want to juice it a little more?"

This guy was going to bite, Grigsby had to try to goose it a little. Grigsby had seen enough of this blowhard by now to know. These types were his bread and butter. His Pops called them trout bait 'cuz they were always on the line, and you could always reel them in. No need to fish, they were in your boat to begin with.

"No, $5400 will do. How do I know you have it?"

"Don't you worry," he said, opened up his golf bag and dug to the bottom. He pulled out a bundle and held it up like the roll from his cookie jar. It was a bunch of blanks, but it would do, "Good enough?"

"I'm gonna feel bad taking a geezer's money, a strange geezer at that. It's only the 12th of the month. Social security doesn't come for almost another twenty days."

Grigsby was going to beat his ass. He clenched his fists in his mind and grinned on the outside. A good sport through and through.

"Pick your club, old man."

Jesus, I'm only fifty, Grigsby thought, that guy was like thirty-five. Though Grigsby loved it when they thought they could rattle him. It motivated him.

Grigsby surveyed his bag as if he didn't know what club it'd be, running his hand and eyes over his sticks. Finally, he grabbed the 1 iron from his bag and handed it off. Even God can't hit a 1 iron.

The bully's friends yacked and laughed.

"Hey, Billy, you know what they say, even God can't hit a 1 iron!"

"Suzanne is gonna kill you!"

Billy just grinned and took the club.

"Loser ball," Grigsby said.

"This ain't basketball," Billy said. In one-on-one basketball, often the guy who is scored-on takes the ball for the next chance to score. In golf, it's the pleasure of the winner of the last hole to tee off first on the next.

"I know the rules. But I figure a guy like you would cry something fierce otherwise," Grigsby said.

"Don't you worry, I'll be fine."

Billy grabbed a broken tee off the tee box and placed his ball. He surveyed the 400-yard hole, a straight one, took two practice swings then hit a worm burner, 200 bouncer, like a little leaguer grounding down the middle.

His boys laughed. "You're so dead."

Billy still looked pleased with himself. Something was up.

"My choice now," Billy said as he walked to his bag.

Grigsby was used to this. It can go a lot of ways. Some guys give you a driver figuring you can't hit your short game and putt with the long ass driver. Others will give you a sand wedge or a 51-degree wedge figuring you wouldn't be able to hit the ball far enough to make it in time. Their choice was usually a reflection of their own game.

Long ballers will give you short game and short gamers, the driver.

Billy had already decided.

He walked right to his bag and picked a club.

It looked like a 7 iron.

The perfect club for this. What the hell?

His boys laughed and he turned around with the club aloft.

"Not the 7!" the friends both said over each other.

Billy held out the 7 iron and gave it to Grigsby.

Grigsby had been thrown off by his confidence and his friends' excitement until he held the club himself. It was a 7 iron, alright.

A left-handed 7 iron.

Some guys, guys like this one, will carry a left-handed club in case they get a lie, where the ball lay, next to a tree. Sometimes with the ball next to a tree, or another obstacle, one can't stand on the proper side of the ball. Rules state you can't move that ball and when you play for $$, people want rules followed.

This was Billy's ace in the hole: a left-handed club. Most people can't swing a left-handed club. Nine out of ten are right-handed. Meaning, one out of ten are left-handed and Billy'd watched Grisgby play a whole round, well seventeen holes, right-handed. What he didn't know was that in those statistics there is another group that was even more rare. More special. Better equipped for a situation just like this. Only one in one thousand is ambidextrous. Can use both sides equally well. To be honest, Grigsby wasn't really ambidextrous. But tell you what he was: a switch hitter. He played baseball all his life and one time, as a kid, Grigsby tried hitting left, was surprisingly good and kept it up the whole time through high school. Hitting from both sides made sure he got playing time on competitive teams. In fact, his power numbers were always worse, but his average was better left-handed. In short, no problem.

Grigsby grabbed the club with a glint, down-turned lips, checked the grip then smiled like the shark in that kid's movie, ear to ear.

"Blood in the water, boys," Grigsby said. "No need to tee it up."

He dropped the ball on the manicured grass of the tee, surveyed the hole by standing behind the ball, feigned going to the wrong side of the ball, then stepped there like a leftie and knocked the ball 185 yards straight down the middle of the fairway.

He grinned at the group, "Everybody loves a switch hitter."

"Fuck."

You know why they call it golf, right?

'Cuz fuck was taken.

"Now this is getting good," the fat friend said. Now that Grigsby gave him a good look, the guy resembled Jonah Hill in Wolf of Wall Street. But not like he was on all that Adderall and quaaludes.

Billy dragged his ass to his sorry shot and stepped around the ball. He bent over to look at it. The other guy, the one who looked like a long-haired old skater guy said, "Don't touch it, Billy. It's August, not December."

The ball sat in a shallow puddle with a touch of mud.

A tough shot.

If it were winter, Billy'd get relief and may be able to

move his ball if Grigsby felt any sympathy, but in summer: no such luck. Besides Grigsby wasn't into charity.

"I know the rules," Billy said. "The lie is fine anyway."

Billy stepped up and pured a shot. The ball flew straight and clean right off the iron. It really was a beautiful shot, especially when it flew over the green too long and burrowed into the sand trap like a sea turtle laying eggs on a tropical beach.

"Fuck."

Grigsby stepped up and knocked another one 185 yards and rolled just up to the fringe of the soft, brightness of, and not quite on, the green.

There are a lot of reasons why there are so many different types of clubs in golf. The driver, or wood, has that big head and long shaft made precisely for you to hit that ball as far it can go. As the number gets higher so does the angle of the club so that a 4 iron is meant to fly lower and longer while a 9 iron is meant to fly higher and shorter. Golf is a game of parabolas. Power, height and distance all even out with your swing and club. One of the most specialized clubs is the sand wedge. It is a shorter club with a high angle plus it is often a touch heavier than other short clubs to help you swing through a situation like Billy was in.

That extra weight helps you dig the golf ball out of the sand that cannot be touched by your club before swinging or suffer a one stroke penalty. After all, golf is a gentleman's game. Bets and all.

All of this is to say, a 1 iron is not built or easy to use in a shot like this. One could swing and never move the ball. One stroke. One could hit it too well and too hard sending that ball halfway back to the tee box. Not likely in this case but still 1 stroke plus the effort to get close again.

One of the most frustrating aspects of golf is that a 300-yard drive equals the same stroke as a 3-foot putt. As the saying goes, "Drive for show, putt for dough."

Billy was 20-feet deep in the trap with at least 60 feet more of green.

Billy settled his feet, a fair way to see how soft the sand really was. He gave his ass and feet a final wiggle and struck the sand two inches behind the ball with his club and all his might.

A full wave of sand flew double overhead and halfway across the green and the ball dribbled across the sand, hit the lip the size of an ostrich egg and just barely spun onto the grass and stopped.

"Fuck."

There's that word again.

Billy lies 3. Grigsby 2.

Since neither was on the green and Billy was further, golf courtesy stated it was Billy's turn.

Billy addressed stern and, if Grigsby wasn't mistaken, was breathing a little fast. He wiped the sand from his hair and off his palms, closed the face of the club and took a nice easy chip at the ball.

The ball undulated over a hill and broke left and right and headed straight toward the hole.

Jonah Hill screamed; skater dude squeaked as Grigsby remained steely eyed. If he made it, Grigsby still had at least a stroke advantage here, but it put pressure on him, and he didn't want to get into some sort of play off scenario putting on the practice green or some arguable long drive crap at the driving range. This needed to end now.

He thought all this while he watched this damn ball take a miniature golf route; there might as well be a windmill and popcorn.

The ball caught the lip and circled around the hole like it was a drain. It made a full revolution before it dropped in the damn thing for par. Four shots.

Grigsby ran his hand through his barely salted, deep pepper hair and figured he could just bump it close and putt for par for the playoff which could go either way.

Nope. This was "Go Big Time". No safe plays.

He stepped up to the ball and executed a bump-and-run Pops had taught him when he was playing on these big courses at 8 or 9, racking up a full 15-20 shots on a hole like this. Pops didn't let him pick up. He was here to play, and he would respect the game and its rules and customs. That was always important: to respect the game.

That bump and run never had any doubt. He knocked that thing straight in the cup for a birdie 3 and $5400.

Billy said it. "Fuck!"

Yep, golf because fuck was already taken.

29

Main Beach: Reserved

Grigsby felt pretty good. Cruising PCH, his top down, the wind flowing. This was how his life had been. Ups and downs, balls and strikes, but it always worked out in the end.

Like he told Tony, "It'll all be okay in the end, and if it's not okay, it's not the end."

Grigsby passed the Verona Beach Art Museum with its gleaming windowed entry on a hill overlooking the ocean. He rolled down that straight hill overlooking Main Beach, downtown and the damn theater in front of him. That place would've worked out great.

There, walking past the place, was Brodie. Might as well save a trip. Grigsby stopped at the light, one of a half dozen lights in that short stretch, and called to Brodie.

Brodie looked over and gave him a chin. He was eating an ice cream.

"Hop over, would ya? I got something." Grigsby pulled to the side and stopped at a red curb.

Brodie crossed through the stopped traffic, "Whaddya want, Grigsby?"

Grigsby handed the $5G he just pulled off that idiot to Brodie., "Can you pass this to Tony for me?"

"Already?"

"It's a good day, Brodie. It's a good day."

"Good for you." Brodie took the cash with a salute and continued wherever he was going with his ice cream.

Grigsby took in the beach, the waves, the swaying palm trees for just a moment and enjoyed how picturesque it all was. Who wouldn't want to live in a place like this? He wanted to take a picture right here.

Holy cannoli, he had to set up the Finals at Main Beach.

He was gonna have the damn Finals right here.

He called Nacho. "I need a permit for Main Beach."

"For what?"

"The Finals."

"How many people?"

"Couple thousand."

"Never going to happen."

Grigsby knew Nacho was right. When Grigsby dreamed this whole festival up, he never really thought it'd make it this far.

"Okay, how about for the Semis? Maybe a couple hundred people."

"Pendejo, I told you they don't do that at Main Beach, besides the whale."

"The whale's gotta be gone soon, the Semis are in a

couple weeks. Hell, just get me a permit for a protest. I've seen those there before."

"You're insane."

"We'll call it a First Amendment gathering. We have a right to gather. Look at the Constitution."

"They might not be able to deny that, actually."

"By the time they realize, we'll be done, or it won't matter."

"What are you gonna show those movies on?"

"Don't worry about that, I got a plan." He could see it now. It'd be amazing. The beach, the people, the movies. All perfect for pictures and promotion.

"No shit," Nacho hung up.

Grigsby was feeling pretty good about himself. He headed home.

Orange sat on the sofa, swiping, while Freckles laid on the floor with her feet on the sofa, swiping.

He didn't manage to say a word, because Katniss and Adam rumbled in the front door behind him.

"Do you have a line on where we'll have the Semis?" Katniss said.

"Have you looked at what BeachieGurl has done?" Adam said.

"Nacho is on it," to Katniss and, "No," Grigsby said to Adam. He barely had his bearings. He was still celebrating the chance at getting Main Beach. He wanted to congratulate himself for thinking up another solution for this racket, but the kids were fired up about something.

"Well," Adam said. "Beachiegirl's pumped up the event and is creating big demand for the Semis." That sounded perfect. Demand translated to value, and value was cash.

"There's also crazy bidding going on for that charity spot," Katniss said.

Freckles pulled up the site and displayed it on the holo in the middle of the room. Coke and Pepsi seemed to have gotten into a bidding war like East and West Coast rappers. The buzz on social gave them attention for free. Bids don't cost anything, and the chance to screen one of their commercials at the event that, to Grigsby's mind, would reach as many as the Super Bowl for probably half the price.

"Shit, we left serious money on the table." To his surprise, Grigsby was having trouble grasping the scope of his concoction.

Katniss had no problem keeping him on task. "Dad, we're helping Save the Oceans. Not everything is about cash."

That's what they think. The only fund Grisgby cared about was Save my Kids. As the other four continued to discuss the festival, it occurred to Grigsby that Katniss was dressed comfortably, like a beach girl. No character, no affectation, just a kid. And with that realization came another. Adam hadn't pulled one of his stunts in weeks. The two of them looked relaxed, happy and engaged. Grigsby never would have dreamed this con would bring him closer to the kids. More importantly, he never imagined the kids would feel closer to him.

30
City Council

Forced to find a legitimate and approved space for the Semi-Finals, Grigsby did something he found distasteful and unsanitary. He went to the City Council meeting. The Semis were next month and, apparently, there were some things Nacho couldn't do for him. Nobody was buying the Free Speech protest at Main Beach, and nobody would let any of this flow through back channels. Nacho got him squeezed onto the agenda, but it would be a long haul.

The chambers were perfectly antiseptic with indoor / outdoor carpeting of blended gray on gray with a wooden pedestal for the five council members and the dull buzz of too many open microphones. The chairs for the public were limited by the sign on the wall that said the capacity was 80 people.

Most of the meeting was dry with following the Robert's Rules of Order, calling roll and accepting the previous meeting's minutes. However, after all that rigmarole, Grigsby was surprised to find the meeting somewhat interesting. If you dug through the decorum to what was really happening, Grigsby realized the underbelly of a city was revealed to you. Before Grigsby even had a chance to plead his case for his latest idea, he learned there was no better place to see the combination of grand master level maneuvering blended disconcertingly with crackpot screamers. There were even three tweenie girls with #PoorDickie posters with what Grigsby considered impressive artwork for a city meeting.

As he waited for what he was sure was a quick approval of his plan, he watched the council discussion, and the public comment, on, what to do with the whale. Poor Dickie. Grigsby took some pride in his Moby Dick remark having some staying power. The public had many thoughts for Poor Dickie. Bury it? Cut it up and take it to the dump? Tow it back out to sea? It was all on the table.

Bio was present and was not only asked her opinion but gave a presentation detailing the whale's place in the food chain and the importance of a *rotting hunk of meat*, words and emphasis my own. She detailed conversations with NOAA, the National Oceanic and Atmospheric Administration, with several specialists chiming in from Scripps and Monterey Bay National Marine Sanctuary, who had handled similar man-made whale falls, and whose thoughts and opinions coincided with Bio's recommendation. Bio proposed the creation of a whale fall that would bring a benefit to the scientific community to better understand the underwater life in the Verona Beach Bluebelt, a protected marine refuge. The amount of food that a whale such as this provided could sustain a plethora of species for, in some cases, decades. From the flesh and blubber that feeds large animals from sharks to hagfish to the bone burrowing, marrow sucking Osedax worms. All of the meetings and reviews made the whale fall more difficult to sink, because time allowed the gasses to expand, and bloat made the carcass more buoyant.

A few citizens simply wanted to bury the carcass, but the combination of the small, popular beach and the scientific possibilities aligned with an eco-friendly, water sports loving city made the whale fall all but inevitable.

However, this type of event also excited another certain type of citizen. Every crackpot had an equal opinion, and the crackpots influenced the process, too. This was how voting worked. And, most times, the only ones who showed at local government were the crackpots and the developers. In this case, the crackpots wanted instant answers. And for the problem to just go away.

They wanted to blow up the whale.

This shouldn't have been to Grigsby's surprise, but this was not Bio's first run-in with the general public. She was prepared for this line of reasoning and shared a video from a previous news report. Having spent time at the Arts Festival recently, and those city meetings, she looked to know all the players. Also, smart.

The whale video was from decades before but must have come in the biologist's dead whale starter's kit. The news report covered the entire process up to the attempt to blow the thing up in Monterey County in Northern California. To the surprise of many and entertainment of most, the use of dynamite to rid the beach of a corpse tends to be a messy affair and destructive to more than the whale. Chunks of the beast flew high enough to travel to the adjacent parking lot and flatten a wood paneled green station wagon as well as cover the spectators with a spray and splash of rotting meat, blood, digestive material and feces. After the tasteful completion of the video, the issue was settled. Bio had carte blanche. They'd tow the carcass out to sea, sink it and allow said carcass to act as a feast for the surrounding marine life.

Next on the docket was the Verona Beach Film Festival. The council debate surrounded the usual suspect: There's too much interest. Great. For once in his life, Grigsby was suffering from too much success. Except, of course, with Cox. Cox took joy from ensuring everything about the festival sank the same way they hoped that whale would sink to the bottom of the ocean and rot, forgotten.

After Grigsby laid out his plan, setting the scene of a picturesque moment straight from a romantic film with Verona Beach as the hero, Cox began, "Clearly the city wouldn't allow this festival at Main Beach and downtown. An event like this would create too many traffic problems."

Grigsby needed the beach. "Councilman Cox, you miss the point. We can showcase what nowhere in the world has, except maybe Côte d'Azur."

"We are not the French Riviera."

"We are not. Our weather is better, and our beaches are cleaner."

"Beside the point. That amount of traffic is untenable."

In his mind's eye, Grigsby had only imagined Main Beach so far, but they weren't wrong about the traffic now that he thought about it. Improvisation is a skill and, as you know, Grigsby had practice. He needed a showcase. He quickly ran all the beaches in town against parking. There were only two he pictured working. The first was Siccomoro Beach, which was a State Beach. Even more bureaucracy.

Second was a place he was surprised he hadn't already considered himself. There was a hospital across the street with ample parking, it was secluded. It was adjacent to the big store. A place where he could charge for entry, but still picturesque. A cove with pearl white sand, crystal blue waves overlooked by sandstone cliffs. Why hadn't he thought of this before?

He pitched Thousand Steps beach.

"We will have a bus come from the hospital parking across the street and bring people to the steps. The free city bus already drops off there all summer for everyone around the city. It'll work like clockwork."

Cox piped in again, "We want a cut of the gate." That was all he had? Even this asshole was picturing it.

"I'm already prepared to pay a large permit fee and am shining a light on our gem of a city, isn't that enough?"

Councilwoman Williams-Shaw took this one. Self-made, she owned her own business. "The permit is enough. The city has no part in the success, or failure, of this venture, Councilman."

That was it. The rest of the council saw a chance to take some credit for something. And when he saw their interest, Grigsby pulled out the poster. He knew most people lacked the ability to imagine what wasn't there, so he would make it real and tangible. The poster had a circular eye with a lens iris. The iris overlayed red, green, and blue to blend with sunset above the beach and silhouetted palms. A smart sans serif named and dated the event.

That closed the deal. The entire council supported the event with the dissent of Cox, of course.

As Grigsby made his way out of the boardroom and into the jasmine scented night, he found Bio waiting for him. Or, at least, standing outside the doors in the courtyard. He approached her. "You seem to have your way with councils."

"Thank goodness that's over," Bio said. "I never look forward to these types of events, just having them behind me."

"Well, you seemed comfortable enough to me."

"You, Mr. Grigsby, seem to have a talent for pulling victory out of defeat yourself."

"Do you mean the beach adjustment?"

"I do," she said with a shake of her head. "I was sure you were sunk."

"Not the first time for me, either."

"At city council? I wouldn't think so."

"No, that's my first council meeting, but I've made a life out of adjusting on the fly."

"It shows."

"I'm going to take that as a compliment."

"Suit yourself," she said with a laugh. "Now that this big step is behind me, can I take you up on that coffee?"

Grigsby had wanted to get back to the house and fill everyone in on the location change, and begin to figure out logistics but that wasn't necessary. Orange, Freckles and the kids must've been watching the government stream because, immediately, they posted images and promotional text to all the socials and pushed a banner and more info pages on the site. Then there were those promotional posters, the kind they used to glue on walls around town. Freckles printed them in the afternoon against Grigsby's worry it'd jinx him. Those beautiful promotional sheets popped up in a few windows almost as soon as that meeting ended, including Jah Lounge, where Grigsby and Bio went for coffee.

"A poster out in the world already? You work fast," Bio said as they walked past the Bob statue with the concert-sized festival poster in the window.

"Deadlines are a good motivator, but I can't take credit for that," Grigsby said. "I don't think I've accomplished something like that poster in my life." He smiled at Lisa behind the counter, who tilted her head with a slight question, and Grigsby ordered a Café Mocha and Bio got a peach, green tea and honey concoction.

Bio agreed, "You can't do it alone. I wouldn't be where I am without mentors or mentoring my grad students. Many hands make light work."

"I'm starting to see that." Grigsby was not accustomed to anything happening, good or bad, without doing it himself. The couple took a seat outside, next to each other on a couch beside a glass bead fire pit that shimmied and shined. A young lady in the corner played her own songs on an acoustic guitar with a small amp for her instrument and voice. She had two tables of intense fans which helped pull along the rest of the crowd.

"She seems to be getting a little help from her friends," Grigsby said.

"That was a little on the nose."

"Sometimes it's the cliches that work."

They listened to the music and chatted over their drinks until the end of the set provided a nice breaking point. The evening ended with a chaste hug but not entirely without longing. Grigsby caught himself chuckling as he ran over their exchanges on his drive home, like a teenager. Doesn't the heart ever change?

By noon the next day, the street team had distributed the posters throughout town and the shop owners were in. How could the businesses turn down the street team? The street team were the groms. The kids delivered the posters on their skateboards all afternoon while collecting emails and cell phone numbers. As soon as the approval hit, a communication went out and the townies responded. So did the whole internet. Never underestimate the need of a small business to increase revenue or support another local. Plus the value of virality. They sold the tickets through a slick event plug-in on their website and those babies moved. The Fest sold out. But the craziest news was, by midnight, a secondary market developed where the $6 tickets sold online for $200. No joke. This festival was real, and the momentum built.

31

PREP THE WHALE

You wouldn't think it, or maybe you would, but I didn't think it: there was a lot of work involved in towing a carcass out to sea and sinking it. First, they had to get the darn thing back into the water, which involved Nacho's heavy machinery, high tide and a firm, yet gentle, pull. Don't forget, this thing had been sitting for a bit and might break apart easier than you'd want.

Another issue was the tie-down that attached the weight to the beast and forced it to sink to the bottom. In other parts of the county, they had used old boxcars as artificial reefs to some success, so it was determined to use boxcar wheels as they would, more or less, surround the carcass and trap the body on the bottom.

Bio led the charge and, being a local expert with diving, boats and the ecology of the area, Ali was enlisted to help. Grigsby came down to watch, because, what else was he going to do? He needed to be out of the house and, along with a couple dozen others, wasn't about to miss the spectacle. BeachieGurl offered a wave when she came, videoed, and left. The grommets all had their phones out taking video of the event, as they were wont to do.

At low tide the day before, Nacho and the city's heavy machinery, namely a bulldozer, created a shallow trench running up to the whale. As high tide approached, the scientific research boat and a medium sized fishing vessel broke the one-hundred-yard rule, but not by much. They ran two booms around the whale. Ali and another guy pulled a line out from boat to shore with a couple Zodiacs. As the carcass began to float on that approaching tide, the boats slowly pulled the whale against the propitiously flat surf. Hence the journey began.

Two miles from shore, a working boat with a long-armed crane saddled alongside the carcass and held the old train wheels in place, while Ali and a team of underwater welders (who else knew how to work underwater better?) strapped the three wheels to the thing and got the hell out of the way.

The scientific boat had a drone-submarine which traveled a safe distance away and recorded the event from underwater. When the last set of wheels was released from the crane, the whale floated for a moment, then gently lulled its way to the sea floor as peacefully as a crab on any unnamed day.

Unfortunately, the whale settled on a space that had a crop of rock jutting from the floor and placed the carcass at a slightly bent angle like a kid in a beanbag chair. The wheels on the high side of the whale settled down the whale a bit. It probably wouldn't change anything. They needed the carcass at the bottom of the ocean and that's where it was.

32
All Together Now

The sun beat down through the swirling wind of Grigsby's convertible as he headed back to his house after the whale and a few minor errands. He found himself going out for quick trips during the day because he couldn't relax with the place full of all his "house guests". But things were looking up. He bought a little time with Tony with his golf win the other day, he had another meeting coming up at a studio and, it turned out, this festival would be worth more than any of it.

If he could only get that contract from that marketing lady. All he kept hearing was: it's on its way. "It's on its way. These things take time. I'll check on it."

He didn't have time. What cash Grigsby kicked over to Tony was a welcome surprise, but it wouldn't buy him much time in the grand scheme. That lady, this huge multi-national corp, that place was like the Queen Mary, took 'em two miles to turn right. Grigsby preferred his leaky boat. It was small and powered with oars. He had to empty it with a rusty coffee can, but it was his coffee can. And his boat.

The house was buzzing when he arrived. It was the kids, Orange and Freckles. And some guy with clean cut hair and a measuring tape making notes in his living room.

Katniss was closest to Grigsby, sitting on the wingback, so Grigsby asked her. "Who is this guy?"

"Some general contractor. I thought you were getting some things fixed or something because Mom's doing all that work at our house."

A grimace punched Grigsby in the mouth, and he wasn't sure if it was this contractor or that comment about Posie so he took it out on the guy who shouldn't be here. "What the fuck gives?"

The guy smiled, "Are you Grigsby?"

Grigsby didn't expect the contractor to be polite, that put him on his heels a touch, "Yeah."

"I was instructed to give this to you." It was a cream, starched paper envelope with Andrew W. Grigsby hand- scripted in deep purple on the front, sealed with wax. Grigsby had a not-so-sneaking suspicion who this was from. When he opened it, the hunch was quickly confirmed. A large *16 Days* filled the page in a fancy script similar to the cover. This had to stop.

"Your designer told me to look at knocking out these two walls. Everybody wants open rooms now 'cuz of these Home and Garden Network shows. But you could probably keep this one to save some money, it's load bearing."

"My designer?"

"Yeah, the guy, southern accent, that sent me out here."

It wasn't his fault. The contractor seemed a nice enough guy but what the fuck was Grigsby supposed to do? "Get the fuck out of my house. That guy is wasting your time and he's wasting mine."

"Whoa. I didn't mean nothin' by it."

"It's me, not you. Just pack it in and tell Sorenson to eat shit."

"Suit yourself." The contractor pocketed his tape and walked straight out the door like a pro. Was this not the first time he'd done that?

Grigsby took a seat on his couch and, in an attempt at some zen, soaked in the sky with the slightest horizon line of ocean visible, dark blue below and light blue above. He didn't even acknowledge Orange right next to him.

The sun was four fingers from setting, not even golden hour yet. Fuck that guy. Sorenson. Plenty of time for whatever he needed. It was going to be alright. It'd be good.

Orange sat quietly for a moment, the length of a long kiss. She took in the sky, considering.

"You know there's some really great story lines coming through this ridiculous concoction of yours."

Did she just change the subject for him? She just complemented the bullshit he'd been pulling. There really would be a way out of it. Sixteen days. Asshole. Okay, focus on what's in front of you. Grigsby turned to Orange and worked to find some footing. Talking about things out loud always helped Grigsby get grounded. "We are story telling animals." He held out his hand, thumb extended. "People say it's the thumb, but I think it's the stories. We're able to learn from the mistakes and successes of others. That's why we have this tech," as he dug out his phone. "Millions of years of technological advancement made this phone possible."

Orange was amazed. "You really think we can have it all, don't you?"

"We can have it all, Orange. We, you and me, will be the first to turn a con into a legit legacy. Not for ten grand and a name on the street but for a million and something that lasts forever. A FILM, our names in lights. No talk and no death threats. No hiding. Fame and Fortune."

"I still don't know, Grigs."

"We just need to keep doing a little every day. Like Aristotle says..."

"Excellence is a habit."

"...Excellence is a habit. Let's beat these bastards at their own game."

Orange looked at the horizon calculating her own equations.

Grigsby wasn't sure how far along he'd take Orange, but he'd need her. He could tap dance on conference tables like the best of them, but he needed someone to pitch. He needed the tech. He needed these girls.

"Did I tell you about this meeting I went to this week?"

"What'd you do?"

"Just a wannabe looking for a deal."

Now Orange was doing calculations to his face, so he said, "Not me the wannabe, the meeting."

"And?"

"Well, she seemed like podcasts are making her some money, but she wants to get to the majors."

"Like us."

"Like us. But she took one look at me..."

"And decided you were an olde."

"Absolutely. That's fine. Whatever. They can underestimate me. That's what's gotten me this far."

"But."

"But I got a real meeting at a studio and I can't risk being dismissed out of hand."

"As an olde."

"As an olde. We have numbers and credibility because of that website but their game, the studio game, the entertainment game, is youth."

"And you want me to come along."

"I want both you and Freckles to come along. We need your pitching skills and Freckles' tech. Then I'm gonna close those bean counters."

"All right. I'll think about it. Now that you've had your Big Dreams talk, we need to talk festival, because our man Gong is getting excited."

"What does that mean?"

"It means what it sounds like, he's beginning to see the possibilities."

"He sees the possibilities, that's great. Why are you acting like it's not great."

"Because of the tech we are skirting the edge of his sphere of experience. He imagines he has something to contribute," she finally addressed him straight on. "He has a lot of energy. He is excitable, that's all."

What was she not telling him about Gong? She would tell him when he needed to know, Grigsby could trust her to do that. Gong's involvement was needed and necessary. The involvement also meant he'd be contributing in the only way Grigsby cared about: monetarily.

Grigsby had a thought and asked Orange something with more excitement than he meant to, "You ever see The Sting?"

"Redford and Newman? With the guy left at the beginning with the cut-up magazines?"

"Yeah, when they pull the switch?"

They both laughed.

"You ever pull that off?" he asked.

Orange stopped, "It works?"

"The classics always work." Now Grigsby got thoughtful, "But you can't take the unwilling."

"Nobody gets something for nothing."

"The word of the lord."

She laughed, "Thanks be."

33
THE QUARTERS

The ocean offered its waves to the sand and took the waves back each time. Grigsby watched the tide's pendulum with barely a thought. Unobstructed peace for just a moment as he leaned his forearms on his prickly railing outside his bedroom. Inevitably his worry intruded like the splinters in his forearm. Today they would have the Quarter Finals.

After all that had happened, Grigsby could barely believe they'd reached this point. The top vote-getters got in and the first round was under way, shorts competed against each other.

Grigsby realized he better know what was in this competition. At least he would have to know the favorites.

The breadth of ideas and styles astonished him. He had never truly considered the different types of movies in any real way. Movies were entertainment, a way to pass time. But when Grigsby traveled, he was always struck by the difference in the bodies of water. Not only did the Pacific look different outside his window every day, if he went an hour north there were dunes leading to a light blue. Hawaii offered a very different tropical feel from St. Thomas or the Canary Islands, for that matter. South Carolina's coast didn't even feel like it faced the same body as Dover.

These flicks, he now realized, were the same as the bodies of water: they were all completely different. There was a German full of silhouettes and machines and another with amazing, stylized costumes.

An Italian that loved the circus, with its clowns and spectacle. Life was a circus.

A Brit who offered a couple flicks. They loved to somehow trap the characters in a public place and force them to react to an unexpected conflict. Like one of them, he was just a regular guy and was suspected of being an international spy.

One in New Jersey created a stir by telling the story like it was a news report and some people believed it.

Another had a cute alien as his childhood friend, and another had aliens eating people while a different one had the alien burst out of his stomach.

There were horror flicks with toddlers crawling across the ceiling and panoramic, painterly Samurai movies.

One kid dropped a whole side of a building around himself and a kid from Mexico City created a whole underworld of fantastical, magical demons that threatened a child and the world. Another from New Zealand used so much blood, Grigsby thought he might work as a butcher.

This New Yorker kept submitting all about gangs and the mob. They were great but Grigsby felt they were a little too close to home.

There were the inevitable LA kids all about noir with wet streets, cocked angles and high contrast, a handful of black humor and mysteries, but with a laugh. And another New Yorker who kicked his ass with a pizza parlor and a trash can.

This other family drama had a girl from New York. Her Gramma's dying, and no one tells the Gramma, but the girl goes to China to say her goodbyes.

Another one Grigsby really got into. It was a con that spun into dreams and consciousness, messing with reality, time and space. Now that's a new way to run a job.

Did they come up with all these ideas by themselves? And did they just make these up when they found out about this competition? So many stories and ideas and looks and feelings. Some of them were better than good, they were great.

Downstairs, the whole place already hopped with anticipation. It wasn't until now that Grigsby realized his home had become the de facto hub of the festival like he was running some sort of startup. Adam was on a call with Gus handling some sort of configuration issue for the livestream. Katniss was editing a montage of hero shots from all the films he just scanned / screened with a pretty good piece of music that built to a big finish. He didn't know the song, but it was working.

Orange came inside from the courtyard as she put her phone in the back pocket of her jeans, "You've really done it now."

Grigsby didn't really have the patience, nor did he want to deal with another thing, "What."

"Gong's coming over for part of the stream. He wants to see all the action."

"Not here."

"Yes, here."

"He can't come here. I don't want the mark here while we do this."

"Well, I'd have him come to the theater but that doesn't seem to be an option, anymore."

"Aren't we past that, Orange?"

"I'm never past anything, Grigsby. My memory is long and spiteful." She held his gaze.

He held hers right back. "I'll remember that. When's Gong coming?"

"When he feels like it." She gave in, looked away.

"You know it'd do us a bit better if you had better control of your mark."

"In this configuration, he's looking more like a partner, Grigs."

"I'm not sure how comfortable I am with that."

"It's not what I envisioned either, but here we are. You made the bed..." Orange tucked some hair behind her ear.

"At least his muscle doesn't look at us like meat anymore."

"Cold comfort."

Freckles picked up the guitar and plucked at a Johnny Cash song.

"What does she do again?"

"Don't worry, she has her uses."

"I don't mean as your fun toy."

"This is one of those times you'll just have to trust me."

The Quarter Finals. The montage of the most popular films as an intro with music, the touch of a finger on a cheek, the gears of a bicycle, movement against stillness. And the big finish went over well in the comments. The full films rolled. Adam continued to monitor and work with Gus on the livestream. Who knew you had to babysit this stuff so much. Grigsby figured the computers did it all these days.

Each film ran and was voted on. Each piece was a separate event to allow people to watch together and comment in the Discord server or on the YouTube comments in real time. He didn't need some Simon Cowell, people rallied and criticized on their own while the best rose to the top every time. They've said there's the wisdom of crowds. The more Grigsby experienced this online world, the more he understood that this community was real. Actual bonds and friendships were made. Users and comments racked up exponentially. Katniss said the new social function allowed the people to stay on the site and changed the way she promoted the festival. She had devised an approach that promoted the events and the movies on site and, in social media, she focused on new users, pulling them to the site based on the excitement, competition and quality of entertainment.

Gong opened the front door slightly, peeked his

head in and surveyed the room, then burst in and went straight to Adam. Now two things struck Grigsby at the same time. First, he didn't like this guy near his kid or at his house. Second, Gong seemed completely different. Instead of the cold; calculated billionaire he was loose, even a bit bombastic. He was also engaging.

"How is the stream? Do we have enough bandwidth?" Gong said.

Orange moved directly to him, "Mr. Gong. So good to see you."

"I saw all the people on the site and all the comments and had to come over. This is impressive."

"We are pleased," Orange nodded and gave a 'how about that' look to Grigsby.

Success breeds interest and it must've motivated this change in Gong. Grigsby didn't always want to take things at face value but having a motivated billionaire in your corner couldn't possibly hurt their chances. Grigsby thought he'd cozy up to him with some of his research and if he could learn more about how deep the well they seem to have tapped was. Why not get straight to it?

"Your father must've been very rich to have so many children."

Orange gave Grigsby a look that said: where is this coming from?

Gong turned with a look that told Grigsby he was somewhere else. "We were privileged. He paid some of the bureaucrats off but with the business, even before the limited privatization, he traveled. The family traveled. Of the seven of my siblings, five of us have foreign passports."

"What number are you?"

"I am the seventh."

"Seven! That must be lucky for your family."

"Not for the Chinese. I was simply a step closer to the eighth son. Eight is the lucky number in our culture."

Gong's entire demeanor changed. He'd also lost his accent.

"If I may, you seem to have lost your accent."

Gong side-eyed with a squint, just slightly, "You've caught me. The accent is just to scare people. I attended university at Berkley and got a master's in computer systems at Stanford. And, like much of the world, I've watched American movies my whole life."

"I hadn't considered that." Actually, Grigsby knew about his degrees with the research on him, but it was a special person who could affect a perfect accent in whatever language he spoke. There seemed to be a lot that he hadn't considered about this man.

They watched the film on the live stream about a record store guy obsessed with music and avoiding his life. Funny.

Gong took the lead now and started to lay out more of the business, "so, we're taking copyright on all these things."

"Yup."

"Is it enforceable, the copyright?"

"It's enough to scare the entrants and when the real deals come down, there'll be a new contract. Close enough for the internet."

Gong gave him a broad smile, "We have a million movie ideas and, with the winner, we'll have one that is market tested and proven. A stroke of genius."

This guy was too much. Grigsby turned around and walked straight into Brodie at the front door. Jesus. "Hey, Brodie."

"Grigsby, Tony's missing."

"What do you mean Tony's missing?

"I don't know where he is."

"You don't just lose your boss."

"It don't look good."

"What do you mean it don't look good. He's the boss."

"All I know is I can't find him, and we both know that never happens."

Was something really wrong or was this an over-reaction? Tony was a grown man, he could do stuff on his own once in a while, for Pete's sake. But Grigsby also knew that if Tony was gone, somehow, Sorenson would be officially in charge. It also meant the hot seat was hotter. Both Tony and Sorenson being out of town may give additional room to navigate, but he wasn't getting out of this without cooking up something really big, really fast.

A text popped on Grigsby's screen: We see your

event on social. Looks amazing! Come in Monday - we want a meeting.

It was Kate at the studio. The long shot hit! He knew this was going to work. AW Grigsby had a meeting in Hollywood. He went from nothing brewing to a meeting with bigwigs in tinsel town because of a silly idea on a shoddy website. That little meeting was one thing but a meeting with a studio was another level. Should he tell Orange? He might be able to work both angles. He was going to share this but now? He's gonna need the money to keep the kid alive.

Well, having help was something he might be able to get used to. Not having to do every little thing. What was he thinking? Forget stealing the advertising money, he needed Orange and Freckles for that meeting.

34

Another Morning

Grigsby walked downstairs ready for his meeting. The place was empty but for Adam drinking a coffee at the dining table swiping his phone, a plumber under the sink and a calligraphy note to AW Grigsby in dark blue on the counter. He knew the contents, but before he even yelled at the plumber, Grigsby looked at the *12 Days,* because he had to see, and dropped it in the junk drawer next to the others.

"Why are you under my sink?"

"I got an order to fix this leaky faucet," the plumber said, creaking his head out of the cabinet. "And then I'll check the whole house plumbing for leaks. Thanks for leaving the door open." He went back underneath for a couple turns then came back out. The plumber turned the faucet on and off. No leaks.

Grigsby considered and wondered if this one truly pissed him off or not. There may be a bright side. That sink was a thorn in his side. Until the guy said, "You know, a consistent leak in the plumbing of a house like this can cause serious damage to the foundation. No joke, you could end up in the ocean. Those drops over time create erosion. Grand Canyon was made with water, you know."

That was enough, "Great. Thanks for fixing the faucet. Get out."

Wiping his hands, the plumber was confused. "You don't want me to do the inspection you paid for?"

"That'll do. Thanks for the help," and Grigsby waved him out the door, out the courtyard and out the gate for his single second of silence before the girls came back through the garage and Katniss banged the gate. Alright, reset.

They had work to do. Katniss and Adam needed to update the website and push the content to their social media people.

Just as important, Freckles needed to get some of that same info into the presentation before they left, and they had to close the sponsor with contracts.

"Do you have contracts?" Orange said.

"Not back from Lawanda. I don't know why I had Arlo is draw them up."

"You had the lawyer do it?"

"If we're going legit, I guess the answer is, yeah."

Grigsby was feeling like Arlo just cost him money now. Grigsby couldn't decide if he was on the fast track or if there was no future in this. All he did was make money so he could pay it out to other people.

35

The Meeting

It was a big couch, hell, the room was big considering it was one of these bungalows on this old movie lot. Grigsby sat on the couch next to Orange. AW always wondered what it'd be like to get inside one of these places.

Orange said there's an old saw about Speilberg sneaking in and taking over an empty one of these bungalows. He did it so long, the guards thought he belonged there. Grigsby doesn't think that's true. Never let the truth get in the way of a good story, though.

Now, don't get it wrong, Grigsby is from a beach town and a big believer in flip flops, even bare feet, but he'd never seen people take a meeting in their bare feet. Weird fuckers.

Grigsby also imagined he'd see all sorts of clowns and soldiers and show girls and stunt men walking around the lot when he got on but it was pretty quiet.

He did like the feeling of the old buildings from the 30's and 40's though. The dust and old silt mixing with the cold cement even in summer, deep down. The corrugated metal, the peeling chipping paint. Nothing was as cared for unless it was on camera. The rest was fine, but it wasn't pristine. Not from lack of care, of course there was some of that, but from too much traffic. Except for today, he guessed.

The skinny guy in his tight jeans and no shoes, who looked more like a music guy than a movie guy, was on a land line complaining about Bobby not wanting to show up for line readings. His people say he's too big for that. But skinny guy said you're never too good to practice and no, that doesn't kill the freshness. Faking sincerity is what he's paid for.

The one next to the skinny guy was a suit. The guy had the chubby glow of too much wine, too much paté and too much money. Orange said he was part of the Harvard mafia. Freckles said there was a gay mafia, too. The only mafia Grigsby knew was the one he owed a cool mill to. They needed to get to work.

"Let's get to work," Grigsby said as the two movie moguls hung up their phones simultaneously.

"Huh, magic sync, amiright?!" said the skinny guy, Juan. His name was John but he thought Juan made him sound cool. Grigsby didn't know that for a fact but this fucking guy was Juan like the KKK were into civil rights. Those glasses he wore were just glass, no adjustment, either. A facade. Grigsby could tell because he could look right through those glasses with everything behind perfect.

"Tell us about this festival," the business guy said, all business. His name was Gore. For real. He had the money to prove it.

When in walks a tiny woman, short black hair, black jeans, black tank and 4-inch black heels, "Sorry, I'm late." New York accent. "How are YOU" - she said to both of them." An affectation but somehow sincere all the same.

She sat down, demure and focused. "What'd I miss."

"We're just starting," Juan said.

"They're going to tell us about the festival," Gore said.

"Yeah, what's the pitch?" Kate said. "What's to like?"

"Picture Cannes but in English," Grigsby said. "Outside on one of the world's most beautiful beaches."

"Verona?"

"Yes, Verona Beach, Home of the Arts."

"Why not Malibu or Santa Monica?" Gore said. "It's closer to everything."

Orange jumped in, "Because it's close enough to be easy and far enough to get away."

She hit her phone and the holo projector floated the graphics into thin air six feet in front of them.

"What's this?" Kate said, gesturing at the holo.

"It's some cool tech we've licensed," that's a lie, "for exclusive use in North America and parts of the EU," another lie, "excluding GB, of course," Orange said. All lies.

"We have secured use of the entire city," lie, "utilities" lie "public transportation" lie "hotel" lie "fire" - lie - "police" - lie - "and the full cooperation of the Coastal Commission, city council and mayor." Lie. Lie. Lie.

"You've done a lot of groundwork."

"Years of it." Lie.

"Why haven't we heard of it before?"

"We wanted to have proof of concept."

Kate swiped at the holo. "And, judging by these numbers, you've done that."

Freckles had set the numbers to update on the screen in syncopated beats to give the feeling of real time updates. The numbers were coursing upwards before their eyes. Followers, engagement, participants. Every wonderful and innocuous marketing buzzword you could think of was splayed before their little MBA minds. They wouldn't, couldn't, turn them down with this type of engagement.

"We have to listen with these types of numbers," Gore said. See.

"What's the creative side, then?" Skinny jeans guy.

"It's actually the strongest part of the presentation," Grigsby said. "Grassroots. Consumer generated content. But not like the old days. These kids have cut videos on their phones since they could walk. It's sophisticated, smart, real filmmaking. Take a look."

Orange started Katniss's short - just the precipitating incident. The horses and carriage - deep, gloomy, foggy, a casket. Original music.

Really great.

They stop at a cliffhanger.

"That's a start."

"There's one other thing," Orange said and looked around the room with a smile. "We own copyright to every single one of them."

"Did you put it in the language?"

"Yep. Not only that, they agree to it, explicitly, twice in the process and the language is the same as a typical work for hire or start up. It's what the film schools do to them anyway for using their equipment."

"Does it stick?"

"Why do you think Stanford's endowment exploded? Google and all the rest were graduate seminar studies. Everybody's got a piece. How about you?"

"We just might want a piece," Kate said.

"We'll need $250,000," Orange said.

Grigsby jumped in, "To start. With subsequent weekly installments over the next month until the event."

"Well..." Gore wanted to dig in his heels.

Then Grigsby got nervous but knew how to dangle

the line, too.

“Of course, if you’re willing to write the check now, we can offer a 5% discount on the entire amount.” MBA types. Always about the bottom line.

“Bennie!” In walked a six-foot two blonde who seemed to have just rolled out of bed with an ache in their head. They had on a summer dress and high-top converse painted by a local graffiti artist. They stopped and waited, pen poised over a note pad, but not a word. Kate handed them a sticky note, “Get a check made out to these two. I need it in NOW. My next meeting is in five.”

Grigsby and Orange were scared to even look at each other. Clearly, Freckles stayed quiet.

“Just sign here,” Kate said as she flourished contracts in front of each.

Grigsby scanned and Orange reeled. Of course, on page 3, section 15b there it was: “Studio corporation will own copyright in all places, galaxies and universes known and unknown.”

The check came in an envelope. Bennie handed it to Kate, who looked at Grigby then Orange expectantly.

This fucking thing was going to work. They did it. And legitimately.

Well, mostly.

“Just sign.”

“As this is written, you’re buying the festival and we don’t own anything.”

"That's right."

"You're just buying us off."

"Mmhm. Isn't that what you wanted?"

"I thought so. But I'm not signing it." Grigsby was getting attached to the idea of being legit. He wouldn't give it all up. He had a purpose; a team and his kids were involved for once. Was he really going to scuttle the deal? Plus, $250,0000 wouldn't cover the nut he owed.

"This is as good as it will ever get. The price goes down from here."

"I already discounted five percent."

"Yep, and you'll discount more. You need this, I don't."

"Eat shit."

Kate smiled and tore the check in half.

Grigsby's heart melted.

Then roared like a smelter in a steel mill, "Fuck you, Kate."

"We'll see. I have my two o'clock. Bennie will validate your parking," and she picked up her phone to swipe, cool and demure.

On his way out of the office, Grigsby couldn't tell if that loud whining in his ears was the intern squealing the cappuccino machine or his blood pressure piping through his jugulars.

He smiled cooly at Bennie as they stamped his

parking ticket and waived to the receptionist.

Once outside, the asphalt had gotten hotter. Grigsby stepped in a puddle of tar that could be patch, could be seepage from the tar pits. He looked around at the tan, yellow buildings and felt them growing higher and higher somehow closing in. Assistants rode bikes along the road that wasn't a road, Grigsby smelled the asphalt and tar again before feeling the bright yellow sun singe the back of his neck. Summer inland.

Grigsby had to get back to the beach.

But it wasn't going to be much cooler there.

The big yellow buildings rose above him like an outside wave in a South swell and he was caught inside. Paddle though he might those big fuckers broke over him and he tumbled and gasped. Usually, you can relax and let the wave carry you. You'll float to the top most times if you don't fight it. But on those specials days when the back of the wave is bigger than the front of anything you've ever surfed before? Getting caught inside means drowning and fighting. Duck diving didn't get you deep enough. Those walls were swollen and breathing, reaching a peak before they curled and broke and tumbled you into the ground. Sand was once rocks and corral, so to, Grigsby used to be whole. No more. Grigsby was crushed. There was nothing he wanted more than to get that deal but the deal needed to cover everything. The only thing that would make him whole was enough money. The entire amount made his kids safe, not a contract.

36
Dinner

Without noticing, Grigsby relaxed for a moment. As he strolled down the street downtown in shorts and sandals, with Bio, on the way to Salerno's the stress dissipated like antacid in a cup of water, if even for now.

They were seated and ordered their meals and wine in the cute little Italian place that smelled lovingly of garlic and basil and tomato sauce. They nibbled hard crusted, soft centered Italian bread dipped in olive oil and vinegar.

"So, tell me more about how a beautiful name like Violet became Bio. There must be more than syllables to it." As the waiter passed again Grigsby apologized and also asked for two waters, "Now, about Violet to Bio."

"It happened way back in my undergrad," she grinned ready to bust out a well-worn tale. "When I was in the field at the Monterey Bay Aquarium."

"Is that where you went to school?"

"We drove down from Berkeley."

"That was your start?"

"Yes." This was solid footing for her. Grigsby enjoyed seeing the wall come down just a bit. She continued, "I tagged along on a crew with a PhD and his grad students one day where they were studying the effect purple sea urchins have on kelp forests."

"As in eating their roots."

"Precisely. They basically eat the stem. The loss of their natural predators, top of the food chain types, like sea otters and California Sheephead, meant a proliferation of the urchins that, like you said, were depleting the kelp forests." She took a bite of bread and out of the corner of her mouth said, "I'm boring you. I always babble too long about my science stuff."

Picturing her as a college student laughing with her friends, all dreams and visions of the future, gave Grigsby a warm feeling in his stomach. He took a bite of the bread, too. Where was the water? And wine?

"Don't fret, I love the ocean. You can't live next to it and not care," he coaxed her. That's not exactly right, he wasn't coaxing her like he did with most people, he really was interested. "But you're just getting to the point of the story."

"Well, I knew two of the grad students pretty well on the boat and they had taken to calling me Vio."

"Because syllables are expensive."

"Extremely expensive on a student budget. And the ship's crew misunderstood them and called me Bio a few times. My friends loved it because we were all Bio majors and college kids love nothing more than a nickname."

"Hence: Bio." Where's the waiter?

"Yep. I stayed at Berkeley through grad school. So, by the time," here she listed these things off on her fingers, "I went down to Santa Cruz to be closer to Monterey for my PhD, had gone to classes, conferences and published papers, people were more surprised to see my name written as Violet than they were to call me Bio." Her biography completed; she crunched the crust then focused on him. "Enough about me, tell me about AW Grigsby."

This was always a bit awkward as Grigsby's entire life balanced on walking the line between not enough truth and too much. "Well: divorced. Two kids, grown in college. Lived in town all my life."

"This isn't a class reunion. What do you like to do with your time?"

"Work. Some golf. Don't surf much anymore, my knee's too wonky. And I play music. The first Tuesday of every month some old friends and I play as a jazz quartet at the Snowy Plover."

"I would love to see that. What do you play?"

"On those nights, the piano. I also dabble a little in guitar."

"A Renaissance man!"

"If running your own gig and playing makes me Michelangelo." He liked that comparison. Where're my drinks.

"Clearly," she grinned. "Now, tell me about the film festival. How did that come about?"

"Are you sure this isn't an interview?"

"Aren't all dates?" There was that smile in her eyes.

"Okay, okay," he was embarrassed and distracted now, so retreated to the canned answer. "It came out of a love for film and art and the community. I wanted to add something to the town that had given me so much."

"So, money," she laughed.

It startled him, she didn't know how right she was and because the real truth sometimes startled people. "Yes," he laughed. "For the money."

A moment of comfortable silence like they experienced right then can be quite rewarding. Grigsby munched the last piece of bread as the entrees arrived, he thanked the server, "Can we also have our water and wine, please?" Now, to Bio, "The Semis of the fest are soon. Would you like to come down?"

"And be your guest?" There they were, those eyes again. How does she do that?

"Yes, as my guest. You can see some of the surprisingly terrific films."

"I've seen some of them."

"Have you?"

"To be honest, that one with the Vespas might win it all. I voted for it."

Now, he liked her even more. But could Katniss really win this thing? That would be so great and so bad.

And the water finally came with their drinks.

37
ARTS FEST THEATER SET UP

With sparks arcing over him, Nacho held a lawn mower blade to a grinder. Grigsby came to see him in the city maintenance yard because Nacho wasn't picking up his phone. Must've been bad service.

"Nacho, I have an idea and why didn't you think of this? For the Finals."

Nacho stopped what he was doing. "What?"

"Arts Festival theater - You gotta get it for me."

"And why would I help you now G?" Nacho inspected how sharp the blade was.

"Our friendships gotta be worth something."

"It was." Now he looked up, "But I don't know if it is."

"Nacho. Pendejo. C'mon." Grigsby flashed his Grigsby smile.

"Man, you screw us out of the starting funds. You muddy the waters with all these extra cons. I don't know which job we're working. Is it the Chinese guy with the long play? Is it Orange? Are you working movie studios with this festival? It's even starting to look like this festival is for real. Grigsby, I don't know which way is up with you."

"Nacho, they are all in play."

"Brother, that's some three-dimensional chess that nobody is smart enough to manipulate."

"It'll work. I can see it coming together. But I need the theater. It's the only place."

"They close it for winter, you know that."

"For what? Maintenance?" Grigsby swiped his hand around the yard.

"It's the way it is, Grigsby."

"I'm willing to pay for it. No freebies. No deferred payment. If I can get the ten grand by tomorrow, can you get me that theater?"

Nacho was going to agree because that's what Nacho does and convincing him is what Grigsby does. The scorpion always stings the frog. "I can do it."

"I knew you could."

"You're a pendejo, you know that?"

"Always have been. Gracias, amigo."

"You think the only two Spanish words you know will do it? 'Gracias, amigo', 'dos tacos', 'una cerveza'," Nacho went back to work. "Get out of my yard."

Grigsby knew when the getting was good. He left Nacho to do whatever he did and chased the next step and then the next one. First Orange then the Studio. All of that will settle the Chinese. Maybe.

38

SORENSON SHAKES MOB SIDE

Sorenson was back. It was obvious because Sorenson was lying with his feet propped up on Grigsby's couch in his living room.

"Making yourself comfortable?" Grigsby said after he hung his car key on a hook at the front door. Sorenson looked like he was at his freaking shrink laid out like that.

"As a matter of fact, I am very *un*-comfortable," Sorenson said without even moving his eyes off the toes of his boots. "You know the loss of a loved one brings up many difficult emotions. Particularly a parent. A father."

"I..." Grigsby had to choose his words carefully. He hated this guy to the core, but this guy had Grigsby dead to rights, and his kids for that matter. "I heard about your loss. My condolences."

"Oh, your condolences don't matter but thank you for expressing them." He still hasn't looked at Grigsby. "As you may know, when people experience a traumatic event, like losing a parent, they often lash out or act irrationally."

"I've heard that." Where the hell was he going with this?

"Also, one of the five stages of grief is anger. My main one. And I don't believe in bargaining with my lessers." Sorenson rose and fixed his pants. "My father was not one to suffer fools, barely suffered his little children. Same with me."

Wherever he was going, Grigsby didn't like the tone.

"Eventually, we're all deserted," Sorenson said as he walked across the room. He had a thought and turned his full attention, finally, to Grigsby. "You know, you won't always have Tony around to protect you. Things happen. Lives change. Or end."

"That's neither here nor there," Grigsby said and touched his shirt pocket for the cigarettes that weren't there.

Sorenson proceeded to the bay window, and looked down on the beach below. "When I was little, I liked watching the birds in my house entry. One spring, a family of sparrows built a nest in a cross beam. Eventually, there were eggs, then squeaking babies."

Grigsby wasn't going to interrupt wherever he was headed with this story. Sorenson had a trapped audience and would make some sort of point with this. "The three of them waited for the mother to bring food. They jockeyed for position, squeakin' and squawkin', chirpin' and bitin'."

Sorenson worked his way back through the living room to the foyer. "Soon enough, it became difficult to get enough food. Of the three, the biggest got bigger and the runt? Well... Next time, the mother came with food, that little runt was bumped out of the nest and tumbled to earth."

Sorenson picked up the Virgin Mary statue, investigated then set it down. He continued. "A cawing crow swooped and grabbed the little thing. The big black bird flew so high and dropped it. This tiny bird fluttered as it fell but... That crow feasted."

Sorenson walked back to the center of the room, flipped his pen through his fingers for a dramatic moment. "I've already talked with them back east about it. I stopped there on my way back from my father's funeral. I will get my way on this."

And he probably would. Grigsby couldn't believe they'd choose to let this blowhard to carry the load instead of Tony. He had to believe they made better choices than that. "Where's Tony?"

"Don't worry about Tony. Worry about your own skin," Sorenson said. "Worry about your children's skin. Your hatchlings. Time is short Grigsby."

Fuck this guy. "Tony's gone." No, not a question.

"Yeah, he's on retreat. Like in those big companies. A leadership retreat."

As much as he didn't want to face it, Tony was missing, and Grigsby could assume who had the power. He knew.

Sorenson sauntered to the entry, "We all reach that unfortunate end, AW Grigsby. Don't forget, it's your choice which of your children will suffer the consequences of your inability to back your words with actions. That's not a malady I suffer from." He quietly closed the door.

Grigsby ran through his options again. He could just kill the son of a bitch. But Grigsby wasn't a killer. He would've leaned on Tony, but Tony didn't even own the loan anymore, had no power and was missing. That line of thinking ain't gonna help. Grigsby could grab the kids and run but they wouldn't do that unless he told them what was going on and if he told them what was going on, they wouldn't come along. Grigsby could pay his loan. All that took was this deal. If Grigsby could hook up this deal, everything would be alright. The deal was the answer. Get the money. He'd been through this before. Get the money. Grigsby will just have to get the money.

Orange and Freckles entered the front door. Orange said, "What did Sorenson want?"

"You know what he wants."

"I mean why was he here? Are you double dealing with this?"

"No, Sorenson wants to rattle me." Grigsby didn't have the patience for this.

Neither did Orange, "Never trust a cornered animal. And not only are you cornered, you're smelling desperate. Desperation isn't exactly where rational decisions begin."

"Don't you worry. I'm a rationalist."

"You haven't made a moral decision in your life, Grigsby. You're the opposite. What doesn't work for Grigsby doesn't work."

"I'm always true to the game."

"The only point of the game is the payoff, Grigs."

"The point of the game is the playing. It's the juice. Every game has a winner and loser, so I say damn the consequences. I just gotta play the best game I can, and the results will follow."

"Is that what you're doing turning down that money at the studio?"

"They'll come with more and better."

"They will? You a playa? You know this as a master negotiator?"

"You don't? A first offer always means there will be another offer. Did you see how fast they cut that check? We must be worth ten times that much to have closed on us so strong."

Freckles spoke up, "He's not wrong."

Grigsby wasn't sure if he was more surprised that Orange shut up or that Freckles spoke up.

39
THE SEMIS

To Grigsby, reaching the Semi-Finals in this festival seemed an accomplishment in itself. As people arrived, the crowd buzzed about the colors of the early sunset. You could never get jaded to that beauty. The crowd also debated where or how the festival would set up the screen. This location was tailor-made for the panoramic images the people online would gush about. A few umbrellas scattered through the crowd while most sat on multi-colored Mexican blankets, or towels and beach chairs.

Some had picnics and wine or beer while the few cops and lifeguards looked the other way. Younger kids chased each other, sand arcing behind their feet as they ran. The teens laughed and showed off for each other in their perfectly imperfect hair and outfits. As always, the chatter followed the surf forecast among some. The summer south swell was coming. Peeps were stoked. Grommets were chattering. It was looking 6'-8' and they wanted to believe there was going to be an off-shore breeze, making the waves glassy and barreled. The only thing that compared to the buzz of a surf community with a big swell was a ski community with a big snowstorm coming. Epic weather brought epic fun.

Our group of skater grommets did as always. They shot videos of each other and videos of the crowd while slaloming through it all.

Grigsby was pleased to see Stewart had his coven seated and ready to watch. They came down from Stewart's house in the 1920's funicular and he looked to be lubricating them with gin and tonics, sweet, tart and strong from the sound of it. Maybe, Grigsby did give him enough to chew on. Was Stewart's blow up at their meeting the other day a negotiating ploy? Stranger things had happened.

When Grigsby decided to have the Semis at the beach, he thought of it as an opportunity to pull another thing off that no one expected him to pull off. He figured enough people would show to make nice shots for the website and social. The stolen shots would last a lifetime, but he sold all the tickets, BeachieGurl liked the idea, and he promoted. Great thing was, just her post alone garnered millions of likes and #dreams #Paradise #VeronaBeachFilmFestival and #CinemaVerona. That last one would make Orange happy.

As it had a habit of doing, the sun slowly settled into the sea with a green flash. The water boiled and the sun disappeared for this time in the rotation.

The orange and red sky bled to purple as the stars peaked out, sparkled in the canopy above the full beach. Grigsby turned to his audience one more time and admired the wool blankets of pink, orange, yellow and red that dotted the sand, beach chairs in semi circles, and umbrellas coming down. Parents and children, groups of boys, girls, couples all awaited the extravaganza.

The time had come, and Grigsby succeeded at producing a legitimate event. He pressed some more flesh and walked around the sand. Everyone wondered where the screens were but Grigsby promised they shouldn't worry. There was another trick up his sleeve.

It was about time he got back to the house to check on Gong and Orange, so headed over with a little hope in his heart that maybe these things would work out.

On the veranda of the beachfront home, Grigsby and Orange stood with Mr. Gong as he enjoyed the spectacle.

Gong broke the silence, "All the arts have become silo-ed and self-referential. When have these films been influenced by another art, other than film adapting literature? Kurasawa and his painting? The Italian Neo-realists with people off the street as actors?"

Who was this guy?

"There are those that argue film cannot be art because the crew are paid. The end result is meant for commerce. Any piece of art can be made for purchase. Jeff

Koons also makes large scale installations. Are these not art because he has apprentices paint and sculpt for him as Koons directs? Even books take a team to make those books. The writer is not the only one who touches the characters on the page, not to mention design and production. Art is made to impart a thought or point of view on others. We should not judge someone's attempt to communicate, only observe it."

"Ingmar Bergman says that each film should be treated as your last. I like the winner-take-all mentality of that."

Smiling as he turned to the other two, Mr. Gong said, "The Finals better deliver."

Grigsby didn't know if he should be proud, offended or scared. Orange was unreadable. Gong hadn't given reason, yet, for Grigsby to fear him other than the bodyguards. But the man seemed to be a dangerous quarry. Fact was, between Tony, Sorenson and this guy, Grigsby wasn't sure he'd make it to Halloween and almost didn't care. He could live with that, so to speak. But the thought of his kids? Do the sins of the father truly curse the children?

The kids arrived and delivered Bio from the crowd. Grigsby changed gears, "Orange, can you double check on the backup generators? I don't want to be stranded if a circuit pops on us." Gong almost blended himself into the scenery, but Grigsby wanted him engaged, "Mr. Gong, we have a special seat for you just over there."

Adam volunteered to help Orange. Katniss decided to check on the ticket spot now that she delivered Bio, but Grigsby wanted her to entertain Gong, which she happily obliged. The kids'd never been more involved or interested.

Bio gave Grigsby a light hug, "I hope I'm not interrupting."

"Are you kidding?" He just didn't know if he had the energy.

"All of this is so picturesque," Bio marveled.

Out on the single-yard-width pier, Freckles set up the projector, which suffered her final wire and power checks as she prepared for the show with wireless headphones on her head run from the soundboard. Grigsby hoped they were from the soundboard.

Behind them on small beach platforms, two kids manned a spotlight each, swinging them around in the sky as if warning of an air raid.

"The festival looks ready to roll," Bio said.

"The icing on the cake is that projector. You know that thing Disney does at California Adventure?"

"How they project the movie onto a water spray?"

"One of Adam's friends has a dad who is an engineer for the mouse and the guy borrowed a prototype from the back lot. All we needed were water lines to spray."

"As long as they stay constant, the movies reflect back. Clever."

"We have the whole ocean of water before us."

Grigsby was happy for a chance to impress her, especially on something legit.

"So, you seem to have assembled quite a crowd, and a crew," Bio said, standing shoulder to shoulder with him assessing the event.

"I have to say, there's a certain pride in getting people together like this," Grigsby said. "This job keeps surprising me."

"There is a lot to be said for the greater good, Grigsby."

"Maybe."

She raised an eyebrow, "I'll go take a seat."

Orange came back and said, "Let's get this show on the road, Grigs."

The sun had set behind him to darkness and the windows of the houses up on the hill twinkled behind the crowd as he welcomed them with a mic in hand and the two spotlights upon him.

"Thank you for coming out!" Everyone quieted, gave him a space to address them.

Grigsby soaked in the energy as he surveyed the crowd, he could get into this. "Welcome to the Semi-Finals of the Verona Beach Film Fest. A quest where the shorts produced by our contestants compete head-to-head until we have a single victor in the Finals." Grigsby ignored Sorenson's appearance to the left, looking expectant. "This winner has the opportunity to develop the short into a feature film with a major player in Hollywood." Brodie showed up on the right with a chin to Grigsby.

The crowd gave its round of applause until a single voice yelled, "Give us the flicks!"

Grigsby agreed after he took a peek at Bio, who

didn't seem to like the look of either of those guys and Grigsby lost track of her. He had other things to worry about, "With no further ado, our Semi-Finalists."

At the very moment the color bled from the sky, a projection appeared just over the horizon line of ocean to sky. Like magic, the set up worked.

An orchestral chord was struck and held in tremolo. Rolling was the teaser Katniss cut together of eye-catching moments from the Semi-Final films. Shots of love and adventure, humor and tragedy. These flicks really had it all. And Grigsby couldn't help but think Katniss had a knack for the edits.

Sorenson had other things on his mind. Or, he had exactly the same thing he always had on his mind as he made his brusque way up to Grigsby, "Where's the next payment?"

Shit. Seriously? "You know I'm working on it."

"I'm considering moving up the timetable." Sorenson felt extra confident and needed to dig a little more. Grigsby thought he might be a little jealous of their success. "I have been wondering, Grigsby, which one is it going to be?"

How could Grigsby get his hands on that advertising money? Would it come in fast enough? All this ticket money went right back to these security guards the city made him buy. It's bad enough he owed the money, why had this asshole put his kids in the middle? "What is the matter with you?" Grigsby finally said out loud.

"Nothing is the matter," Sorenson said and gestured around. "I am just doing my job like a good employee."

"Putting my kids on the block is what a good employee does?"

"Sure."

"I have made payments through the years; I have toed the line for your bosses and their bosses."

"You shouldn't take this personally. This is just business."

"That's where you're wrong. Nothing is just business. I gotta take care of my kids. I gotta take care of this thing we're setting up. I've even followed the code. I protect our own. Even protected your bosses and the thanks I get is to have you threaten my kids."

"I am just doing my job and protecting the bottom line. No more. You shouldn't confuse the relationship with the business."

"The relationship is the business, Sorenson."

"No, AW Grigsby," Sorenson said, spinning his ridiculous pen. "It is not. You are too old and from a time long past. It is never about the relationship, it is only, and always, about the money. You are in too deep, old man."

Grigsby looked away to the projection. The montage was coming to an end. The movies would start but this guy made Grigsby want to burst. Maybe Grigsby should just kill him. He couldn't take it any longer. Any of it. Grigsby turned back to Sorenson, but he was gone like a ghost.

No sooner had that asshole left then Grigsby heard a big, "Uuuuuh," from Gong's direction. With a look past the projection then to Orange, Mr. Gong said, "Is that what I think that is?" He had smelled what the rest soon would.

A stench rolled across the beach and the crowd murmured.

We all knew that stench by now.

The lifeguard jeep searched the waves with the spotlight then settled on the corpse as it drifted toward shore, lurching and swaying with the breakers.

Freckles ran over then hit one of pier spotlights as the whale took out the water screen and drifted toward the stanchions of the pier. It was like a slow speed train wreck.

Everybody knew what would happen and nobody could stop it.

The kids ran from the spotlights as Freckles frantically unplugged the projector and soundboard. The spotlights froze in the air as they ran from the old little pier jutting into the small breakers as the whale was pushed by wave and tide, coursing into the spindly legs anchored to the sand. The century old wood crumbled with a creak and fell like a snake swallowing a rat.

The projector was saved but the light descended into the waves under the spotlight coverage of the lifeguards.

The music stopped and the whale rolled onto the sand. Flopped once and from inside the belly fell a man's bloated and long dead body.

The crowd inhaled.

The crowd exhaled and the most adventurous ran to the body.

The first to reach was the county coroner Dr. Inklehoffer who quickly extended his hand to the body's neck almost touching the wound but feeling for a pulse. Inklehoffer pronounced him dead.

The crab crawling out of his mouth had done that for the rest of the crowd.

The body's bloated midsection gave the impression of a distended stomach. Grigsby's eyes were drawn to a dark purple puncture mark on the left side of his neck at the jugular then he noticed a similar mark on the other side like a whale sized vampire had tapped the juiciest veins when the doctor pulled the fallen chin and his purple face in Grigsby's direction. Grigsby wasn't sure but it looked a lot like Tony. It really better not be Tony. But Grigsby was betting it was Tony.

Oh, God, how is he going to close all of this out. The crowd would leave, he'd lose his audience.

The bullhorn dialed up, Grigsby said to the crowd, "This won't stop us. Please stay. We will set up the projector and we can watch on the hillside."

But he had lost them. The whale was enough, but a dead guy was too much. It was so bloated, and water soaked, you couldn't identify the deceased. Although the bald crown set above the hairline suggested someone Grigsby couldn't bear to see gone. For many reasons the loss of Tony was gut wrenching.

The crowd already traipsed up all the so-called thousand steps and as Grigsby surveyed the crowd, Sorenson made sure to make eye contact with him. It was then Grigsby was sure it was Tony's body. Sorenson was capable of killing people. Most importantly, Sorenson was in charge and was going to kill one of Grigsby's kids. If there had ever been a question, there was no question anymore who ran the show. Sorenson had taken over. Now, the only hope Grigsby had was that Sorenson wouldn't fly off and take out one of the kids simply to further prove his point.

With a desperate check of the audience, Katniss was over with Orange and Freckles, but Adam was nowhere to be seen. Well, maybe Grigsby just missed him. It was a sizable crowd.

Included in the group was Stewart with his group of purple haired old ladies and flamboyant old hags riding the funicular up to refresh their beverages and forget the show.

The grommets all scrambled up the path next to the stairs, ignoring the screams from parents and grumbles from the men.

The teenies and their mom's all flooded 'gram with selfies of #DickiesBack #WhaleStench.

There was nobody left but the crew and the police patrolmen and Inklehoffer, who had been off duty ready for film under the sky. Now, Inklehoffer had called in the dead body.

40

NO DEAL, NO FEST, NO KIDS, NO HOUSE

Walking back along the beach, Grigsby skirted the tide tight up against the sea wall as he approached his house. A wave rolled up and he got knocked right into the damn wall by the force of the water. This was one hell of a high tide. Now covered in sand and wet, Grigsby noticed the waves were pumping, but they hadn't even registered before. Too focused on watching his feet in the sand, counting his obstacles.

He could feel every nerve clench around his heart just thinking about it.

Katniss must've been six or seven when a wave rushed up this very beach, sweeping along the sand like a viper. The water took Adam's feet out from under him. He was three or four, and Katniss grabbed his fat little armpits with her chubby little hands and helped him up while he cried. She wiped off his legs, patted his head and ran back to the water before Posie or Grigsby even got out of the chairs and to the kid.

How could Grigsby choose between those two beautiful little things? How was he going to save this mess? What has he wrought?

That Sorenson asshole.

What a failure. His marriage, Tony Jr., the cons.

How did he lose it all? No deal, the city won't let a suspected killer use the Arts Festival theater, no fest, no kids, no house and The Choice. Tony gone, sponsors surely gone, Orange surely out. All he had was this fucking house. How was he going to get out of all this?

By pushing. His pops told him that old story about his great grandfather up in Long Beach who invested his life in an oil well. During that time, as he drilled for years, some big oiling outfit, the name changed every time, so the name was lost but it could've been the Gettys or the Bixbys or some other of those families that built California on oil (not gold like they say in the history books).

Well, those rich bastards made offers to buy. They knew old man Grigsby had to be low on funds, which he was. He spent money building the damn well, on parts. He spent money on helping hands and lost the ring finger of his right hand to it. He even spent money once, then two more times, on a surveyor who said the oil was there just to be sure the oil was still there. He had a family to feed and clothe and not only did money not grow on trees, it also didn't appear out of the earth. That big company with salary men, it wasn't the families he talked to, it was their hench-men. They low-balled him with pennies on the dollar time and again. Until, eventually, he ran out of his money and his patience. He just couldn't see the damn well paying off like he imagined for all those years. He pitched his dream into the Pacific and he gave up on the well. Nothing there, never would be. Old man Grigsby sold the damn thing and moved from a shitty little clapboard house next to his well to a shitty little clapboard house next to nothing.

What happened next was told over and over but how could he have known? He just didn't, couldn't, see it.

What is known to happen in the past was an unknowable, unseeable future in the present. The week after the old man sold out, the well that pumped air for twenty years, that he fixed and prayed over, sweat, cried and failed with, that God damn well, a week after he sold it; that fucking well hit oil. That fucking well still pumps to this day, printing money for that company. Money that was rightfully earned by Grigsby's family. Sold for a clapboard house that was rolled over the day the old man died. He must have stopped twenty feet short if it was an inch.

The old man was known to visit that pump when he was down just to watch it roll. He knew he was right. He knew it would work and the proof was right there. The clear problem was that he gave up. He couldn't have known. But that didn't mean he forgave himself for giving up on his dream. How he envisioned his future and his children's futures would be safe from money worries. No, he gave up and never forgave himself that weakness.

When he was younger, Grigsby always swore he'd persevere. He'd never give up like old man Grigsby. But now. Now that he was older and knew. Now that he could see what it looked like from the other side. What failure felt like. How the depths of darkness surrounded you, leaving you nowhere to go with no relief in sight. Grigsby knew why his kin gave up because he was there. It wouldn't work. He couldn't do it. It was all a fucking farce.

Grigsby climbed the house stairs from the beach, worked his way to the living room so trapped in his head, he didn't notice the other people in the room.

First up: Bob. "They got you pegged as a suspect, Grigsby."

"What are you talking about?" Grigsby couldn't focus on the problem at hand, but he did know the truth. "Tony was my friend."

"And your loan shark. They all know about the hole you're in."

"They do not." The dealing and the conning were a secret. Only those who knew, knew.

"It's no secret what you owe, Grigs. C'mon."

How could it have come to this? "But I'm no killer." Grigsby needed to get a handle on himself. He couldn't let his fear rattle in his ribs and multiply.

"You and I know you wouldn't kill someone but the powers that be see motive and opportunity."

"That's not me." The waves crashed below but there was simply darkness outside those bay windows.

"Well, anybody that's read Agatha Christie knows that's all you need."

"A Story." Grigsby turned on the patio light and focused on the peeling paint of that rotting railing.

"You bet. A story. I recommend you find one about where you've been these last couple days, or they'll concoct one about how you did this."

Grigsby walked to the railing as Bob followed. "I need an alibi." Grigsby picked at the peeling paint.

"Sure as shit you need an alibi," Bob needed his attention. "This ain't no fucking around. As much good as you've done with this fest. Money. Visitors. People see tourist dollars and promotion for the city right now but that body falling out of the whale? You know people. They're gonna hang the good and the bad on you but it's only the bad they remember."

Grigsby got a sardine sized chunk of paint off the railing, "Well, I didn't do it." He snapped that chunk in half.

"You better find someone who did. What about that prick Sorenson?"

Grigsby paused and thought on it for a minute, Grigsby couldn't peg it on him. "Sorenson doesn't have it in him."

"He doesn't have it in him?"

"No."

"Grigsby, you know there's no honor among thieves, don't you?"

"What? Bob? No." Why would Bob call Grigsby on this now? Grigsby couldn't focus.

"It's me. I'm a cop but I'm your friend. We go way back. Don't protect that piece of shit, especially to me."

"Why would I do that?" Habits. We all fall into habits.

"That's exactly what I'm asking you. Why would you do that?"

Grigsby couldn't help it. He defaulted to protecting other crooks to cops. It's how he was brought up. It was the only constant he'd had; that he believed all this time. "I'm not protecting the guy."

"Yeah. Sure. Just come up with that alibi, the guys at the station will take care of the rest. We've been friends too long; they're keeping me a mile away from this investigation. Murder is serious business."

"Did you see those weird holes in his neck?. You saw the holes, right?"

"I'm sure they saw them. It's what they do."

Grigsby threw the chipped paint off the edge. "It was strange how purple the holes were."

"Sure, Grigsby. Just don't waste your time protecting that prick, Sorenson." Bob headed towards the door as Grigsby followed him inside.

"Sure thing, Bobby." Grigsby sat on his couch. "Thanks for the heads up."

"Yeah, sure thing, Grigs." At the door Bob faced Grigsby, "Take care of yourself." The door closed with the receptive click of the latch into the strike plate.

Frozen on the image of the door from his couch, Grisgby knew he needed to get rid of Sorenson. But pegging Tony's death on him just didn't feel right. That type of action simply brought on bad juju. They always talked about that time Jimmy the Face ratted out that lug in Philly and Jimmy went down for a job he didn't even do three months later. Karma paid its debts even if nobody else did. Grigsby wasn't giving up anybody else to the cops. If someone was sloppy enough for the cops to be able to draw a line between the crime and them as a perp that was their problem. Besides, there's no way Sorenson would do that without the approval of back east. All these educated new school kids were rule followers. At least, Grigsby was pretty sure about that.

That's when something in the room shook. He smelled something hellish. There was something else, someone else, here. The tickle at the back of his mind finally made it to the front. He looked to the dining table and sitting on top of the corner was Adam's head on a platter. Kale surrounded his neck like a 18th century puff collar, blood pooled to the lip.

Grigsby gasped and whispered, "Adam." It took all of his determination not to collapse. His son.

"Dad!" Adam never imagined this would be the one to work.

"Dammit. Why do you have to always do this?"

"I didn't think this one would do it, of all of them."

"You gotta stop these things. Shit." Jesus, he thought Sorenson did it. He reached for the cigarettes that weren't there.

"What were you guys talking about?"

Grigsby couldn't even look at him. He walked past him into the kitchen to the cookie jar and picked it up.

Adam wriggled out of the piece of table he hid under and came into the kitchen with the tablecloth still around his neck like an Italian clown, ruffle collar and movie blood trickled down all sides.

The cigarette pack came right out of the Garibaldi cookie jar in Grigsby's hand, a single cig was knocked out and Grigsby lit it on the tic, tic, tic of the stove. He inhaled like a drowning swimmer.

"Grigsby, what were you talking about all that money you owe Tony?"

"Of course, I owe Tony, Adam. I haven't hit a decent score in years."

"I didn't know."

"Why would you? You with your mom, and off to school and pulling your fucking pranks."

"I thought it was our thing."

"OUR THING?"

In walked Katniss, "What's with all the screaming?"

"I got Dad."

"You got Dad!" She noticed his get up and looked between the two. "With a head on a platter? Where!"

"Dining table."

"Nice."

Grigsby smoked his cigarette and contemplated if maybe he should be the one to kill these two. Tony's body shows up, this Sorenson asshole is ready to kill one of them, Grigsby's gonna lose the house and probably get thrown in the ocean with cement boots and they're celebrating this fucking prank.

"You two are the most spoiled, self-centered little fucks I have ever seen in my life."

All the noise stopped. "Dad?"

“Do you owe that much?” Adam.

“Owe what?”

“Bobby came by, and the cops think he killed Tony because Dad owes him a bunch of money.”

“Did you? Do you?” Katniss.

“No and yes, K.” At the end of his rope and for once unable to control what was coming out of his mouth, Grigsby spilled the whole thing. “But I don’t owe Tony anymore, that prick Sorenson owns the loan. I owe him now and I gotta pay by the first or else.” He just caught himself. He already said too much.

“Or else what? He’ll kill you?”

“He won’t kill me. Corpses don’t pay debts.”

Katniss took this all in, “If he isn’t going to kill you, who’s he going to kill?”

Adam leaned against the cabinet with a clack, “He’s going to kill us.”

“He’s after us? Is that why Adam finally got you? You thought he already did it? Went on a killing spree and cashed his chit.”

Grigsby looked between the two of them, nary a word.

“Fuck, I’m getting the fuck out.” Katniss stormed to her room, Grigsby was going to have to pull some shit here, “Wait!”

41

THE KIDS ARE PISSED

Katniss and Adam were pissed like he'd never seen them pissed before.

Katniss packed her over-nighter while Adam stuffed his duffel bag then waited on her bed, his feet resting on the bag.

Grigsby wasn't going to lose them again. At least, not this way.

"I can't believe you'd risk us like this," Katniss said as she reached in her purse then lit a cigarette with the snap, vrrrp, clack of a mirrored chrome zippo.

"Of course, he did. Haven't you been paying attention?" Now Adam had opinions.

"I thought you didn't smoke," Grigsby said in a ploy to change the subject and search for a place to put his own cigarette butt. He gave a real look at her. She looked like a young woman at this moment not one of her characters; something of Grigsby's grandmother in the scoff of her eyes transitioned on top of a little film school goth but her own touches, even a bracelet he and Posie bought her for her sixteenth, showed the makings of a woman.

"Whatever," she answered with smoke in her eye then a bigger blow of smoke.

"Just follow me." Grigsby walked out the door.

They didn't move. Grigsby walked back to the threshold, "Please." The two exchanged a sibling glance then wordlessly, reluctantly followed as he led them to the garage and flicked the butt in the bushes. He stood over practically the only thing in that place besides the car with his open hand directed at the 5-gallon paint bucket with so much dust on top it that it must not have been touched in years. "Look."

"At the paint?"

Grigsby looked to God above then bent to open the bucket by popping the top off.

Katniss said, "Great, Andrew, paint."

It was true. What sat right there looked like a full container of wet white exterior paint. Grigsby dipped his finger in, and it bounced right off the top.

"It's latex. A movie trick. I'm not the only one who pays attention around here." Grigsby unscrewed a one-inch topper that was threaded on the inside of the plastic. Beneath were bundled rolls, Grigsby-style, of what looked like cash. He grabbed two and threw one to each kid.

Katniss grimaced and raised an eyebrow. Adam busted his open. "Dad, these are all hundreds," he said counting them. "Must be fifty grand in just this wad."

Grigsby nodded and pursed his lips. "Yep."

"And the bucket's full of these?" Katniss asked.

Grigsby silently, continuously nodded.

"Just twenty of these would make a cool mill. You got that?" Adam said.

"Why didn't you pay Tony, or the crazy Texan-"

"Georgia." Adam interrupted.

"...redneck - off?"

"Then I'd have no wiggle room, no safety valve. No pad. It's better this way. Like I always say, I've got it. Don't worry. Now you go inside and put your stuff back. I'll pack this away."

The kids left the garage, and he reassembled the bucket. He reached into a small bag of dry wall joint compound and sprinkled it lightly over the thing by rubbing his hands together like getting flour ready for some pizza. Then he grabbed the spray bottle off the shelf and misted seven or ten times slowly at head height and watched the water settle and wet the compound like a light fog in the morning. Within a couple hours it'd dry hard and look like it hadn't been touched in months, or longer.

Grisgby closed his eyes in a silent prayer for the length of a tiddle on the piano then shut the door to the garage on his way through the courtyard. Something had to be done about the cops trying to peg this on Grigsby.

As he bent to sit at the iron two-seater table in the courtyard, Brodie opened the front gate with some hurry in his step. Didn't it ever stop?

"Brodie, my god, what happened with Tony?"

"You and I both know what happened." Brodie cast around the place. "Where's everybody else?"

"Inside." Why is he so nervous? "You know they're trying to peg this on me?"

"Well…"

"Jesus, Brodie. I'd never kill Tony."

"I know, I know. That's why I'm here," Brodie said then waited, thinking, weighing something. "There may be a way to get rid of this whole mess. Get you out of this - but you gotta sit tight."

Now, Grigsby weighed and considered as Brodie continued. "I'm not quite sure of the steps but I need to know you are on board."

"Why wouldn't I be?"

"Because if it goes sideways, you're done for."

"Looking like I'm done for anyway, Brodie."

"True." Brodie nodded, walked to the gate, pulled it open and made eye contact with Grigsby. "I'll let you know." He left.

Grigsby nodded back and wondered what he was cooking up. But, let's be honest, anything he had that involved getting rid of Sorenson? Grigsby was in.

42

We Can Work it Out

Smoking another cigarette, out on the balcony strumming his guitar, Grigsby wondered what the next wave in the storm would be.

Orange was slow getting back to the crib. Honestly, Grigsby hadn't expected to see her or Freckles ever again when Orange blew in the front door with Gong and Freckles in tow which was weird. Why would the billionaire Gong allow her to lead anything?

She must've parked outside and didn't expect him home. They went straight to the extra room and the sound of them packing their things rattled back there.

Oh my god. Gong wasn't real. The gears of the vault lock clicked into place. Orange and Freckles and Gong were a team. His palms sweated at the realization. He always knew they didn't have their shit together. A nauseous lump scurried up his throat. They pegged Grigsby as a mark, easy pickins, low hanging fruit. Looking back, it was obvious: the unexpected visits, the bodyguards that disappeared, Gong's accent that disappeared, the Bentley only on the first visit. A fucking rental. Even that wig at the card show. Boy did they read Grigsby wrong. And now they were as wrapped up in this as he was.

Were they really going legit? Another big fish disintegrated in his hands with Gong in on the grift. The existence of large bank accounts was ephemeral. This proved Grigsby's conclusion that no matter the size of the front people put up, or the size of the company, other than a rare few, the whole web hung by that single thread of silk, ready to snap with a strong breeze.

It made more sense. They hadn't hit their mark on enough of the issues to take him for anything. It also explained why she stayed around in the first place when she should have split after he messed with her theater con. Grigsby was a sunk cost and they had nowhere to go. She should've walked.

He could have saved this for another time or a better play but it just popped out when the thought arrived at the door to their room. "So, how long did it take you to realize I wasn't a worthy mark?"

Gong, or whatever his name was, and Orange froze but, admirably, didn't look at each other. Freckles continued packing.

Gong started, "Look, Grigsby-"

Grigsby interrupted him, "You shut the fuck up. The adults are talking."

Orange sat on the bed and crossed her legs, calm and collected. Grigsby had to admit, he admired her resolve. She wasn't going to show her hand. Then she said, "You've got a body now. I'm not going down for a stiff."

"You know I didn't do that."

"But you're on the hook for it. Tony's body showing up at the beach blows up the whole operation. We couldn't even hold the event. I'm sorry, Grigs."

Grigsby considered for a moment then said, “Drop the act. I get it now. You guys were pretty good to have gone this long. I’m not mad. A little sad to have lost a funding source, but if Gong hadn’t ponied up, yet, he never would. All the clues were there.

“But before we move on, I need to know about this job’s past. All of it. Maybe there’s a way forward but I need to know your plot points along the way.”

He led them back out to the living room and made himself comfortable in a corner chair.

43

ORANGE

Orange started, “Well, I was flipping through Instagram-“

“Wait, I want the full story. Parents?” Grigsby said. The whole crew spread around the room in chairs, sofas and the floor like it was story time at kindergarten.

Orange looked around, “Seriously?”

Grigsby leaned back in his chair and lit another cigarette, “I like backstory, it gives me perspective.”

“My father, though, he moved us constantly, was also, as often as not, gone on deployment. The family in military housing," she paused with a grimace. "The family. Mom and me."

"Army brat."

Orange nodded and told her story.

She flipped through Instagram and came upon this town with this perfect little theater and her wheels a-started turning.

Orange had just met a Chinese magnate making more money than legally possible, because it wasn't legal. Even after the government payoffs he lived like an emperor far above his peasants. The guy called himself Gong like he was an English duke or something.

The magnate, Gong, wanted to show off. He wanted to make even more money so his mistress could drive a second Rolls like his wife drove a third.

Verona was this idyllic little town, had a theater perfectly situated close to LA but not too close. Clearly it was Los Angeles to someone halfway across the world but strictly behind the Orange Curtain to any Los Angeleno.

Orange got a quick lease on the theater and got to town to get the lay of the land. Lots of tourists and plenty of money but parochial.

She worked a tourist for a few bucks and met this guy at the bar. Grigsby.

Orange thought to herself, *He seemed he might be a player.* As a matter of fact, the fucker was checking her calls that night like a pro. Every chess move had a response. She felt Grigsby out. They played the game pretty well together.

To mix a metaphor, she'd serve, and Grigsby hit the ball right back over the net like he knew where she'd go.

Problem was, these parochial mother fuckers in the town had a bro network. Small towns do, don't they?

Orange had never really fit anyplace having been an army brat, just learned to not trust institutions. What they did to her dad in the name of patriotism wasn't much different from her Chinese magnate. They dropped chemicals on them, made them take bunko pills then forced them to chase a disappearing enemy into a firestorm or raining oil. Her dad died of cancer and lung disease like they did from Agent Orange before him.

He had even called her that when she was a tyke. Agent Orange. Because she ran through the house destroying things like that firestorm rained down on the jungle in the other never-ending war. Sorry, police action. Intervention.

So, Verona was full of townies, that's what they called them on base back in the day. These locals had a solid grip on what happened here, and it was incredibly tight and impressively impregnable and invisible. She needed a local.

And this guy at the bar fit the bill. Grigsby dressed like a local and carried himself with the assurance of a local. He didn't wonder if he was wearing the right thing to look like the people from around or look sideways at what other people ordered. The bartender knew him, he walked directly to a seat without a thought. He was local. He knew the routes. He would know the people.

Orange had made some good money over time but not the BIG score. She had drive. She had ambition. And she owned it. She wanted to make a score that would be talked about.

Like Bobby 3-ball had made. It's what that old Paul Newman movie was made about. No, he didn't get a free ride in the red district. He wasn't talented like that. Bobby was so good, every time he played a pocket of games, he always found a way to sink three balls with one shot. Every time. He was so good, hustlers still talked about him, and that guy had to have died seventy years ago at this point.

Orange was going to make her mark.

And she knew the world around her. Her mark would be so big, they would more than remember, they'd talk about it in the movies. They were gonna make a movie about her someday, someone like Jennifer Lawrence would play her, or Amy Adams, but black. A bad ass like Lupita Nyong'o but from that time they make it.

Orange was going to make her mark.

Because she spent so much time alone on Army bases across the world, she spent a lot of time watching movies.

But Orange was different.

Most of the kids went one of two ways. They watched a ton of anime and when they weren't watching it, they were reading it. The other kids bought full force into the patriotism with war movies and blockbusters like Top Gun, Braveheart and Men in Black. Don't take that the wrong way, she loved both of those types of movies. It's just that she loved all movies. Whenever they went to a new country, she made it her mission to dive as deep as she could into the movies of that country. Japan, Germany, South

Korea. Even areas in the country. She'd get real specific like Mississippi or Georgia. Not just LA and New York. Nothing was off the table.

Up until now, she hadn't thought about it until she met that magnate, Gong, at that rooftop pool in DTLA. She teed him up and they started talking movies. He was in LA and loved the idea of it. Even started out with jazz and La La Land. The more they talked, the deeper it got. The magnate assumed she was a producer and said so. Orange didn't deny it.

Now, she was a producer. She figured, she saw The Producers; had seen those guys lose money. But, like everyone her age, had seen tech companies, too. Figured it worked the same in movies. Get the money to start, then keep taking money to keep going to pay for getting it started. She could start a never-ending train of money without ever having to make a product. In fact, that was part of the myth: Only 10% of scripts ever get made. They didn't even have a script. She could spin ideas with this guy for at least six months before he wanted to see anything at all. Once that tap turned on, many people have no idea how to step away from a sunk cost.

Conventional wisdom says, "In for a dime, in for a dollar."

Real wisdom says, "That money spent, is sunk. I'm not losing more, I'm out."

But once emotions are all wrapped up in it, people don't see straight. Money and emotions. Greed and avarice. These are Orange's currency. Once she had that type on her line, they never let go. They can't. Because they can't admit they're wrong and can't imagine that they were duped. Not until Orange has disappeared and they're left with a bag full of cut up magazines and a phone that doesn't pick up.

Once the theater was lost and she was in Verona for too long, Gong disappeared. He just stopped taking her calls. He must have picked up the scent or dug deeper. He had connections because he had money. When you have that much money, people take your calls.

In her mind there was a bright side, she had started with this Grigsby character. Maybe he could be worth a quick score. He had that big house and a solid network.

She brought in her old buddy to play Gong's son - the idle son - and would work out a way to get Grigsby to pony up starter funds for this big play. She sweetened the deal with the last of her funds that day at the theater then held on for dear life. When you have nowhere else to go, you take risks and she felt like one of those people holding on to the C-17 as it took off from Afghanistan. She'd committed. Once we were fully wrapped up, you can figure out the rest. It was fun. There was nowhere to go and if she let go, she'd just drop to the ground.

44
THE ISSUE AT HAND

"The only real question then, now, is: how do we move forward and get the cash." Grigsby could feel it rolling again; the juice that made this worth it. He laid it out quickly, "We will keep Gong in the loop as the high-end investor. It's best for the play, for now. The large investor looks better for the studios."

"The jig is up." It was Freckles. Everyone's head swung in her direction, annoyed and confused. "I've just always wanted to say that at an important moment. Y'all need to take a look at Instagram."

Of course, nobody had looked at their phones. There were bigger fish to fry.

Checking out their socials they discovered, Tony's corpse notwithstanding, it couldn't have gone better for the Verona Beach Film Festival.

There's no explaining what people will respond to. Not only did people gravitate to the #PoorDickie #whalestench stuff, one of the groms had caught the body rolling out of the whale's mouth, watermarked the festival and the thing had gone viral with that festival watermark and tags. God bless those kids.

Of course, BeachieGurl did her thing on top of that. She created a story on her feeds highlighting the grom's vid and the damn thing not only went viral, it was number one trending on Twitter. People were making memes mixing it with new dances, as a punch line, some Finding Nemo and Pinnochio call backs. Even marketing gurus were already posting case studies about the value of monopolizing the negative to present and accentuate the positive like it was the Tylenol thing or something. There's a lot of creative and opportunistic people in this world.

The Festival finally had its true viral moment. The experts were right, you really can't manufacture what will go viral. But, a surprise dead body didn't seem to hurt.

"We have leveled up into the attention economy." This time it was Gong. "We have mindshare."

"You sound like those fucking marketing gurus," Grigsby said.

"Where do you think I learned the con?" Gong smiled. "This attention is going to light a fire in the studio. When you deal in attention, you only have it for so long but when you have it, you have to strike."

Grigsby was feeling the juice. He could make it happen. It had to happen. "Orange, we still have a play."

Orange had that sour look on her face. "And what do you propose to do about Sorenson?"

"If I have to, I'll fucking kill him," Grigsby said.

"That simply will not play in the papers," Katniss piped in as she entered the room.

"Too many moving parts," Adam said.

"Maybe," Grigsby said as his kids settled in the

room behind him. "Or, maybe I'll just pay Sorenson off enough to extend the whole charade. Corpses don't pay debts."

"He seems to like your house a lot." It was Freckles.

Grigsby ignored that and addressed Adam and Katniss, "We have too many parts. You need to pick up some of the slack or the fest won't go off." He was proud of his kids for not bringing up the other cash.

"That's what we've been here for all this time." Katniss was dressed in a 1930's full length dress, her hair bunched in the back with a hair clasp. "You have to let us help. We are involved, anyhow. We'll get on the horn and make sure everything is tip top."

Grigsby grimaced, "Not this again."

"No, no, no," Orange laughed. "I got this one. You're Hildy Johnson. *His Girl Friday*."

"The fastest talker on film, sister," Katniss nodded. "And if you need us to get things done, well, we'll do it. Won't we, Adam?"

"Yes." Adam had the sibling demeanor that there was nothing he could do about Katniss's behavior, he'd watched this most of his life and was going to do nothing to encourage it either.

Grigsby liked it for once. The great thing about Hildy in that movie was she was a newspaperwoman who got things done. Nothing stopped her from getting what she wanted and Grigsby needed some more of that gumption around here. He needed the help.

The whale video carried the internet that night and the rest of the next day. In twenty-four hours it had two hundred million views. People couldn't look away. And those eyes also stampeded to the Verona Beach Film Festival site. There was a downside, the servers got hammered. Gus had to up the server load capacity again and the top three videos in every category were gaining views like they'd paid for the attention.

45

Tickets and Art and Cops

This big event looked to be worth more and more money. With the washout from the whale, Katniss had the bright idea to push all the Semi's movies to the Finals. Grigsby realized moving those Semi's upped the interest in the final reveal. After watching the tickets sell out and go to a secondary market where they were making 1000% markup, Grigsby figured he could get in on the deal. Good thing he had held back 20% of the tickets in the beginning for eventualities. Katniss convinced him that at least half had to go to stars wanting in, influencers, etc. He capitulated but he took half of those for himself, too. He marked the event as sold out and used the local scalpers to sell the rest at a massive markup, giving the scalpers their cut, of course. He clearly needed more cash, but Grigsby just couldn't leave money on the table, pocket money was pocket money.

Besides, to his mind, it was really no different than the crime committed against painters. Secondary markets. Do you think guys like Picasso made $50 million on a painting? He sold his pics for like five grand then these rich people 'invest' in art, drive up the price and add to their already sizable pile of cash. The artists die starving (not Picasso) and the rich simply feast, then leave the art to The Met. Well, Grigsby wasn't going to starve. Or die. Not yet. He still had time and you don't get credit for paying early.

Of course, that small section of tickets Grigsby held back ended up going to stars and insiders. These people added value to the event and Grigsby had to capitalize. Pictures of stars at his event would lend credibility and verve. Those stars posting to increase their appeal helped all of them. This became like a sporting event. Or the Oscars. People had to be there. Like a Lakers game. Or the Super Bowl. Playoffs. World Cup. You might be able to see these online, but you wouldn't see the stars participate in the experience.

Tickets were only the beginning of the event responsibilities, but Grigsby wasn't worried about the other issues. That's what he had Adam and Katniss for. They took care of it. Grigsby had Orange manage. Gong took the load on social from Gus. The kids were there to make sure Freckles didn't fuck up any of the tech, which she wouldn't, and if any of the studio people actually appeared, they would ensure the VIPs were liquored up and ready to spend.

Grigsby could see a point of sunshine at the end of the long dark cave of his existence. Hope.

That's when some guy poked his head in the front gate. Grigsby went out to meet him. "Can I help you?" he said as he opened the gate.

"Hi, I'm from Majestic Landscape-"

"You're just playing courier," Grigsby said. "Give me the note."

The guy, a little confused, handed over a beautifully scripted envelope with Grigsby's name in purple and orange inks.

"This is pretty nice in here," the guy said looking around. "Are you considering another space on the property?"

Grigsby ignored him and opened the note to *2 Days*. "Nope," he threw the note on the ping pong table and escorted him out. "Somebody is wasting both of our time." Two days until it was all done. Festival. The house. The kids. His life.

As Grigsby closed the gate on the landscape guy, the cops showed up with a search warrant. And it was serious. The chief himself showed up. Either seriously or the jerk wanted to be there when they pegged this on Grigsby because, with Grigsby a suspect, they searched for the murder weapon. They tore the house apart which pissed everybody off. They even grabbed the letter opener and pens from his desk. Grigsby had followed them around downstairs then gave up. The cops would do what they would do.

Back upstairs in the courtyard, Grigsby took a seat and the chief followed and leaned on the ping pong table. Grigsby pulled out a cigarette and offered one to the cop, who passed.

Grigsby had to find an angle. The clue to save him. That's an idea! "Where's Bobby?"

The chief quietly watched his men through the window, without looking at Grigsby he said, "Bobby's off this case. You two are too close. I won't allow that type of relationship to interfere with the investigation."

"It was Sorenson, Chief."

"You're the suspect here, Grigsby."

After all he'd done all these years, Grigsby wasn't going down for some other chump's gig. Especially killing Tony. It had to have been Sorenson. Grigsby had to find a way to link him to this murder. Drop a line, always drop a line. "Chief. You know it wasn't me. Why would I do it?"

"Cuz you're in hock, AW."

Grigsby stood out of the chair and joined the chief against the ping pong table. He watched those cops rummage in the house. Pick up the Virgin Mary and look all around it. They opened and closed all the cabinets in the kitchen.

"What? In hock? That little thing?" Grigsby said.

"Have been for years. Everybody knows it." The chief stood and motioned to the men inside to wrap it up.

"I don't know where you get all your information. Besides, we go -went- way back. What about Jr.?"

The chief focused on Grigsby. "Exactly. What about Jr.? You two got him shot."

"Yeah."

"You're bad luck, AW. Born under a bad sign. The writing's on the wall. We just need to find the answer."

As the crew came out the door into the courtyard, Grisgby stopped listening to him. *Writing.* The last pin on the lock clicked and he had to hope something would bring it together. Maybe Bobby could still do something, or, more likely, maybe the balance of justice was actually true. That scale would even out. He had to trust something, someone, somehow, would know what to do with it as long as Grigsby could put his finger on that scale.

Grigsby reached behind him on the ping pong table. "Did you see these?" He held up the numbered note on the ping pong table.

"Practicing caligraphy?" the cop said.

"No, they're from the prick, Sorenson."

"No kidding?"

"No kidding. He delivers these things to torment me."

"What? Fancy numbers? Get out, Grigsby."

"Sorenson keeps sending them." Grigsby needed him to see. "He's threatening my kids. Chief, he took Tony out."

The chief nodded, "Sure, he did."

"Chief. He did."

"Sure he did. And these are going to link him to it." Not a question.

It was worth a shot. "It sure will. Trust me. Take 'em. You'll see."

The chief clearly didn't know what to do with them. Obviously, they didn't find the murder weapon and all they had was motive. No proof. Grigsby could give him a start.

You don't make the shots you don't take, kids.

"You got anymore?"

Grigsby went toward the kitchen. The cops had taken all sorts of things from the kitchen like his knives, a screwdriver, and pruning shears from the junk drawer when one of the beat cops came out of the kitchen with the small pile of the handwritten notes Grigsby'd been saving and handed them to the chief.

The chief studied the different notes all written in blue and brown and orange and purple. "These are all from Sorenson, right?"

"That's what I said."

"O'Hara add these to the evidence, too. I want them checked for prints and the whole battery of tests run."

"Sure thing, boss."

"You'll find what you're looking for, Chief."

"Don't you worry about it. I'll worry about my stuff; you worry about yours." The chief bumped Grigsby on the shoulder and followed the cops back out of the courtyard. Before he closed the door, he said, "Think about finding yourself a lawyer, AW."

Grigsby sighed. He entered the foyer and closed the front door. He turned and gave the Virgin Mary statue a rub on the head, plinked the piano as he walked by and plopped on the couch.

They may have left the house like a monsoon tore through, but they left him there. At home.

Not in jail.

Maybe things were looking up. It would work out. He didn't know how. But they needed a link to Sorenson. That prick did it. Pointing the finger at Sorenson had to work. Those cops had to be smarter than they looked, right?

"Look at me," Grigsby said to no one. "Trusting the cops to help me out."

46

The Last Supper

To set the scene Grigsby cleaned up the house and moved some things around. With the table extended and pulled into the middle of the living room, Grigsby wanted everyone to share the same space and eat, talk. A lucky thirteen plates were set with chairs from throughout the house. He even cut down a double dozen bouquet of yellow, white and pink alstroemeria at the center, to nicely fill his mother's crystal bowl which he had bought back at Brodie's favorite pawn shop. Besides, Heather at the flower stand said these flowers represented wealth, prosperity and fortune. Couldn't hurt.

This was the only way Grigsby could close this chapter down properly. Convincing the kids to stick around forced him to face the fact that he had a lot of important people who had contributed not only to the job, but his life and he hadn't recognized any of them in entirely too long. A lot of the people had been telling him things he didn't want to hear and maybe he would start listening better.

The Finals were here, and he would celebrate his last and only effort at legitimacy. The money was not going to be there. The deal was not going to be there. None of it. But, he was AW Grigsby, he'd persevere because what he would have was his family. He would keep them safe regardless of what happened to him.

Katniss and Adam.

Orange and Freckles plus this Gong character. He wasn't family, yet, but he was wrapped up in the gig.

Bobby and his wife.

Nacho and Delores. Sure, they never married but come on.

Ali plus one. He could bring whoever he wanted. The man had earned it. Grigsby never knew he dated a guy before this night. Why would he have hidden that for so long? It's the twenty-first century in Verona Beach for crying out loud.

Bio, too.

The night started with a drink he'd been experimenting with: the Petralia.

He named it after the town his grandfather had emigrated from in Sicily. The only grandparent he could track much beyond the grandparents themselves.

Anyway, the drink was made from gin, Campari, Pellegrino water and a lime wedge. One part, one part, two parts all over the rocks. What a drink. But not for the sweet ones in this world, you needed to handle a little of the bitter. He tinkled the ice in the glass and Freckles, across the room, tinkled it back.

After that he broke out some wine and more Pellegrino while he cooked. Don't worry, you don't have to drink to have a good time. The food is part of the wine which is part of the festivities. The drink is not the point, or ever the point. The people were.

Now he prepared a nice meal. A mix of tradition and cultures, techniques and temperatures. Grigsby tried something new this time. All these morning breakfasts proved the kitchen worked for other people, too. So, he enlisted some help. Or more truthfully, he allowed others to help. Adam got the tri-tip duty.

They could have used the gas grill, but they were going in style, last meals and all. Grigsby had Adam pull out the wood fire grill and got an oak fire started. Together they made the rub from garlic, dry mustard and California chilies to await the orange and white-hot coals that would cook the hunk of beef.

"There's nothing like the oak fire for these things."

"Don't screw it up, son."

"Dad, I've got it."

"I know you do," Grigsby said. "I know you do."

While Adam cared for the fire and tri-tip, Katniss prepared for their Spanish frittata. She thinly sliced two handfuls of potatoes, a pair of onions and some roasted red peppers. Grigsby liked them so thin you could almost see through them, and, to his surprise, she had done precisely that. They layered this all together in olive oil to get started.

"I love these."

"Me, too," Grigsby said.

They turned over the potatoes once and scrambled a dozen eggs. When nicely cooked, they soaked the combination with the eggs in a large bowl long enough to make another Pelligrino then placed the concoction in the large pan to cook.

Now, Grigsby loved a Spanish frittata because it was delicious, but it may be just as much because he cooked it like his grandmother's peppers and eggs. The trick was to slide the whole egg, potatoes concoction out of the pan onto a plate, cooked side down. They needed to flip the frittata onto the frying pan to cook the other side. But here you flipped the pan on top then turned the whole thing over again, dropping the frittata into the pan and onto the stove for another few minutes of cooking.

Delores made a cool little lima bean salad with radishes and mint that Posie used to make, and Nacho prepped the Chimichurri sauce; a mix of a basil, bay leaf, oregano, mint, chilies, olive oil, vinegar cut and blended to be eaten with soft crusty bread and later on top of the tri-tip. Chimichurri may not be from California, but it should have been. There was a green salad and for dessert he planned espresso over ice cream and cappuccino if they wanted. Dairy and nondairy because that milk kills some people. Specifically, Bobby, who had an allergy to milk that resulted in anaphylactic reaction.

The night was a chance for Grigsby to acknowledge all of these people. To spend time with them not because of business or money or responsibilities but because he loved them.

And because if things didn't go right, it was going to be the last time he'd ever do something like this again.

Before Grigsby spoke, he looked around the table at all the smiling faces and soaked it in. He had his kids, who got along with each other and spoke to him. Reason enough to celebrate. His oldest friends and their significant others, who have done so much for so long; there were no weak links there. He had this new crew with bogus names, hearts of gold and nerves of steel. And last, a woman he could reasonably see a future with.

"Some of you have known me longer than others and those who know would probably tell you that I don't appreciate them."

Nacho, Bobby and Ali toasted to that.

"Well, tonight I change that. I've brought you all here to do two very simple things. To thank you for what you've done and for what you will do tomorrow."

"What, are you dying?"

Grigsby grimly continued, "In my dotage, I've realized I should show some appreciation before I don't have the chance to do it, that's all."

"So, to say it out loud for the first time in my life, I say, 'Thank You'. Thank you for everything seen and unseen. Thank you for enriching my life and my bank account. Thank you for being here. Sharing a meal may be the oldest way we humans have displayed trust and teamwork. Any pack animal can only eat through the efforts of the pack. The group surrounds and weakens the prey before the kill. There are very few predators that hunt alone. And I am proud to be part of this pride of lions, this pack of wolves. Now, let's eat."

Orange stood and held her glass for a toast. The gathered family lifted their glasses again. She looked them each in the eye on her way around the table, gave a slight nod and said, "Don't fuck up."

"Saluds!" and "Cheers!" and "Chin-Chins!" and "Here-Heres!" echoed and the motley crew enjoyed a fine meal, in a fine place with reasonably fine friends.

After the eats Bio sneaked up behind Grigsby as he put a pile of dishes on the counter, "I'm really touched by all of your friends gathering together to celebrate."

"I'm probably just getting soft getting so close to the festival, so don't be too touched."

"Well, I choose to be. You seem a bit emotional today, but I can see you usually take these people for granted and you should know, not everyone has a group of people they can count on when everything is on the line."

"You have no idea," Ali said as he walked in the kitchen.

"Ali, my friend," Grigsby didn't want him saying too much. "Bio was just saying how lucky I am to have such terrific friends."

"And I'm agreeing with her. We have saved your bacon so many times, I've lost count."

Orange entered the fray, "Kate's coming."

That stopped everyone in the kitchen.

"Don't fuck with me." Could that buy him time? "Why didn't she call me directly?"

"Bennie just called with a request for two pair of tickets to the final."

Bio, "I thought you were maxed out?"

"Not for her. They get tickets. We'll come up with some VIP something or other."

From the back corner Freckles chimed in, "We'll set up a dais to the side. She can be up on the pedestal like the queen. She'll love that shit."

Grigsby looked around and all the people he cared about in the world were right here. With the good news, they were either in the kitchen or peeking through one of the doorways. No matter what happened, Grigsby was sure: In life, he won.

Even so, looking forward, one of Grigsby's plans included everything not ending well, which forced him to consider doing something drastic about Sorenson. This was the end. Like coming to the last chapters of a book, there wasn't much left that could happen. If that million didn't come in, he was going to kill that son of a bitch before he ever got close to his kids.

47

The Festival - The Finals

The scene was set. A classic California outdoor amphitheater on an early October night. The light glowed from the stage on out. The grommets silhouetted as the group of kids ran to reach their perch at the rim of the bowl to sneak views of the people and the films. They had tickets but the fun was in the act of getting away with something, not walking where they were allowed.

The cats ran through the bushes away from the kids and down into the crowd where Stewart and his girls caroused in their over-sized Chanel glasses, sipping the rich rose colors of their Aperol spritz.

Tonight, history would be made.

The charity auction may have been the biggest surprise. After Coca-Cola and Pepsi had battled it out in their new world version of the cola wars, NFTcryptoCash.com swept in and outbid them both. Doubling the price. Grigsby's greatest regret may be making the amounts public. He wasn't going to be able to swindle any of that cash he needed so badly. They hadn't cut the check yet, anyway, but the kids would never let him take from SaveTheOcean either.

Studio executives made the trek, agents chatted, and stars shined before the papparazzi, influencers sparkled for their own phones, capturing, and shaping the event with their own perfectly crafted narrative. Katniss had smartly suggested a space to the side. She created a festival, and advertiser, branded wall with television level grade lighting and plenty of space where those social media mavens and warlocks could spin their yarns.

BeachieGurl was in her glory, big sunglasses and decked out in an all white jumpsuit. One hand in her pocket, she said, "Hey Guys! I am so pumped to finally have the chance to show you the Finals of the Verona Beach Film Festival! I was the first to bring you news of the fest at the beaching of that poor whale and now I'll bring you the winners and losers. Well, nobody is really a loser at this event. If they made it as far as the Finals for consideration, heck, like they say at the Oscars, it's an honor just to be nominated. You didn't hear it from me, but I've heard that more than a few of these finalists have the studios sniffing at their flicks whether they win or not! How freaking cool is that??!"

The celebrities and execs all hushed almost imperceptibly when Kate took her spot on the dais to the side. What followed was the jealous rumbling that accompanied a less exalted spot in the pecking order. Kate had three assistants trailing her like little puppies, Bennie and two other young women. Kate took her seat and watched from her perch like a queen over her subjects, just as she liked it. Grigsby couldn't help but think the V.I.P. treatment would clinch for him. She not only got the special spot, the others didn't. It could just as well have been building blocks or tricycles.

After she gave an acknowledging wave to Grigsby, a skinny little twerp bailed mid-sentence on a B-list starlet Grigsby had seen on Netflix the other night and sidled up,

"You have to be Grigsby! This is the grandest, greatest idea for movies since Cannes and Sundance. I'm Jeremiah Jones, I'm head of production at Rattling Locks. I don't know how you imagined such a terrific idea."

It was what Grigsby had been working towards. The attention, recognition, but this guy was a star fucker. And worse, there was nothing Grigsby hated more in this world than a kiss ass or having to kiss ass. It was probably the root of at least ninety percent of his problems if he ever cared to think about it. One thing all of the ass kissing proved to him was they were weak. The weaker you were, the more you wanted your ass kissed. The strong don't need sycophants. It's the weak ones who need to be propped up like a water trough in Egypt in an Indiana Jones movie.

Before Grigsby could get beyond an introduction he saw Bio at the entrance. He exchanged a last pleasantry with Jeremiah Jones and excused himself to meet her. Bio brought that sly-grinned grad student with her, and Grigsby still wasn't sure if that was a positive or negative towards his chances. He still didn't have a read on Bio's feelings for him and it may have been his attraction was just because he hadn't convinced her to fall in love with him. We all want what we can't have. He met them at the entrance to the amphitheater and couldn't break beyond small talk with sly-grin there. Not that he had time to deal with romance tonight, but he at least wanted to impress her.

The small talk filled the time it took to escort them to their prime seats, the better to impress her with. Not only did they have a perfect view of the screen, when it lit up, but with the hubub around them and media celebrities pressing flesh, he knew they'd be entertained. As much as he hated the star fuckers, he wasn't above using those stars to impress. Grigsby excused himself with the need to attend to all of his duties but not before having a crisp Pinot Grigio delivered to Bio and her cohort.

As this festival came closer to the line, Grigsby wasn't sure about anything. When the deadline had been set a month ago, Sorenson didn't seem like a true threat. Tony was in charge; Sorenson was just an upstart little prick. Now, Tony's gone, and Sorenson just might take out one of the kids. Grigsby was going to make sure he took the hit before one of the kids. They wouldn't suffer for his sins. Grigsby was still holding out that they would get that studio signature which would get them that cash infusion, which allowed Grigsby to pay off the prick and allow everyone to live happily ever after. Because, c'mon, it's the movies, we can all have a happy ending, right?

That pen came swirling over Sorenson's fingers, a casual walk with cunning eyes approached Grigsby, "I am sure I don't have to remind you, but the time is at hand. You choose a child tonight. And choose you will. If not, I will kill them both."

Grigsby's focus washed away like he was trapped under the pounding waves, scrambling for air. He thrashed but couldn't find escape. Couldn't find sweet, sweet breath. He'd been fooling himself that he could avoid this. Or that he would kill the bastard. After the wave broke over him and Grigsby found his feet, Sorenson went in again.

"You could almost call it a witching hour, huh?" Yes, Sorenson felt it tonight. The surge of power and dominance, of how he owned Grigsby and Grigsby couldn't do a thing about it, except of course to pay him. Really, either way, Sorenson won. The payoff gave him money and power, killing the kids gave him credibility and power. "Are you sure this excess will even save your children? Looks like you took your eyes off the prize. It's a shame really."

When the cops arrived, Grigsby was sure they were here for him. If it wasn't the scheming and the money, it was something as mundane as his permits and license. Did Nacho take care of everyone? He couldn't rescue the kids from jail.

Grigsby flailed adrift. His breath left him; the abject terror shut his system down. His lizard brain failed, his most basic functions, the neurons and synapses that fired without conscious direction failed as the police chief and two pair of uniformed officers strutted with purpose directly at him.

What a beautiful moment when those cops walked right past him without an ounce of acknowledgment. Grigsby couldn't fathom what they were doing. At the time, it just didn't compute.

Bobby, in uniform, trailed the group. And he passed. With a wink.

The chief addressed the psychopath facing Grigsby.

The authority of the badges and the policeman's numbers kept Sorenson's bodyguards back. Or the fact that Sorenson's a prick.

"And under what grounds is this arrest?" Sorenson said as he spun that pen over his thumb.

The chief nodded with a raised eyebrow at the pen and threw a chin directing his charges. The officers acknowledged their boss and took possession of Sorenson and the pen.

"Sorenson," the chief said. "We have an arrest warrant for the murder of Tony Gandalfo."

"That's your opinion?"

"It is more than my opinion. This warrant means a judge agreed with our assessment of you as the murderer. I suggest you save the talking for your lawyer." The chief used that smile Grigsby had seen directed his way so many times before. "Unless, of course, you'd like to confess."

Sorenson clammed up and held out his hands for the cuffs.

The cops cuffed Sorenson, taking him into custody. Grigsby almost couldn't believe it was someone else having his Miranda rights read to him. Almost. He knew there was a way.

Grigsby felt a surge of relief. He burst through the water and gulped a mouthful of air between waves. It had happened. Sorenson was under arrest for the murder of Big Tony.

Everybody knew that Sorenson had done the dirty deed but how would, could, they tie the killing to him?

Brodie appeared at Grigsby's shoulder.

Sorenson mad dogged Brodie as he was marched from the amphitheater. The two watched as they escorted him through the gates then Grigsby looked at Brodie for an answer. For a moment, Brodie paid him no mind.

Then Brodie beamed at Grigsby and had that answer. "It was the pen and ink," he said.

Grigsby pushed up an eyebrow and nodded

deliberately then said, “Clearly.”

“Yeah, apparently, not only does that pen he’s always spinning make a distinct cut when used for punctures, that pen is filled with an extremely rare ink made from a combination of squid ink... sap, nuts and berries, I don’t know, a million other things. The point is, nobody but that jerk has both the pen and the ink. At least not in this town.

Besides, Bobby tells me you simply have to prove beyond a reasonable doubt.”

“Assuming Sorenson would still be in the country to go to court,” Grigsby said.

Brodie looked thoughtful for just a second. “He won’t be making it to court. There’s some guys who owe me and have recently been admitted to County Jail.”

One of those high end real estate agents gave Brodie her million dollar smile and that put a sparkle in his eye. He put an arm on Grigsby’s shoulder and said, “There can be some menacing people. Mysterious things happen in places like that.”

Brodie laughed and walked toward the agent with a wave. “I’ll be seeing you, Grigsby.”

That was an incredibly big check mark off his list. Grigsby believed in himself, always, but even he had a hard time believing this one would work out. You know what? The long shots hit, too. And it feels like nothing else when they do.

Now, what was next on that list? He gained some space to think again.

Grigsby looked over to the dais and Kate was nowhere to be seen. He couldn't allow this one win, that wasn't really even his, get in the way of what he had to do. Shit, this dog and pony show still needed to deliver. He made eye contact with Orange and gestured for: "Where the hell was Kate?"

Orange texted: She's introducing Gong around.

Grigsby: No shit?

No shit.

He would learn. He would trust Kate to be taken care of and with that out of his hands for the moment he peeked around for Bio, but she was nowhere to be seen. Did she see the whole mess with Sorenson?

Of course. Everyone here saw that go down. That, too, would have to wait until later. He wanted to catch a little of the show with her but maybe she wouldn't want to deal with all of Grigsby's issues. Or maybe she went to the little girl's room.

One could hope.

The murmur of the crowd reached a crescendo when the lights dimmed, injecting silence as the darkness rolled over the amphitheater.

48

SUCCESS

A title card faded up with fans hooting and hollering for the start of the show. Music played as the projection displayed multi-colored Vespas pulling a hay wagon with a coffin on top through an old cemetery and coming to rest before a mausoleum.

Grigsby had pulled a lot of cons and made plenty of money on most of them but they had never felt like this. To sit in this amphitheater with the stars above, the stars all around, an audience cheering and, to top it off, his little girl's movie leading the charge? This was quite a moment to savor.

The winning documentary was from the grommets with an iPhone doc about the beached whale, snippets of all the characters, from the kid's perspective, all looking like good citizens doing good deeds (we all learn about what we look like from the outside / from a child's perspective / an appeal to our better selves). The original had done fine but this one finished with a surprise ending they had recorded just days earlier. They overtook everyone in the competition. This latest version couldn't win because of the way the rounds worked but, suffice to say, they had more views than all of the other videos combined times ten.

Their bit of genius was to include the dead body rolling out (you can't beat the viral lightning strike). They had worked a deal with Bio to record Dickie's final voyage.

Concerned that this thing was going to disintegrate, they tied up to the whale tail with half a dozen ropes and waited for the high tide to float Dickie again. Once she had full buoyancy, they slowly began the long tow back to the designated fall spot.

This time they used a couple tons of rusty chains they sequestered from the old naval yard in Long Beach and gently settled them on the carcass. A bulge gathered near the tail as they hoped and waited for the chains to win the battle of solid versus gas. After watching the bubble slowly move then explode for the biggest longest fart you could ever hope not to hear, the gas and intestines sprayed away from the boat, then Dickie sank. Fortunately, this moment was captured for posterity in the documentary. As a matter of fact, the lauded science photographer who had insinuated himself on the trip, placed the image in none other than National Geographic because, apparently, even PhD's think farts are funny. This time, with any luck, Dickie was down there for good.

Katniss and Freckles stood at the very back, on each side of the projector, and watched the movies, cringing and laughing, fully enjoying the fact that they had made and completed the damn festival.

They were watching in front of a crowd just as they had promised.

Kate watched beside them, too.

These shorts weren't going to win an Oscar or even get a movie deal, but they were good. They were true and real.

It was beautiful.

Grigsby sidled next to Kate. Orange was directly on the other side.

"To be honest, I expected the two of you to be scammers. But this is a very nice, somewhat impressive display. You just may make something out of this, yet."

"Not bad," Grigsby said. They both nodded their heads in agreement.

"I have some notes," Kate said.

"Do you?" Orange said.

"You do?" Grigsby said.

"I do."

"We have a deal?"

"It's a start. If you can get this thing off the ground and get all those people here," she spread her hands to the crowd, "and get me here, you can get a movie off the ground. That's all a production is-"

The murder of cats ran through the walkway, one side to the other and disappeared into the bushes from whence they came.

"-it's herding cats," Kate finished.

"And apparently, you have learned to do that. You also got the crowds to come out. We need people like you in this world. Too many bean counters not enough carnival men. It's the storytellers that make the movies what they are not the line counters. It will work because you can weave a story like a wizard weaves a spell." She considered her next words as she looked over the crowd as they laughed at the right time. "No. Let's be honest, you will weave the design, I will pay for it. We will find someone to weave the spell. It is the auteur who carries that load with the help of his producer, writer, and the rest."

Grigsby would keep on keepin' on. Maybe he really could make a go of the movies and the fest with the kids and everyone else. For the first time in a long time, Grigsby knew things were going in a positive direction. He said, "We'll make a hell of a team."

"That we will," she said as she waved to Bennie who had been waiting to the side, unnoticed. "I'll have legal draw up a contract. Bennie will send them over." She walked away, "Bennie! Where the hell did you go?"

49

Everything Has an End

Our whale corpse, Dickie, sunk and rotted at the bottom of the ocean not far from San Clemente Island, adjacent to the Banks. The Banks was the spot in the middle of the ocean where underwater mountains rose in the sea plain and created forty and fifty-foot waves. Surfers of a certain sort came out here to be towed in by Jet Skis and SeaDoos and surf the massive waves. This handful of guys were supported by a score more riding, wiping out and risking their lives to catch that high of riding a massive wave. Risking their lives to ensure they were remembered. Risking their lives to secure that sponsorship so they could continue risking their lives.

Meanwhile, a full league beneath those waves above, the whale that finally settled on the sea floor had served its first visitors. A planted camera captured three great white sharks as they took turns attacking the body and tearing pieces off. At first, once all the commotion ended, the sharks circled, unsure if there was a threat. Eventually they settled into a rarity in their struggle for existence: a feast. An opportunity to gorge themselves and have more than they could handle.

As the sharks feasted, ratfish and hagfish from just a bit lower on the food ladder rungs came to do the same. Pecking and biting, they pulled the meat and fat from the bones. The scavengers got smaller and so did the other partiers. Squid and crabs swarmed to the easy meal, seated at the table with other fish and members of the community. Mollusks, crustaceans, and worms feed on leftover blubber. After weeks and months, the carcass was merely the framework of what it once had been. A skeleton with more scavengers atop that scraped the bones of the last protein from without and within. Worms sucked the marrow and ate the bone itself and microbiological entities broke down what we could not see until the body collapsed on itself and fully joined the world from which it emerged, as all things must do.

Bio stepped off the research boat, the *Trudie*, onto the dock and recalibrated her sea legs.

Grigsby waited to get into a more personal distance before saying anything.

When she saw Grigsby, the spring in Bio's step disappeared before she made it over the gangplank. She greeted him with a cursory wave and a reluctant smile.

Oh.

He had been dumped enough times to know the signs. He'd dumped enough times to know the signs. There had been enough good right now, he always girded himself for the inevitable swing of the pendulum. She wasn't up for this.

"Did you learn anything new?" he asked

"We extracted some specimens and will see what's there. Science is slow."

"I took a look, and your livestream of the sub had a heck of an audience."

"This whole dead whale thing took on a life of its own. To be honest, I just want to sit in my hammock and rock. No, strike that, I've had enough rocking for the moment, I'd go for a nice solid chair with the ottoman holding my stretched-out legs. All alone and quiet."

"I thought maybe I could take you for a bite to eat."

There's the look. She was going to drop the hammer.

"Grigs, I can't do this."

Maybe he could talk her out of it.

"It doesn't have to be this way," Grigsby said. "I've changed. You see it don't you?"

"I see it but I'm not twenty anymore. I don't have to settle for a smile and charm. You just don't have enough for me."

"I just closed the biggest deal of my life. I'm hopping on the fast track."

"Exactly. And I have the department and my crew and studies to complete. I'm not going anywhere. And I don't want that. I don't want what you want."

"But I want you."

"I don't want you, Grigsby. I don't want the lies and the manipulations and intrigue. I just want someone to share a glass of wine with at the end of the day. Or a slice of cheese and saltines standing at the kitchen counter."

"I can do that. I like saltines. I've changed, Bio."

"A shark can't stop hunting. And I wouldn't want it to. That's what makes sharks wonderful. I won't ask you to stop either. We're just too different."

Grigsby took in her eyes, the color of the ocean today. Green and blue and deep. He'd never be here again, this close, surrounded by her attention. The breeze rattled her gray and blonde strands of hair that had fallen from her salty, bent cap. He captured an image in his mind to remember her this way.

Bio patted him on his left shoulder with a squeeze, a last look straight into his breaking heart and walked past. Well, broken might be too strong a word. But it was dented.

As she said her goodbyes to the crew getting into their vehicles, she got into her own car and drove off. Grigsby walked to the corner of the dock away from everyone. The tide pushed the sun-streaked water into the harbor and the seagulls hung still above him riding the wind under their wings.

A pair of dolphins intermittently surfaced for air.

A horn blared and he saw Bobby at the helm of Harbor Patrol. Bobby laughed at Grigsby's startled jump. Grigsby waved back and watched the waves lap on the stacked gray rocks of the jetty, chloroform-filled sea grass waving hello just underneath. He turned back to the mostly empty parking lot and his convertible.

Welp, right now, he had a party to prepare for.

50

Back at the Patio

The entire crew was there. It was nice.

The kids brought in the tin containers with everything from Papagayos: carne asada, carnitas, pollo rojo, beans and rice. Guacamole and chips. They had everything, but they needed a big bowl for chips. Grigsby was on his way to the garage when Brodie showed up. So excited, he grabbed Grigsby by the head in the entryway. Rough housing, really. Brodie couldn't contain himself. They won. Well, Brodie won. Brodie was the boss now.

As Brodie threw Grigsby free from the ruckus they knocked over the Virgin Mary statue in the alcove and it shattered on the floor. Plaster everywhere.

It was Freckles first, "I thought that thing would be full of rubies, diamonds and emeralds."

Orange agreed, and so did the kids.

"Jesus, what'd you think it was? Rosebud?" Grigsby picked up the cross that had been embedded in the hand on her heart. "The cross was Jr.'s."

"Ohhhh," said both the kids. Brodie, too.

Grigsby looked at Orange, Freckles and Gong. "It's a long story. Besides, I have a special relationship with Mary. I'm gonna get the broom."

Adam picked up the big pieces while Grigsby went outside.

"While you're out there get the bowl," Katniss called and went back to the kitchen.

Just inside the garage he grabbed the short broom and dustpan. The first bowl, he couldn't reach, so he grabbed the bucket. The paint bucket with the cash. When he stepped on top of it to reach and lift the thing from the rafter, the bucket tipped.

Grigsby took a small spill and the bucket was on its side wide open, the rolled chunks of cash in plastic - saran wrapped rolls with duct tape - clearly marked in denominations in Grigsby rolls - tumbled out. He picked himself up, brushed himself off, like it's everyday, and put the money back - 1, 2, 3, 4 ...twenty chunks that looked to be fifty grand each. Only two of the rolls were cash. The rest were blanks. He double checked 'cuz you never know, there was always a chance for a little magic somehow. But, he knew. He always found the magic, but these were marked up paper empties.

You can't teach an old dog new tricks. Grigsby would keep working the old tricks until the end. Or, maybe you can teach an old dog new tricks, but he was still the same old dog.

With the bowl in hand Grigsby headed inside and handed it to Freckles to give it to Katniss. Gong took the broom and swept up the remnants with Adam's help. Orange offered another "Salut!" for the group through the kitchen, through the living room out to the balcony.

After they grazed on take-out, everybody enjoyed the spot they were in. Freckles sat next to Katniss on the outdoor sofa, guitar in her hands. Katniss had taught her the chords to "Rivers of Babylon" as they both sang it in the broken language of a newly learned song; not birdsong and fluid, but full of missed notes and messy and full of the joy.

Adam lazed on the hammock on the balcony and took it all in, slowly dipping into a relaxed nap. Comfortable and content.

Brodie leaned on the balcony railing. Grigsby joined him and thought he really needed to paint this thing. From the patio they overlooked a supreme sunset of oranges, reds and purples when, finally, the green flashed as the sun dipped into the sea.

In the end, Brodie took over the book. All seemed good. But Brodie wanted the money, too. He couldn't be made to look weak to the guys back East.

"But I thought it would be different?" Grigsby said.

"I said 'might' be different," Brodie smiled, then flat: "It isn't."

Grigsby smiled and elbow walked Brodie to the living room to sit on the couch. "Now, you know we have a distribution deal in the works and a director already. Funding is all but set."

Grigsby signaled Orange to sit with them. He nodded to Freckles with a silent pour in one hand and a tinkle-tinkle glass in the other with 'that' grin across his face.

"How about I give you a cut of the movie in lieu of payment, Brodie?"

From above in a drone you would've seen it like a BBC nature documentary. From Brodie's vantage point, he couldn't see the sharks circling him like an adolescent sea lion fresh on his own. The sea lion swimming, feeling free, fast and in control. Little did that sea lion know a great white shark just may charge at full speed, breach at the surface, and take that little sea lion in its jaws as lunch.

"I don't know, Grigsby. I like cash. Tony always said that you get the cash."

Grigsby spread his arms. "Tony was old school. We're new school. Look at what the old ways got Tony."

"A pen in the neck," Brodie said, then, quickly, "Rest his soul."

"Rest his soul," Grigsby nodded agreement.

Orange booted the hologram presentation while Freckles brought the batch of Campari and Gins. The

Petralia.

Grigsby settled and smiled wide, "Now, this movie could be worth ten - TWENTY TIMES what I owe by the end of next year. Did you know some of these movies make a billion-plus dollars, that's with a 'B', in the box office? Let alone streaming or merchandising. Licensing. Did you also know YouTube just contacted us about a streaming deal? Don't even get me started on IPO's."

Darkness settled over this part of the world as the waves lapped on the smooth sand of the shore. The telltale briny smell told the story of another red tide algae bloom. The red tide that fueled the bioluminescent blue of the breaker's whitewash. The waves that are the constant pulse of our living planet.

ACKNOWLEDGMENTS

Life throws some difficult pitches. Look for a good one and take a hack. After all, we can only control our effort and attitude, not the outcome.

Tina, you are the best, plain and simple. Without your support and belief, I would be nowhere.

Joe and Mike, you inspire me daily with your efforts and ability. One step at a time...

Many people read, commented, and improved this book: Thank you.

Lastly, to you, the reader, thanks for spending time with my imaginary friends. They may be flawed but they're doing the best they can.

See you next time!

About the Author

If Jeffrey Messineo isn't hunkered down writing his latest thriller, he is probably reading one. His love of blind curves and unexpected twists expands beyond the page to the local hiking trails where he invents many of his story concepts. After reading California Hustle, you can devour Reaping Independence, another thriller. He is working on a new novel.

Sign up for Jeffrey's Newsletter

at

JeffreyMessineo.com/newsletter

And get a copy of a rare short story.

You can also follow him

On Twitter: @jeffreymessineo

On Facebook: https://facebook.com/JeffreyMessineo

If you enjoyed California Hustle, please take a moment to review this book

on Amazon and/or Goodreads.

www.ingramcontent.com/pod-product-compliance
Lightning Source LLC
LaVergne TN
LVHW100517110826
845146LV00002B/671

* 9 7 9 8 9 8 7 1 9 2 4 3 6 *